PRAISE FOR EKATERINA SEDIA'S ANTHOLOGIES

"The action of the stories of **Paper Cities** occurs, in some manner or another, in an urban setting. Their other aspects are as various as one could imagine. Other stories are about street kids, doomed love, the children of office workers and photocopiers, and ghosts; their settings range from the suburbs to the city of the future; and their approaches to the idea of the urban, what urbs are, and how we might interact with them as they become ever more fantastic, are wildly varied, intensely satisfying."—*Booklist*

"Together with eight other stories of cities and their people, this vital collection pushes the envelope of the urban fantasy genre, reaching beyond the standards made popular by Charles de Lint, Tanya Huff, and Jim Butcher to create an ever expanding definition of the term." —*Library Journal*, for **Paper Cities**

"**Paper Cities** is a delightful and absorbing read. In coming years, as the talents collected herein, including editor Sedia, become better known, this quirky anthology may take on even greater significance."—*Publishers Weekly*, starred review

"Sedia collects twenty-two tales that look at werewolves from a multitude of different angles. The stories veer from comedy to horror and from tragic love story to coming-of-age tale, showing the richness inherent in the idea of shifting shapes and animal strength."—*Publishers Weekly*, starred review, for **Running with the Pack**

"Sedia has chosen twenty-nine original and previously published stories featuring shape changers and werecreatures to showcase the variety of tales about humans who can take the forms of animals. This collection should appeal to fans of werefiction."—*Library Journal,* for **Bewere the Night**

BLOODY
FABULOUS

OTHER BOOKS BY EKATERINA SEDIA

Paper Cities
Running with the Pack
Bewere the Night
Bloody Fabulous
Circus: Fantasy Under the Big Top
Willful Impropiety

BLOODY
FABULOUS

———◆———

EKATERINA SEDIA

PRIME BOOKS

BLOODY FABULOUS

Prime Books
www.prime-books.com

For more information, contact Prime Books:
prime@prime-books.com

ISBN: 978-1-60701-360-0

To everyone who forges fabulous disguises.

CONTENTS

—◦◦◦◦—

INTRODUCTION

My last two anthologies have been about shapeshifters and were-wolves, so when I talked to people about editing an anthology dealing with fashion, the reaction more often than not has been puzzlement. But is it really so much of a stretch? We talk about shapeshifter stories being the means for manifesting our secret selves to the world. But is this so different from fashion?

We pay attention to what we wear because style and fashion are among the means of nonverbal communication. And we tell the world what we want to be today. It's not a secret that we use the sartorial signifiers in fiction—we know the noir detectives by their fedoras and trench coats, we recognize paranormal investigators by their skin-tight leather. Princesses wear yards of chiffon and ballerinas have tulle; pirates enjoy ruffled shirts, and businessmen have their Brioni suits. So why not write a few stories in which the outfits themselves, the aspirational skins of our inner selves become the characters? Why not let those who create those garments for us tell their stories? Because who is better to explain how important our clothes are than those who spend their days immersed in creating them and imbuing them with meaning!

I think it was Ru Paul who said (and I am paraphrasing) that we come into the world naked, and everything else is drag. I want to agree with that, but I also want to think that this drag is not coincidental but magical in a way. We cannot turn into predators, even if there is a full moon outside—but we can wear

11

jackets with metal spikes on the shoulders to feel a little bit more dangerous. Our clothes give us some shape-shifting abilities— from ethereal to tough to glamorous in a single day! They give us the means to tell the world who we are today (or who we would like to be) without uttering a word. And they let us play and pretend, manipulate our gender presentation as well as other aspects of sartorial personas: clothes are the ultimate disguise, alluring enough to bring a shapeshifter out in all of us.

So I hope that these stories will inspire you to look at your clothes with new eyes. There are so many characters here—from sales clerks to designers to fashion bloggers, from fantastical to historical to mundane costumes, from fashion magazines to fashion accessories; and every story offers a new way to look at what our clothes are, where they come from, who decides what is fashionable anyway . . . but most of all, how our clothes cast such a spell over us—and how we can use them as faery glamor, to cast a spell of our own, and to pretend to be our secret selves. Be your clothes shapeshifting or disguise, these stories will be your co-conspirators as you offer the world a sly glimpse of your sartorial heart.

—Ekaterina Sedia

THE COAT OF STARS

HOLLY BLACK

Rafael Santiago hated going home. Home meant his parents making a big fuss and a special dinner and him having to smile and hide all his secret vices, like the cigarettes he had smoked for almost sixteen years now. He hated that they always had the radio blaring salsa and the windows open and that his cousins would come by and tried to drag him out to bars. He hated that his mother would tell him how Father Joe had asked after him at Mass. He especially hated the familiarity of it, the memories that each visit stirred up.

For nearly an hour that morning he had stood in front of his dressing table and regarded the wigs and hats and masks—early versions or copies of costumes he'd designed—each item displayed on green glass heads that stood in front of a large, broken mirror. They drooped feathers, paper roses and crystal dangles, or curved up into coiled, leather horns. He had settled on wearing a white tank-top tucked into bland gray Dockers but when he stood next to all his treasures, he felt unfinished. Clipping on black suspenders, he looked at himself again. That was better, almost a compromise. A fedora, a cane, and a swirl of eyeliner would have finished off the look, but he left it alone.

"What do you think?" he asked the mirror, but it did not answer. He turned to the unpainted plaster face casts resting on a nearby shelf; their hollow eyes told him nothing either.

Rafe tucked his little phone into his front left pocket with his wallet and keys. He would call his father from the train. Glancing at the wall, his gaze rested on one of the sketches of costumes he'd done for a postmodern ballet production of *Hamlet*. An award hung beside it. This sketch was of a faceless woman in a white gown appliqued with leaves and berries. He remembered how dancers had held the girl up while others pulled on the red ribbons he had had hidden in her sleeves. Yards and yards of red ribbon could come from her wrists. The stage had been swathed in red. The dancers had been covered in red. The whole world had become one dripping gash of ribbon.

The train ride was dull. He felt guilty that the green landscapes that blurred outside the window did not stir him. He only loved leaves if they were crafted from velvet.

Rafael's father waited at the station in the same old blue truck he'd had since before Rafe had left Jersey for good. Each trip his father would ask him careful questions about his job, the city, Rafe's apartment. Certain unsaid assumptions were made. His father would tell him about some cousin getting into trouble or, lately, his sister Mary's problems with Marco.

Rafe leaned back in the passenger seat, feeling the heat of the sun wash away the last of the goose bumps on his arms. He had forgotten how cold the air conditioning was on the train. His father's skin, sun-darkened to deep mahogany, made his own seem sickly pale. A string-tied box of crystallized ginger pastries sat at his feet. He always brought something for his parents: a bottle of wine, a tarte tatin, a jar of truffle oil from Balducci's.

The gifts served as a reminder of the city and that his ticket was round-trip, bought and paid for.

"Mary's getting a divorce," Rafe's father said once he'd pulled out of the parking lot. "She's been staying in your old room. I had to move your sewing stuff."

"How's Marco taking it?" Rafe had already heard about the divorce; his sister had called him a week ago at three in the morning from Cherry Hill, asking for money so she and her son Victor could take a bus home. She had talked in heaving breaths and he'd guessed she'd been crying. He had wired the money to her from the corner store where he often went for green tea ice cream.

"Not good. He wants to see his son. I told him if he comes around the house again, your cousin's gonna break probation but he's also gonna break that loco sonofabitch's neck."

No one, of course, thought that spindly Rafe could break Marco's neck.

The truck passed people dragging lawn chairs into their front yards for a better view of the coming fireworks. Although it was still many hours until dark, neighbors milled around, drinking lemonade and beer.

In the back of the Santiago house, smoke pillared up from the grill where cousin Gabriel scorched hamburger patties smothered in hot sauce. Mary lay on the blue couch in front of the TV, an ice mask covering her eyes. Rafael walked by as quietly as he could. The house was dark and the radio was turned way down. For once, his greeting was subdued. Only his nephew, Victor, a sparkler twirling in his hand, seemed oblivious to the somber mood.

They ate watermelon so cold that it was better than drinking water; hot dogs and hamburgers off the grill with more hot sauce and tomatoes; rice and beans; corn salad; and ice cream. They drank beer and instant iced tea and the decent tequila that Gabriel had brought. Mary joined them halfway through the meal and Rafe was only half-surprised to see the blue and yellow bruise darkening her jaw. Mostly, he was surprised how much her face, angry and suspicious of pity, reminded him of Lyle.

When Rafe and Lyle were thirteen, they had been best friends. Lyle had lived across town with his grandparents and three sisters in a house far too small for all of them. Lyle's grandmother told the kids terrible stories to keep them from going near the river that ran through the woods behind their yard. There was the one about the phooka, who appeared like a goat with sulfurous yellow eyes and great curling horns and who shat on the blackberries on the first of November. There was the kelpie that swam in the river and wanted to carry off Lyle and his sisters to drown and devour. And there were the trooping faeries that would steal them all away to their underground hills for a hundred years.

Lyle and Rafe snuck out to the woods anyway. They would stretch out on an old, bug-infested mattress and "practice" sex. Lying on his back, Lyle'd showed Rafe how to thrust his penis between Lyle's pressed-together thighs in "pretend" intercourse.

Lyle had forbidden certain conversations. No talk about the practicing, no talk about the bruises on his back and arms, and no talk about his grandfather, ever, at all. Rafe thought about that, about all the conversations he had learned not to have, all the conversations he still avoided.

As fireworks lit up the black sky, Rafe listened to his sister fight with Marco on the phone. He must have been accusing her about getting the money from a lover because he heard his name said over and over. "Rafael sent it," she shouted. "My fucking brother sent it." Finally, she screamed that if he didn't stop threatening her she was going to call the police. She said her cousin was a cop. And it was true; Teo Santiago was a cop. But Teo was also in jail.

When she got off the phone, Rafe said nothing. He didn't want her to think he'd overheard.

She came over anyway. "Thanks for everything, you know? The money and all."

He touched the side of her face with the bruise. She looked at the ground but he could see that her eyes had grown wet.

"You're gonna be okay," he said. "You're gonna be happier."

"I know," she said. One of the tears tumbled from her eye and shattered across the toe of his expensive leather shoe, tiny fragments sparkling with reflected light. "I didn't want you to hear all this shit. You're life is always so together."

"Not really," he said, smiling. Mary had seen his apartment only once, when she and Marco had brought Victor up to see the Lion King. Rafe had sent her tickets; they were hard to get so he thought that she might want them. They hadn't stayed long in his apartment; the costumes that hung on the walls had frightened Victor.

She smiled too. "Have you ever had a boyfriend this bad?"

Her words hung in the air a moment. It was the first time any of them had ventured a guess. "Worse," he said, "and girlfriends too. I have terrible taste."

Mary sat down next to him on the bench. "Girlfriends too?"

He nodded and lifted a glass of iced tea to his mouth. "When you don't know what you're searching for," he said, "you have to look absolutely everywhere."

The summer that they were fourteen, a guy had gone down on Rafe in one of the public showers at the beach and he gloried in the fact that for the first time he had a story of almost endless interest to Lyle. It was also the summer that they almost ran away.

"I saw grandma's faeries," Lyle had said the week before they were supposed to go. He told Rafe plainly, like he'd spotted a robin outside the window.

"How do you know?" Rafe had been making a list of things they needed to bring. The pen in his hand had stopped writing in the middle of spelling 'colored pencils.' For a moment, all Rafe felt was resentment that his blowjob story had been trumped.

"They were just the way she said they'd be. Dancing in a circle and they glowed a little, like their skin could reflect the moonlight. One of them looked at me and her face was as beautiful as the stars."

Rafe scowled. "I want to see them too."

"Before we get on the train we'll go down to where I saw them dancing."

Rafe added 'peanut butter' to his list. It was the same list he was double-checking six days later, when Lyle's grandmother called. Lyle was dead. He had slit his wrists in a tub of warm water the night before they were supposed to leave for forever.

Rafe had stumbled to the viewing, cut off a lock of Lyle's blonde hair right in front of his pissed-off family, stumbled to the funeral, and then slept stretched out on the freshly filled grave. It hadn't made sense. He wouldn't accept it. He wouldn't go home.

Rafe took out his wallet and unfolded the train schedule from the billfold. He had a little time. He was always careful not to miss the last train. He looked at the small onyx and silver ring on his pinkie. It held a secret compartment inside, so well hidden that you could barely see the hinge. When Lyle had given it to him, Rafe's fingers had been so slender that it had fit on his ring finger as easily as the curl of Lyle's hair fit inside of it.

As Rafe rose to kiss his mother and warn his father that he would have to be leaving, Mary thrust open the screen door so hard it banged against the plastic trashcan behind it.

"Where's Victor? Is he inside with you? He's supposed to be in bed."

Rafe shook his head. His mother immediately put down the plate she was drying and walked through the house, still holding the dishrag, calling Victor's name. Mary showed them the empty bed.

Mary stared at Rafe as though he hid her son from her. "He's not here. He's gone."

"Maybe he snuck out to see some friends," Rafe said, but it didn't seem right. Not for a ten year-old.

"Marco couldn't have come here without us seeing him," Rafe's father protested.

"He's *gone*," Mary repeated, as though that explained everything. She slumped down in one of the kitchen chairs and covered her face with her hands. "You don't know what he might do to that kid. *Madre de Dios.*"

Rafe's mother came back in the room and punched numbers

into the phone. There was no answer at Marco's apartment. The cousins came in from the back yard. They had mixed opinions on what to do. Some had kids of their own and thought that Mary didn't have the right to keep Victor away from his father. Soon everyone in the kitchen was shouting. Rafe got up and went to the window, looking out into the dark backyard. Kids made up their own games and wound up straying farther than they meant to.

"Victor!" he called, walking across the lawn. "Victor!"

But he wasn't there, and when Rafe walked out to the street, he could not find the boy along the hot asphalt length. Although it was night, the sky was bright with a full moon and clouds enough to reflect the city lights.

A car slowed as it came down the street. It sped away once it was past the house and Rafe let out the breath he didn't even realize that he had held. He had never considered his brother-in-law crazy, just bored and maybe a little resentful that he had a wife and a kid. But then, Lyle's grandfather had seemed normal too.

Rafe thought about the train schedule in his pocket and the unfinished sketches on his desk. The last train would be along soon and if he wasn't there to meet it, he would have to spend the night with his memories. There was nothing he could do here. In the city, he could call around and find her the number of a good lawyer—a lawyer that Marco couldn't afford. That was the best thing, he thought. He headed back to the house, his shoes clicking like beetles on the pavement.

His oldest cousin had come out to talk to him in the graveyard the night after Lyle's funeral. It had clearly creeped Teo to find his little cousin sleeping in the cemetery.

"He's gone." Teo had squatted down in his blue policeman uniform. He sounded a little impatient and very awkward.

"The faeries took him," Rafe had said. "They stole him away to Faeryland and left something else in his place."

"Then he's still not in this graveyard." Teo had pulled on Rafe's arm and Rafe had finally stood.

"If I hadn't touched him," Rafe had said, so softly that maybe Teo didn't hear.

It didn't matter. Even if Teo had heard, he probably would have pretended he hadn't.

This time when Rafe walked out of the house, he heard the distant fireworks and twirled his father's keys around his first finger. He hadn't taken the truck without permission in years.

The stick and clutch were hard to time and the engine grunted and groaned, but when he made it to the highway, he flicked on the radio and stayed in fifth gear the whole way to Cherry Hill. Marco's house was easy to find. The lights were on in every room and the blue flicker of the television lit up the front steps.

Rafe parked around a corner and walked up to the window of the guest bedroom. When he was thirteen, he had snuck into Lyle's house lots of times. Lyle had slept on a pull-out mattress in the living room because his sisters shared the second bedroom. The trick involved waiting until the television was off and everyone else had gone to bed. Rafe excelled at waiting.

When the house finally went silent and dark, Rafe pushed the window. It was unlocked. He slid it up as far as he could and pulled himself inside.

Victor turned over sleepily and opened his eyes. They went wide.

Rafe froze and waited for him to scream, but his nephew didn't move.

"It's your uncle," Rafe said softly. "From the Lion King. From New York." He sat down on the carpet. Someone had once told him that being lower was less threatening.

Victor didn't speak.

"Your mom sent me to pick you up."

The mention of his mother seemed to give him the courage to say: "Why didn't you come to the door?"

"Your dad would kick my ass," Rafe said. "I'm not crazy."

Victor half-smiled.

"I could drive you back," Rafe said. He took his cell phone out of his pocket and put it on the comforter by Victor. "You can call your mom and she'll tell you I'm okay. Not a stranger."

The boy climbed out of bed and Rafe stuffed it with pillows that formed a small boy-shape under the blankets.

"What are you doing?" the boy asked as he punched the numbers into the tiny phone.

"I'm making a pretend you that can stay here and keep on sleeping." The words echoed for a long moment before Rafe remembered that he and Victor had to get moving.

On the drive back, Rafe told Victor a story that his mother had told him and Mary when they were little, about a king who fed a louse so well on royal blood that it swelled up so large that it no longer fit in the palace. The king had the louse slaughtered and its hide tanned to make a coat for his daughter, the princess, and

22

told all her suitors that they had to guess what kind of skin she wore before their proposal could be accepted.

Victor liked the part of the story where Rafe pretended to hop like a flea and bite his nephew. Rafe liked all fairy tales with tailors in them.

"Come inside," his mother said. "You should have told us you were going to take the car. I needed to go to the store and get some—"

She stopped, seeing Victor behind Rafael.

Rafe's father stood up from the couch as they came in. Rafe tossed the keys and his father caught them.

"Tough guy." His father grinned. "I hope you hit him."

"Are you kidding? And hurt this delicate hand?" Rafe asked, holding it up as for inspection.

He was surprised by his father's laugh.

For the first time in almost fifteen years, Rafe spent the night. Stretching out on the lumpy couch, he turned the onyx ring again and again on his finger.

Then, for the first time in more than ten years, he thumbed open the hidden compartment, ready to see Lyle's golden hair. Crumbled leaves fell onto his chest instead.

Leaves. Not hair. Hair lasted; it should be there. Victorian mourning ornaments braided with the hair of the long-dead survived decades. Rafe had seen such a brooch on the scarf of a well-known playwright. The hair was dulled by time, perhaps, but it had hardly turned to leaves.

He thought of the lump of bedclothes that had looked like Victor at first glance. A "pretend me," Victor had said. But Lyle's corpse wasn't pretend. He had seen it. He had cut off a lock of its hair.

Rafe ran his fingers through the crushed leaves on his chest.

Hope swelled inside of him, despite the senselessness of it. He didn't like to think about Faeryland lurking just over a hill or beneath a shallow river, as distant as a memory. But if he could believe that he could pass unscathed from the world of the city into the world of the suburban ghetto and back again, then couldn't he go further? Why couldn't he cross into the world of shining people with faces like stars that were the root of all his costumes?

Marco had stolen Victor; but Rafe had stolen Victor back. Until that moment, Rafe hadn't considered he could steal Lyle back from Faeryland.

Rafe kicked off the afghan.

At the entrance to the woods, Rafe stopped and lit a cigarette. His feet knew the way to the river by heart.

The mattress was filthier than he remembered, smeared with dirt and damp with dew. He sat, unthinking, and whispered Lyle's name. The forest was quiet and the thought of faeries seemed a little silly. Still, he felt close to Lyle here.

"I went to New York, just like we planned," Rafe said, his hand stroking over the blades of grass as though they were hairs on a pelt. "I got a job in a theatrical rental place, full of these antiqued candelabras and musty old velvet curtains. Now I make stage clothes. I don't ever have to come back here again."

He rested his head against the mattress, inhaled mold and leaves and earth. His face felt heavy, as though already sore with tears. "Do you remember Mary? Her husband hits her. I bet he hits my nephew too, but she wouldn't say." His eyes burned with unexpected tears. The guilt that twisted his gut was fresh and raw as it had been the day Lyle died. "I never knew why you did it. Why you had to die instead of come away with me. You never said either."

"Lyle," he sighed, and his voice trailed off. He wasn't sure what he'd been about to say. "I just wish you were here, Lyle. I wish you were here to talk to."

Rafe pressed his mouth to the mattress and closed his eyes for a moment before he rose and brushed the dirt off his slacks.

He would just ask Mary what happened with Marco. If Victor was all right. If they wanted to live with him for a while. He would tell his parents that he slept with men. There would be no more secrets, no more assumptions. There was nothing he could do for Lyle now, but there was still something he could do for his nephew. He could say all the things he'd left unsaid and hope that others would too.

As Rafe stood, lights sprung up from nothing, like matches catching in the dark.

Around him, in the woods, faeries danced in a circle. They were bright and seemed almost weightless, hair flying behind them like smoke behind a sparkler. Among them, Rafe thought he saw a kid, so absorbed in dancing that he did not hear Rafe gasp or shout. He started forward, hand outstretched. At the center of the circle, a woman in a gown of green smiled a cold and terrible smile before the whole company disappeared.

Rafe felt his heart beat hard against his chest. He was frightened as he had not been at fourteen, when magical things seemed like they could be ordinary and ordinary things were almost magical.

On the way home, Rafe thought of all the other fairy tales he knew about tailors. He thought of the faerie woman's plain green gown and about desire. When he got to the house, he pulled his sewing machine out of the closet and set it up on the kitchen table. Then he began to rummage through all the cloth and trims, beads and fringe. He found crushed panne velvet that looked like liquid gold and sewed it into a frockcoat studded with bright buttons and appliquéd with blue flames that lapped up the sleeves. It was one of the most beautiful things he had ever made. He fell asleep cradling it and woke to his mother setting a cup of espresso mixed with condensed milk in front of him. He drank the coffee in one slug.

It was easy to make a few phone calls and a few promises, change around meetings and explain to his bewildered parents that he needed to work from their kitchen for a day or two. Of course Clio would feed his cats. Of course his client understood that Rafe was working through a design problem. Of course the presentation could be rescheduled for the following Friday. Of course. Of course.

His mother patted his shoulder. "You work too hard."

He nodded, because it was easier than telling her he wasn't really working.

"But you make beautiful things. You sew like your great-grandmother. I told you how people came from miles around to get their wedding dresses made by her."

He smiled up at her and thought of all the gifts he had brought at the holidays—cashmere gloves and leather coats and bottles of perfume. He had never sewn a single thing for her. Making gifts had seemed cheap, like he was giving her a child's misshapen vase or a card colored with crayons. But the elegant, meaningless presents he had sent were cold, revealing nothing about him and even less about her. Imagining her in a silk dress the color of papayas—one he might sew himself—filled him with shame.

He slept most of the day in the shadowed dark of his parent's bed with the shades drawn and the door closed. The buzz of cartoons in the background and the smell of cooking oil made him feel like a small child again. When he woke it was dark outside. His clothes had been cleaned and were folded at the foot of the bed. He put the golden coat on over them and walked to the river.

There, he smoked cigarette after cigarette, dropping the filters into the water, listening for the hiss as the river smothered the flame and drowned the paper. Finally, the faeries came, dancing their endless dance, with the cold faerie woman sitting in the middle.

The woman saw him and walked through the circle. Her eyes were green as moss and, as she got close, he saw that her hair flowed behind her as though she were swimming through water or like ribbons whipped in a fierce wind. Where she stepped, tiny flowers bloomed.

"Your coat is beautiful. It glows like the sun," the faery said, reaching out to touch the fabric.

"I would give it to you," said Rafe. "Just let me have Lyle."

A smile twisted her mouth. "I will let you spend tonight with him. If he remembers you, he is free to go. Will that price suit?"

Rafe nodded and removed the coat.

The faery woman caught Lyle's hand as he spun past, pulling him out of the dance. He was laughing, still, as his bare feet touched the moss outside the circle and he aged. His chest grew broader, he became taller, his hair lengthened, and fine lines appeared around his mouth and eyes. He was no longer a teenager.

"Leaving us, even for a time, has a price," the faery woman said. Standing on her toes, she bent Lyle's head to her lips. His eyelids drooped and she steered him to the moldering mattress. He never even looked in Rafe's direction; he just sank down into sleep.

"Lyle," Rafe said, dropping down beside him, smoothing the tangle of hair back from his face. There were braids in it that knotted up with twigs and leaves and cords of thorny vines. A smudge of dirt highlighted one cheekbone. Leaves blew over him, but he did not stir.

"Lyle," Rafe said again. Rafe was reminded of how Lyle's body had lain in the casket at the funeral, of how Lyle's skin had been pale and bluish as skim milk and smelled faintly of chemicals, of how his fingers were threaded together across his chest so tightly that when Rafe tried to take his hand, it was stiff as a mannequin's. Even now, the memory of that other, dead Lyle seemed more real than the one that slept beside him like a cursed prince in a fairy tale.

"Please wake up," Rafe said. "Please. Wake up and tell me this is real."

Lyle did not stir. Beneath the lids, his eyes moved as if he saw another landscape.

Rafe shook him and then struck him, hard, across the face. "Get up," he shouted. He tugged on Lyle's arm and Lyle's body rolled toward him.

Standing, he tried to lift Lyle, but he was used to only the weight of bolts of cloth. He settled for dragging him toward the street where Rafe could flag down a car or call for help. He pulled with both his hands, staining Lyle's shirt and face with grass, and scratching his side on a fallen branch. Rafe dropped his hand and bent over him in the quiet dark.

"It's too far," Rafe said. "Far too far."

He stretched out beside Lyle, pillowing his friend's head against his chest and resting on his own arm.

When Rafe woke, Lyle no longer lay beside him, but the faery woman stood over the mattress. She wore the coat of fire and, in the light of the newly risen sun, she shone so brightly that Rafe had to shade his eyes with his hand. She laughed and her laugh sounded like ice cracking on a frozen lake.

"You cheated me," Rafe said. "You made him sleep."

"He heard you in his dreams," said the faery woman. "He preferred to remain dreaming."

Rafe stood and brushed off his pants, but his jaw clenched so tightly that his teeth hurt.

"Come with me," the faery said. "Join the dance. You are only jealous that you were left behind. Let that go. You can be forever young and you can make beautiful costumes forevermore. We will appreciate them as no mortal does and we will adore you."

Rafe inhaled the leaf-mold and earth smells. Where Lyle had rested, a golden hair remained. He thought of his father laughing at his jokes, his mother admiring his sewing, his sister caring enough to ask him about boyfriends even in the middle of a crisis. Rafe wound the hair around his finger so tightly that it striped his skin white and red. "No," he told her.

His mother was sitting in her robe in the kitchen. She got up when Rafe came in.

"Where are you going? You are like a possessed man." She touched his hand and her skin felt so hot that he pulled back in surprise.

"You're freezing! You have been at his grave."

It was easier for Rafe to nod than explain.

"There is a story about a woman who mourned too long and the spectre of her lover rose up and dragged her down into death with him."

He nodded again, thinking of the faery woman, of being dragged into the dance, of Lyle sleeping like death.

She sighed exaggeratedly and made him a coffee. Rafe had already set up the sewing machine by the time she put the mug beside him.

That day he made a coat of silver silk, pleated at the hips and embroidered with a tangle of thorny branches and lapels of downy white fur. He knew it was one of the most beautiful things he had ever made.

"Who are you sewing that for?" Mary asked when she came in. "It's gorgeous."

He rubbed his eyes and gave her a tired smile. "It's supposed to be the payment a mortal tailor used to win back a lover from Faeryland."

"I haven't heard of that story," his sister said. "Will it be a musical?"

"I don't know yet," said Rafe. "I don't think the cast can sing."

His mother frowned and called Mary over to chop up a summer squash.

"I want you and Victor to come live with me," Rafe said as his sister turned away from him.

"Your place is too small," Rafe's mother told him.

She had never seen his apartment. "We could move, then. Go to Queens. Brooklyn."

"You won't want a little boy running around. And Mary has the cousins here. She should stay with us. Besides, the city is dangerous."

"Marco is dangerous," Rafe said voice rising. "Why don't you let Mary make up her own mind?"

Rafe's mother muttered under her breath as she chopped, Rafe sighed and bit his tongue and Mary gave him a sisterly roll of the eyes. It occurred to him that that had been the most normal conversation he had had with his mother in years.

All day he worked on the coat and that night Rafe, wearing the silvery coat, went back to the woods and the river.

The dancers were there as before and when Rafe got close, the faery woman left the circle of dancers.

"Your coat is as lovely as the moon. Will you agree to the same terms?"

Rafe thought of objecting, but he also thought of the faery woman's kiss and that he might be able to change the course of events. It would be better if he caught her off-guard. He shouldered off his coat. "I agree."

As before, the faery woman pulled Lyle from the dance.

"Lyle!" Rafe said, starting toward him before the faery could touch his brow with her lips.

Lyle turned to him and his lips parted as though he were searching for a name to go with a distant memory, as if Lyle didn't recall him after all.

The faery woman kissed him then, and Lyle staggered

drowsily to the mattress. His drooping eyelashes nearly hid the gaze he gave Rafe. His mouth moved, but no sound escaped him and then he subsided into sleep.

That night Rafe tried a different way of rousing Lyle. He pressed his mouth to Lyle's slack lips, to his forehead as the faery woman had done. He kissed the hollow of Lyle's throat, where the beat of his heart thrummed against his skin. He ran his hands over the Lyle's chest. He touched his lips to the smooth, unscarred expanse of Lyle's wrists. Again and again, he kissed Lyle, but it was as terrible as kissing a corpse.

Before he slept, Rafe took the onyx and silver ring off his own pinkie, pulled out a strand of black hair from his own head and coiled it inside the hollow of the poison ring. Then he pushed the ring onto Lyle's pinkie.

"Remember me. Please remember me," Rafe said. "I can't remember myself unless you remember me."

But Lyle did not stir and Rafe woke alone on the mattress. He made his way home in the thin light of dawn.

That day he sewed a coat from velvet as black as the night sky. He stiched tiny black crystals onto it and embroidered it with black roses, thicker at the hem and then thinning as they climbed. At the cuffs and neck, ripped ruffles of thin smoky purples and deep reds reminded him of sunsets. Across the back, he sewed on silver beads for stars. Stars like the faerie woman's eyes. It was the most beautiful thing Raphael had ever created. He knew he would never make its equal.

"Where do you get your ideas from?" his father asked as he shuffled out to the kitchen for an evening cup of decaf. "I've never been much of a creative person."

Rafe opened his mouth to say that he got his ideas from everywhere, from things he'd seen and dreamed and felt, but then he thought of the other thing his father said. "You made that bumper for the old car out of wood," Rafe said. "That was pretty creative."

Rafe's father grinned and added milk to his cup.

That night Rafe donned the shimmering coat and walked to the woods.

The faerie woman waited for him. She sucked in her breath at the sight of the magnificent coat.

"I must have it," she said. "You shall have him as before."

Rafael nodded. Tonight if he could not rouse Lyle, he would have to say goodbye. Perhaps this was the life Lyle had chosen—a life of dancing and youth and painless memory—and he was wrong to try and take him away from it. But he wanted to spend one more night beside Lyle.

She brought Lyle to him and he knelt on the mattress. The faerie woman bent to kiss his forehead, but at the last moment, Lyle turned his head and the kiss fell on his hair.

Scowling, she rose.

Lyle blinked as though awakening from a long sleep, then touched the onyx ring on his finger. He turned toward Rafe and smiled tentatively.

"Lyle?" Rafe asked. "Do you remember me?"

"Rafael?" Lyle asked. He reached a hand toward Rafe's face, fingers skimming just above the skin. Rafe leaned into the heat, butting his head against Lyle's hand and sighing. Time seemed to flow backwards and he felt like he was fourteen again and in love.

"Come, Lyle," said the faery woman sharply.

Lyle rose stiffly, his fingers ruffling Rafe's hair.

"Wait," Rafe said. "He knows who I am. You said he would be free."

"He's as free to come with me as he is to go with you," she said.

Lyle looked down at Rafe. "I dreamed that we went to New York and that we performed in a circus. I danced with the bears and you trained fleas to jump through the eyes of needles."

"I trained fleas?"

"In my dream. You were famous for it." His smile was tentative, uncertain. Maybe he realized that it didn't sound like a great career.

Rafe thought of the story he had told Victor about the princess in her louse-skin coat, about locks of hair and all the things he had managed through the eyes of needles.

The faery woman turned away from them with a scowl, walking back to the fading circle of dancers, becoming insubstantial as smoke.

"It didn't go quite like that." Rafe stood and held out his hand. "I'll tell you what really happened."

Lyle clasped Rafe's fingers tightly, desperately but his smile was wide and his eyes were bright as stars. "Don't leave anything out."

SAVAGE DESIGN

RICHARD BOWES

Early one evening last September Lilia Gaines pulled open the metal gates of Reliquary on West Broadway at the shoddy Canal Street end of Manhattan's Soho. As she did, she murmured to herself:

"In the city with sleep disorders styles get old fast. But old styles never disappear. They lay waiting for a kiss or a love bite . . . "

She trailed off. Lilia's copywriting skills had never been a big strength and she found herself groping for a punch line.

A really young couple appeared wearing knock-off Louis Vuitton sunglasses and looking like they might be at the start of a long Nightwalker romp. His jacket collar was turned up; she had a wicked, amused smile.

Lilia could remember being like them, a brand new walker in the dark with eyes just a bit sensitive to sunlight. They waited while she unlocked the door, came inside with her and headed for the relics table at the rear.

In the last few months this kind of eager customer had started reappearing. Twenty-five and thirty years ago, Reliquary was open all night, closing only when full daylight fell on the storefront and the customers fled.

"Reliquary—Boutique Fashion—So New and SO Undead!" was the slogan in those glory days. Then as now one could find capes in a variety of lengths, elegant black parasols to keep the sun at bay, tops designed for easy exposure of the neck and throat. Some of the stock was a bit shopworn.

There had been good years when Nightwalkers were THE fresh thing. Then there were the lean years when Vampires were afraid to show themselves and Reliquary became a dusty antique store while Lilia worked part time jobs and held on tight to her rent controlled apartment on East Houston Street.

This evening Lilia watched the boy select a red silk handkerchief displaying a black bat, the long-ago emblem of Bloodsucker Night at the gay disco The Saint. The girl slipped on a pendant with the logo of the Gate of Night, that brief legend of a blood bar on Park Avenue South three decades back. Reliquary had always specialized in memorabilia of past Undead revivals.

Another customer, a man in running clothes and shades, entered and went over to a rack of capes. A woman stepped inside and glanced around, found a repro of a poster for *Fun and Gore,* a scandalous 1930's Greenwich Village "Transylvanian Review."

As the young couple approached the register, the girl pulled the boy's jacket and shirt off his shoulders. She smiled at Lilia as though offering her a piece of expensive white fudge.

This was very young love. Their teeth still looked normal; the small bites on his neck had barely penetrated the skin. Fangs and puncture wounds still lay in their future.

The boy's smile was blank. He knotted the kerchief over the bites but left one showing. Lilia guessed that his first blood buzz had been last night and that he'd be bitten again very shortly.

The girl looked at the photo behind Lilia, raised her sunglasses and said, "That's you!"

The kid was sharp; Lilia nodded. The picture was from the

1980 Mudd Club Undead and Kicking Party where Lilia and Larry had introduced Downtown Manhattan to Nightwalking.

She was front and center along with Larry Stepelli, the bisexual boyfriend who designed all her clothes. In black with faces white as bone, they stood out among the graffiti artists, stray freaks, and Warhol Factory stars.

Lilia knew she should warn these kids where blood sucking was going to lead. She remembered her own addiction and the horrors of Ichordone Therapy. But too many years of marginal living left her unwilling to risk endangering the chance she saw coming.

Instead she gave them a double discount because they would tell their friends about the place. Then she told the girl that she was hiring sales help and took her name. It was Scarlet Jones (an invention Lilia assumed). The boy was just plain Bret—too paranoid to leave a last name or so blood-dizzy he couldn't remember it.

The phone rang as the kids left and someone with a heavy European accent asked for directions to the store. Lilia felt the good years coming back.

"Staff called in sick?" Even before raising her eyes Lilia recognized from long ago the throaty, sly voice that somehow made every comment sound dirty but also chilling.

The one called Katya must have come in as the kids left. Well over six feet tall, she stood near the door in a jacket and slacks of fierce grey suede and high-heel ankle boots of raw leather.

"Other's shoes are man-made," it was said in certain circles, "but Katya's are made out of men." Maybe it was her imagination but Lilia could almost see the outlines of ears and fingers in the heels.

"Just me alone, tonight," she said though that's the way it had been for a long time. "To what do I owe this honor?" It had been at least twenty years since she'd gotten anything but a fraction of a nod and an amused stare from this woman on those rare occasions when their paths had crossed.

Katya glanced at the Mudd Club photo and frowned. Lilia knew she'd caught sight of her young self, a supporting player in Lilia and Larry's big moment. Katya was off to one side with Felice who had mood swings and Paulo who worked part-time as a professional boy. In that intense instant all five of them were kids without a dime trying to break into the Fashion Trade.

Katya glanced around and Lilia saw her registering the somewhat tired capes on display, the costume jewelry necklaces with what on second glance turned out to be drop-of-blood motifs.

"Happened to be in the neighborhood," Katya said. "Some intriguing things are to be seen in these quiet little nooks. It's the essence of our business, isn't it, keeping an eye on what is being worn on the streets?"

Katya turned to go as a male couple came in. "I'll tell Paulo and Felice about all this," she said. "I know they'll want to see you too."

The time when they were new in the city and broke was well past. Now Larry was the domestic partner of a rich lawyer. Katya, Felice, and Paulo ran Savage Design, which had been a power in New York fashion for as long as that scene's short memory ran.

People in the business went in such fear of the trio that they called them The Kindly Ones and prayed for their help. Before any enterprise was launched it was considered wise to offer them tribute. The Kindly Ones were THE arbiters and always hungry for something new and perverse or at least hot and retro.

Of their little group only Lilia had failed to make it. Katya's visit could mean a break for her, one last desperate chance.

Through the window she watched Katya take in this dark sliver of the neighborhood. A small, elegant hotel a block and a half north marked the end of trendy Soho.

Next to Reliquary was a shop that sold spray paint and other graffiti supplies. The storefronts across the street were dark and empty; the building upstairs was a tenement. This gritty little block was a bit of pre-gentrified New York preserved in a new century.

Next Monday morning Lilia sat in the conference room of Savage Design sipping coffee. She couldn't decide whether she was more ashamed or bitter when she compared her current life to those of the Kindly Ones.

The Kindly Ones' initial expressions when she arrived left Lilia with no doubt that they found her an amusing curiosity. She kept silent and studied the walls which were decorated with photos of last spring's coup.

An emblematic black and white photo taken at what might have been dawn but was more likely dusk showed a blonde figure wearing an ostentatiously plain dark dress and the slightest smile of triumph.

All was shades of grey except for the handbag. That was in the red and orange tones of an October bonfire. *A Satanic Possession of One's Own!* was the caption.

Around the room ads displayed belts, scarves, wraps. A photo was headlined, *For the One Willing to Exchange a Flawed Soul for Perfection.*

Satan's Bag, read the caption on the *Harper's Bazaar* double page spread, *Designer Fashion from inside the Fiery Gates!*

Paulo noticed her interest. He still had the face and body of a kid. But now he had the eyes of an old, bored lizard. He wore a short pants suit of navy blue cheviot wool. A yo-yo spun constantly on his right hand

"Last Spring's triumph," said an ancient voice from inside him. "As of yet nobody knows what to do about next year." His yo-yo slept at the end of its string, looped the loop as he spoke.

Years before, his allowance from a mysterious sugar daddy who insisted he dress like an English schoolboy was often all that kept them in their daily cappuccino and crème brulee.

"The year hasn't even begun," said Felice, whose face today was the mask of tragedy, "and it's already dreary, tired, lacking a defining moment." She was whip thin and dressed in black.

Her mouth appeared to curve even further down. Her eye sockets seemed hollow. It was whispered in the fashion trade that in moments of emotional stress she cried tears of blood.

Katya yawned and said, "Nothing like the designer suicide followed by the show of his work at the Met last year."

"Brilliant timing, yes," said Paolo, as the yo-yo spun through the intricate hop-the-fence trick, "but significant because it was one of a kind. If something similar happened now, would anyone be interested?"

Katya said, "We're being rude to our guest. Lilia, darling, understand that we all change over time. With us, Paulo's Sugar Daddy decided it was easier to become a permanent live-in guest and share Paulo's youth at first hand. Felice got tired of trying to suppress her feelings and allowed them to come forth for everyone to see. I went from thinking men were useless to finding a use for them. Perhaps you never wanted to reach that kind of resolution."

She put her feet with the sling-backs like no others up on the table. "Everyone talks as if we had dark powers. But Savage Design is quite a simple straightforward business. Paulo handles the finances, Felice does the promotion, and I'm the scout."

Then she asked, "How's Larry?"

Lilia's answer was careful. "Still hooked up with the rich lawyer who financed that Gallery he has in Chelsea. They adopted an Asian child, and were talking about getting married now that it's legal."

She left out the fact Larry and she were talking again and that he'd provided money to keep Reliquary open. Lilia wondered how much they knew about her business or if this was just idle curiosity mixed with bitchiness.

Paulo said, "I understand he's breaking up with that lawyer."

Lilia hadn't heard that.

"I brought Lilia here," Katya told the others, "because her shop is still in business and showing signs of life. I've seen a glimmer on the street that could go semi-major. A Nightwalker revival," she said.

Paulo's ancient eyes closed. Felice looked away.

"Round and round we go," Paulo said, "Remember the Boom when everyone was high on blood and being a vampire was utterly hip? Recall the Bust a few years later? Nobody became

41

Dracula and immortal. Everyone was a blood junkie and went into therapy or jail."

"Yes," Katya said, "we've all been there and back. But in one afternoon in Tribeca and Soho I saw a couple of dozen people under twenty-five wearing Blood Sucker artifacts."

"Cyclical but inevitable," murmured Felice but her mouth was now a straight line.

"Before a look can be revived it must die!" said Paulo thoughtfully, "Or at least be presumed dead!"

"Then there's the boutique itself," said Katya as if Lilia wasn't present. "Reliquary is so passé it's almost tantalizing. And it's on a block that's this kind of time bubble from the old, bad Manhattan of thirty years back. The sort of place people who weren't actually there get nostalgic about—all grit, grunge, and decay!"

At the word grunge, Paulo's reptile eyes lit up with old memories and he used both hands to make the yo-yo do "Buddha's Revenge."

"Delicious decay," Felice murmured. The others looked away before her face slipped into the mask of comedy pose. It was said, with reason, that none who saw the laughing mask lived to tell about it.

They discussed what could be done with Reliquary. Lilia stayed very still and alert, determined not to let this opportunity pass her by.

"Reliquary—Open Dusk to Dawn" read the store's new webpage headline: *"Costumes and Accessories For Long After Twilight,"* it promised.

A dozen customers were in her store at 3:30 AM and Lilia stood behind the counter keeping an eye out for shoplifters, watching Scarlet Jones greet friends. Lilia knew all about history—especially fashion history—repeating itself the first time as farce, the second as camp.

She noticed that Scarlet's teeth were changing, getting sharper. Her boyfriend, Bret, worked in the stockroom and looked more pale and dizzy each time Lilia saw him.

The story was unfolding much faster this time than the last. Thirty years back the cult grew little by little. Word was spread in print, *"Something REALLY Old Is Very New Again!"* a *New York Post* gossip columnist had said. *"They Walk By Night—Creepy and DELICIOUS!"* read the *Women's Wear Daily* headline as things got underway.

Suddenly Reliquary's door opened and the room stirred. Magnetic, wonderfully turned out in an antique black cape and dark red top, seemingly untouched by age, Larry Stepelli entered with an entourage of models, minor celebrities and star bloggers—all young.

Thirty years before, Lilia would have been the one beside him. The flamboyant bisexual guy and plain, serious girl was the perfect pairing of that moment. They were in the vanguard of the trip into the night.

Now they were distant friends and the arrangement was financial. A few months before, she'd sensed Larry's boredom. The rich boyfriend, their adorable adopted child, the art gallery in Chelsea, weren't doing it for him.

So she'd turned him on to the Nightwalker revival she was trying to create. It only took a couple of reminders of their initial encounters with the dark mysteries. His curiosity and desire kicked in. Larry advanced money to pay off the back rent and restocked the store.

He walked over and they made kissing gestures. "You must have heard?" he said.

"About your break-up? Sorry."

"Inevitable. I imagine it will all be very civilized. I'll get a settlement and visiting rights with Ai Ling." He looked around. "Business has really picked up."

Lilia said, "Yes. I was even summoned to Seventh Avenue by the Kindly Ones."

"My, MY!"

"Remember when telephone gossip was the fastest news on the planet? Now what any kid posts online, the world knows before the next day dawns."

Larry smiled and turned away. She watched him help a pale young man select a ring with a tiny broken crucifix on it.

Lilia remembered the last Nightwalker scene turning sour. "*BLOODY HELL*" screamed a *Post* headline. "*Nightwalkers in Rehab*," was a three part series in the *Village Voice*. But it was years between those first hints and the morning everyone woke up with hideous addictions to blood and biting.

This time the turnaround would be quick. And Lilia knew she had to ride the wave or go under for good.

A few nights later, the Savage Design trio, complete with personal assistants, photographers, a video crew, and a special secret arrived at Lilia's shop.

Paulo in soccer shorts and jersey repeatedly kicked a ball

against the hydrant in front of Reliquary. The kid's legs did a fast dance step as he stopped the rebound each time then slammed the ball again. Seemingly independent of this, the lizard eyes took in the store and its surroundings.

Felice nodded to Lilia as she went through Reliquary with her face carefully kept in neutral and examined everything while murmuring notes to herself on a hand held recorder.

"Nothing needs to be changed," she said to the production assistant who followed her. "Treat each dusty corner and gauche display as an asset. Pretend you're an explorer stumbling on a mysterious if tacky Transylvanian castle."

Then she said into the recorder, "Time is more precious than blood on this particular project. It's all a matter of DEATH and *death*."

A team of trimmers lighted and dressed Reliquary's front windows. Katya appeared outside shortly afterwards, towering in dark, rough leather platform shoes with dizzyingly high heels that seemed to be watching when you stared. She herded a couple of long-necked professional models and half a dozen Nightwalker kids whom she'd discovered around the city.

The photography crew did shots of them on the sidewalk. "They'll be in here shortly," Katya assured Lilia when she popped into the shop. She also insisted on having Scarlet Jones and Bret in the promotional shots.

"We'll have them behind the counter like they run the place, darling. They exhibit the proper mix of inexperience and incipient damnation."

It went without saying that Lilia herself would stay out of camera range—hers was not the look or age range being aimed for. As the crew began setting up inside, the male model said something to Katya that Lilia couldn't hear. In reply Katya looked down at him and pointed to her shoes. The guy wilted.

Scarlet Jones and Bret wore sunglasses as they basked in the photographer's lights. Felice had them change into white silk tops that rested off their shoulders. Lilia noticed that the bites on their necks were deeper and thought these new blouses looked somehow familiar.

Felice turned to her and said, "Of course you recognize the original Herrault design from the last Nightwalker go-round. Maison Herrault itself OK'd these knock-offs.

"I was afraid we'd have to go to Indonesia for production. Time delay on a fad like this can be fatal. But Hurrah for the Recession! Suddenly there are sweatshops in the Bronx—fast, cheap, and with passable quality."

Lilia looked away lest Felice smile. But she heard the other say, "Reliquary will get a six-week exclusivity period after which they'll be sold at other specialty shops throughout North America and world markets. Then," her mouth turned downward, "Bloomingdales, Macy's, and by next summer, Target." She and the young man adjusting Scarlet and Bret's clothes both shuddered.

"Here's a little surprise," said Katya, "someone you'll remember from the 'good' old days."

Paulo somewhat gingerly ushered in a tiny, ancient woman. As she entered this woman briskly flicked a cigarette butt on the sidewalk while reaching into the formless smock she wore to draw out and light another one.

Lilia looked on amazed. This was the legendary Marguerite,

"The Seamstress Extraordinary," as she'd been called back in the old Garment District. It was said that Marguerite could, without measuring, without even looking, cut a sleeve or a pant leg to exactly the length needed.

That afternoon Marguerite smoked one Gauloises after another. Requests that she stop were met with shrugs, coughs, and mumbles in barely recognizable English, "A vice like any other!"

"Amazed?" Paulo murmured to Lilia.

"That she's not dead," Lilia said.

"Not in the usual sense anyway," he replied. "She's become a sort of curator for Herrault. His emissary in this world."

In the old days Marguerite was employed at the prestigious Maison Herrault's New York branch and lent out to old friends of the late designer. She would always be brought along on fashion shoots in cases of an emergency.

One had arisen in Reliquary just before she appeared. The lapel of the top Bret wore wouldn't lay open at the angle the photographer wanted. Marguerite reached up for Bret's ear, pulled his head down to her eye level and with a needle, thread, and scissors from inside her smock, made three stitches and fixed the lapel in place.

Decades before as a naïve young intern Lilia had first encountered Marguerite. It was in a room slightly larger than a closet at the Studio Building where all fashion photography was done back in that day.

There, with fabric fragments thick on the floor, Marguerite stitched buttons onto a waistband while she squinted at the airshaft outside the window and sipped from a small glass of what young Lilia supposed was red wine.

She had been told to take a pair of women's flared slacks and have Marguerite turn them into culottes. This was an emergency, a great crisis—the shoot was to feature culottes but the garment in question did not yet exist. Marguerite was present for just such moments. She had looked at Lilia with disgust and disapproval as if she was about to send her back to the kitchen with the demand that she be properly braised.

Then, with scarcely a glance at the design sketch Lilia gave her, Marguerite had snipped off one leg, with a second slice snipped the other and cuffed both with a few stitches. She muttered "voila," blew smoke in Lilia's face, and shoved the garment at her.

Recalling this, Lilia watched Marguerite finger the tops Scarlet and Bret wore. "Instant prêt a porter!" the old woman muttered to herself. "For such a venue anything more than off-the-rack would not do."

Herrault had been a contemporary of Chanel, protégé of Schiaparelli, lover of Mainbocher, rival of Dior. His "Sang Chaud" Collection, the master's last great triumph, had defined the look of the prior Nightwalker craze.

His slacks, jackets, skirts, and gowns draped the wearer almost rigidly. But his tops were open, flowing. "The throat too is an erogenous zone," he famously said, "I believe the ultimate one." His firm, Maison Herrault, carried on his cult.

Behind Lilia, Katya whispered, "We're doing it backwards this time. First come these knockoffs with a certain flair."

"Herrault's name will never be officially connected with any of this," said Felice. "But the look will be pushed in places like *Our Daily Shmata*. Images being shot today will turn up in every online post about the dark new trend."

"Next Spring Maison Herrault will put out a line that incorporates this 'street fashion,' " said Paulo. "We aim for a quick kill and exit."

The kid's body, restless, started dribbling the heavy soccer ball on the floor. Even Marguerite noticed and winced.

Lilia concentrated on the six weeks in which these tops would be hers alone to sell.

Late the next day Lilia began seeing images of the shoot on websites like "Stuff I Saw Last Night." One favorite was a shot of Reliquary taken at dusk from across the street. Felice's copy ran with it: *Nightwalkers are all dark glamour, forbidden fashion.*

In the photo, a young guy dressed casually and walking on the sidewalk was caught by surprise and held by the gaze of a woman whose dark clothes seemed to blend into the shadows in which she stood. The silk scarf around her elegant neck flowed over her shoulders as if blown in a night breeze.

The lighted shop windows behind them displayed pairs of manikins echoing the live models' poses. One had the sexes of Nightwalker and potential recruit reversed; in the other both were the same sex.

She scrolled past shots of the interior with Scarlet, Bret, and company caught in moments of beauty and mystery. Interspersed with this was more copy:

They're the newest thing!

They're exclusive, an ultimate in-group.

You rarely see an unattractive Child of the Night! And you never meet a dull one!

Those words came back to Lilia after dark on an evening in the short days of November. A young *Vogue* editor, favored by the Kindly Ones and aiming to steal a prime place in the February book was shooting a secret preview of Maison Herrault's Fall/Winter collection. Marguerite was on hand.

The Children of the Night were trendy again but Lilia, feeling frumpy and old, was shoved once more into a corner of her own shop. She wore a leather choker under her turtleneck sweater.

The leather held evidence of a few token love bites and at least one deep and sincere chomp which customers had sent her way in the last few days. Lilia remembered the soft glow a bite could give both vampire and victim. But she was not going to get hooked like last time.

She was not alone in her corner. Larry had come in as the *Vogue* crew was setting up. Immediately the ethereal young guy with whom he entered was seized by the editor. "Wherever did you find him! Surely he'll want to be part of this!" The young man went with the editor and never once glanced back.

Larry, looking frazzled and worn, told Lilia, "There's going to be a divorce settlement but not as big as I'd thought. He threatens to bring up vampires as regards visiting rights with Ai-Ling."

"You've been down before," Lilia found herself saying, bucking him up just as in the old days. "Like I was until recently," she added to let him know she hadn't forgotten his decades of neglect.

He winced and said, "There's stuff I regret."

"Me too. Nightwalker life was wild fun at first. Then came the pain of kicking the blood habit."

"Ichordone therapy," he said. "Methadone for vampires. It was torture. I came out of that cured and brainwashed into thinking all I wanted was to find a rich mate, have a nice life and raise children."

"You made it clear the future wouldn't include me," she said.

"I wish I was as sure of anything now as I was of EVERYTHING right then," he said. It was as close to an apology as he was likely to give.

Lilia noted with some relish his unsuccessful attempts to catch the eye of the guy he'd come with. But she felt a pang of regret when Larry gave up, said good-night, and exited.

Under the lights Marguerite, cigarette dangling from the corner of her mouth, subdued a recalcitrant ruffle with a swift succession of scissor snips.

Lilia remembered the second episode of their long ago encounter in the Studio Building. A terrible mistake had occurred! The flared slacks had been turned into culottes. BUT the former slacks themselves were needed for a shot that HAD to be done.

The photographer and the art director were afraid to face the Seamstress Extraordinary, so Lilia was sent again. When she appeared and stuttered through her request, Marguerite had glared at her while fingering the scissors. She pointed at the slacks legs on the floor. Lilia stooped and handed them to her.

Marguerite slugged the last contents of the glass down, picked up a threaded needle. Again without looking the ageless woman stitched a leg together once, twice, perhaps six times.

The juncture was almost invisible to the eye and certainly could be to the camera. She handed the slacks back to Lilia. "But the other leg," said the girl.

"En silhouette," said the woman, sank back on a stool and closed her eyes, "one side only," she added.

"I can't take it back like this!"

In a move like a snake, the woman grabbed Lilia's left hand. With scissors she cut the girl's index finger; squeezed out bubbles of blood and avidly lapped them all off. She repeated this a few times then picked up the slacks and again with no more than six stitches created a seamless whole. Lilia, in tears, picked up the garment with her unbloodied hand and fled.

For the rest of that day she floated in a world where light blurred her vision into color patterns, where hysterical photographers and art directors existed in a distant place and nothing touched her.

Only later when she and Larry entered the world of the Nightwalkers did Lilia understand that what she'd felt had been just a small corner of the wonder of the Bite. At that point she also had not faced the horrid downside of withdrawal.

At Reliquary the night of the *Vogue* shoot Lilia didn't notice Marguerite beside her until the old woman grabbed her hair and pulled her head down. With a tiny shears she snipped the leather choker on Lilia's neck and bit her long and deep.

"This is not a game for tourists and amateurs," she hissed as Lilia floated in a blood high. "You will not stand apart and be amused at the workings of my world."

Late that February all was celebratory in the Savage Design conference room. Maison Herrault had triumphed in New York and Paris. The *Vogue* layout, all dark elegance and pale skin, was displayed on the walls.

Marguerite and the Kindly Ones were very pleased with their shares of the proceeds. Lilia sat as far away from everyone as possible. She floated on the remnants of the prior night's blood buzz and gazed at the artwork through sunglasses.

Under the photos were blocks of Felice's copy. One was: *Fashion is a cyclical phenomenon—the newest sensation withers but never dies.*

Another was: *An amazing top found in a vintage thrift store, a haircut seen in the old photo: we are fascinated and want more. A look, a style starts again.*

Paulo had a yo-yo in each hand. His left was slack, his right performed Shoot the Moon. "We found the boomlet and played it perfectly," he said. "By spring it will be nasty and we'll be nowhere nearby."

He turned to Marguerite. "It's always an inspiration to work with Maison Herrault."

Marguerite said, "An old vice gives comfort like any old habit." She got up slowly and went to the door. "Until next time."

The Kindly Ones rose, made little waves with their fingers but kept their distance as the ancient woman exited.

"Remember us to M. Herrault," Felice said.

"In whatever corner of hell he occupies," Paulo added when Marguerite was gone. "Undying but at what cost?" The ancient voice wondered.

"Something to consider as old age closes in," said Katya.

They all looked relieved to turn and see Lilia also on her feet and clearly leaving. "Nice working with you," Paulo said in parting. "Maybe again someday."

Lilia glanced back to see Katya put her feet in glistening

new ankle boots up on the table. They all picked up copies of a proposal.

Paulo's right hand kept on with Shoot the Moon, while his left began doing Skyrocket to Mars. The yo-yos orbited around one another as he said, "Here's a related investment opportunity we might look at."

Reliquary was jumping, if that word could be used to describe the cold, covert way Nightwalkers shop for clothes and stalk each other for blood. In the crowded store each one stared and got stared at from behind dark glasses.

Two cash registers were working. At one Scarlet Jones wore a blood red scarf from Maison Herrault around her neck. Her face immobile, her skin dead white, fang tips visible though her mouth was closed, she racked up sales without seeming aware she was doing so. Bret more or less bagged the purchases.

Just as attractions the two were worth far more than they were paid and even a good deal more than they stole. Lilia calculated that around the start of the summer this would no longer be true.

By then Reliquary and the Vampire Revival would be edging their way into the limbo reserved for old fads and she'd have accumulated a nest egg.

Already the store's customers were largely from New Jersey and outer boroughs. Complaints from the neighbors about the crowds were making her landlord nervous. Building and fire inspectors had put in their appearances and an unmarked car with plainclothes cops sometimes parked across the street.

Lilia sat on a stool and watched it all through a mild haze. The trick she told herself was to keep the nips and bites small and the haze manageable. She remembered the bone-wracking horrors of withdrawal too well to want a repeat.

Just then Larry came in the door looking sloppy and vulnerable. He scanned the customers, all of whom ignored him.

Lilia and he had begun hanging around, talking over old times at CBGB's and the Mudd Club. She'd bitten him once or twice—playfully, with a bit of vengeance thrown in. Her teeth were hardly fangs.

She wanted to make sure he didn't blow the money he got in the divorce settlement. While the Kindly Ones had said their good-bys to Marguerite that last time at Savage Design, Lilia had managed to get a couple of glimpses of the investment proposal on their table.

They were involved in the development of a Betty Ford style clinic for vampires on an estate up the Hudson. Kids like Scarlet, Bret, and many others had families able to pay for their recoveries.

Lilia intended to invest Larry's money. If that worked out she might invest some of her own savings. He crossed the shop towards her and she watched his throat.

BESPOKE

GENEVIEVE VALENTINE

Disease Control had sprayed while Petra was asleep, and her boots kicked up little puffs of pigment as she crunched across the butterfly wings to the shop.

Chronomode (*Fine Bespoke Clothing of the Past*, the sign read underneath) was the most exclusive Vagabonder boutique in the northern hemisphere. The floors were real date-verified oak, the velvet curtains shipped from Paris in a Chinese junk during the six weeks in '58 when one of the Vagabonder boys slept with a Wright brother and planes hadn't been invented.

Simone was already behind the counter arranging buttons by era of origin. Petra hadn't figured out until her fourth year working there that Simone didn't live upstairs, and Petra still wasn't convinced.

As Petra crossed the floor, an oak beam creaked.

Simone looked up and sighed. "Petra, wipe your feet on the mat. That's what it's for."

Petra glanced over her shoulder; behind her was a line of her footprints, mottled purple and blue and gold.

The first client of the day was the heiress to the O'Rourke fortune. Chronomode had a history with the family; the first one was the boy, James, who'd slept with Orville Wright and ruined Simone's drape delivery par avion. The O'Rourkes had generously paid for shipment by junk, and one of the plugs they sent back with James was able to fix things so that the historic flight was only two weeks late. Some stamps became very collectible, and the O'Rourkes became loyal clients of Simone's.

They gave a Vagabonding to each of their children as 21st birthday presents. Of course, you had to be twenty-five before you were allowed to Bore back in time, but somehow exceptions were always made for O'Rourkes, who had to fit a lot of living into notoriously short life spans.

Simone escorted Fantasy O'Rourke personally to the center of the shop, a low dais with a three-frame mirror. The curtains in the windows were already closed by request; the O'Rourkes liked to maintain an alluring air of secrecy they could pass off as discretion.

"Ms. O'Rourke, it's a pleasure to have you with us," said Simone. Her hands, clasped behind her back, just skimmed the hem of her black jacket.

Never cut a jacket too long, Simone told Petra her first day. It's the first sign of an amateur.

"Of course," said Ms. O'Rourke. "I haven't decided on a destination, you know. I thought maybe Victorian England."

From behind the counter, Petra rolled her eyes. Everyone wanted Victorian England.

Simone said, "Excellent choice, Ms. O'Rourke."

"On the other hand, I saw a historian the other day in the listings who specializes in 18th-century Japan. He was delicious." She smiled. "A little temporary surgery, a trip to Kyoto's geisha district. What would I look like then?"

"A vision," said Simone through closed teeth.

Petra had worked at a tailor downtown for three years after her apprenticeship there was over. She couldn't manage better, and had no hopes.

Simone came in two days after a calf-length black pencil skirt had gone out (some pleats under the knee needed mending).

Her gloves were black wool embroidered with black silk thread. Petra couldn't see anything but the gloves around the vast and smoky sewing machine that filled the tiny closet where she worked, but she knew at once it was the woman who belonged to the trim black skirt.

"You should be working in my shop," said Simone. "I offer superior conditions."

Petra looked over the top of the rattling machine. "You think?"

"You can leave the attitude here," said Simone, and went to the front of the shop to wait.

Simone showed Petra her back office (nothing but space and light and chrome), the image library, the labeled bolts of cloth—1300, 1570, China, Flanders, Rome.

"What's the name?" Petra asked finally.

"Chronomode," Simone said, and waited for Petra's exclamation of awe. When none came, she frowned. "I have a job for you," she continued, and walked to the table, tapping the wood with one finger. "See what's left to do. I want it by morning, so there's time to fix any mistakes."

The lithograph was a late 19th-century evening gown, nothing but pleats, and Petra pulled the fabrics from the library with shaking hands.

Simone came in the next day, tore out the hem, and sewed it again by hand before she handed it over to the client.

Later Petra ventured, "So you're unhappy with the quality of my work."

Simone looked up from a Byzantine dalmatic she was sewing with a bone needle. "Happiness is not the issue," she said, as though Petra was a simpleton. "Perfection is."

That was the year the mice disappeared.

Martin Spatz, the actor, had gone Vagabonding in 8,000 BC and killed a wild dog that was about to attack him. (It was a blatant violation of the rules—you had to be prepared to die in the past, that was the first thing you signed on the contract. He went to jail over it. They trimmed two years off because he used a stick, and not the pistol he'd brought with him.)

No one could find a direct connection between the dog and the mice, but people speculated. People were still speculating, even though the mice were long dead.

It was only some plants left, and butterflies. By the next year the butterflies were swarming enough to block out the summer sun, and Disease Control began to intervene.

The slow, steady disappearance of plants and animals was the only lasting problem from all the Vagabonding. Plugs were more loyal to their mission than the people who employed them, and if someone had to die in the line of work they were usually happy to do it. If they died, glory; if they lived, money.

Petra measured a plug once (German Renaissance, which seemed a pointless place to visit, but Simone never questioned the customers). He didn't say a word for the first hour. Then he said, "The cuffs go two inches past the wrist, not one and a half."

"Don't hurt yourself talking," Petra said. "Hold out your arm, please."

The client came back the next year with a yen for Colonial America. He brought two different plugs with him.

Petra asked, "What happened to the others?"

"They did their jobs," the client said, turned to Simone. "Now, Miss Cardew, I was thinking I'd like to be a British commander. What do you think of that?"

"I would recommend civilian life," Simone said. "You'll find the Bore committee a little strict as regards impersonating the military."

When Petra was very young she'd taken her mother's sewing machine apart and put it back together. After that it didn't squeak, and Petra and her long thin fingers were sent to the tailor's place downtown for apprenticeship.

"At least you don't have any bad habits to undo," Simone had said the first week, dropping *The Dressmaker's Encyclopaedia 1890* on Petra's work table. "Though it would behoove you to be a little ashamed of your ignorance. Why—" Simone looked away and blew air through her teeth. "Why do this if you don't respect it?"

"Don't ask me—I liked engines," Petra said, opened the book with a thump.

Ms. O'Rourke decided at last on an era (18th-century Kyoto, so the historian must have been really good-looking after all), and Simone insisted on several planning sessions before the staff was even brought in for dressing.

"It makes the ordering process smoother," she said.

"Oh, it's nothing, I'm easy to please," said Ms. O'Rourke.

Simone looked at Petra. Petra feigned interest in buttons.

Petra was assigned to the counter, and while Simone kept Ms. O'Rourke in the main room with the curtains discreetly drawn, Petra spent a week rewinding ribbons on their spools and looking at the portfolios of Italian armor-makers. Simone was considering buying a set to be able to gauge the best wadding for the vests beneath.

Petra looked at the joints, imagined the pivots as the arm moved back and forth. She wondered if the French hadn't had a better sense of how the body moved; some of the Italian stuff just looked like an excuse for filigree.

When the gentleman came up to the counter he had to clear his throat before she noticed him.

She put on a smile. "Good morning, sir. How can we help you?"

He turned and presented his back to her—three arrows stuck out from the left shoulder blade, four from the right.

"Looked sideways during the Crusades," he said proudly. "Not recommended, but I sort of like them. It's a souvenir. I'd like to keep them. Doctors said it was fine, nothing important was pierced."

Petra blinked. "I see. What can we do for you?"

"Well, I'd really like to have some shirts altered," he said, and when he laughed the tips of the arrows quivered like wings.

"You'd never catch me vagabonding back in time," Petra said that night.

Simone seemed surprised by the attempt at conversation (after five years she was still surprised). "It's lucky you'll never have the money, then."

Petra clipped a thread off the buttonhole she was finishing.

"I don't understand it," Simone said more quietly, as though she were alone.

Petra didn't know what she meant.

Simone turned the page on her costume book, paused to look at one of the hair ornaments.

"We'll need to find the ivory one," Simone said. "It's the most beautiful."

"Will Ms. O'Rourke notice?"

"I give my clients the best," Simone said, which wasn't really an answer.

"I've finished the alterations," Petra said finally, and held up one of the shirts, sliced open at the shoulder blades to give the arrows room, with buttons down the sides for ease of dressing.

Petra was surprised the first time she saw a Bore team in the shop—the Vagabond, the historian, the translator, two plugs, and a "Consultant" whose job was ostensibly to provide a life story for the client, but who spent three hours insisting that Roman women could have worn saris if the Empire had sailed far enough.

The Historian was either too stupid or too smart to argue, and Petra's protest had been cut short by Simone stepping forward to suggest they discuss jewelry for the Historian and plausible wardrobe for the plugs.

"Why, they're noble too, of course," the client had said, adjusting his high collar. "What else could they be?"

Plugs were always working-class, even Petra knew that—in case you had to stay behind and fix things for a noble who'd mangled the past, you didn't want to run the risk of a rival noble faction calling for your head, which they tended strongly to do.

Petra tallied the cost of the wardrobe for a Roman household: a million in material and labor, another half a million in jewelry. With salaries for the entourage and the fees for machine management and operation, his vacation would cost him ten million.

Ten million to go back in time in lovely clothes, and not be allowed to change a thing. Petra took dutiful notes and marked in the margin, A WASTE.

She looked up from the paper when Simone said, "No."

The client had frowned, not used to the word. "But I'm absolutely sure it was possible—"

"It may be possible depending on your source," Simone said, with a look at the historian, "but it is not *right*."

"Well, no offense, Miss Carew, but I'm paying you to dress me, not to give me your opinion on what's right."

"Apologies, sir," said Simone, smiling. "You won't be paying me at all. Petra, please show the gentlemen out."

They made the papers; Mr. Bei couldn't keep from talking about his experience in the Crusades.

"I was going to plan another trip right away," he was quoted as saying, "but I don't know how to top this! I think I'll be staying here. The Institute has already asked me to come and speak about the importance of knowing your escape plan in an emergency, and believe me, I know it."

Under his photo was the tiny caption: Clothes by Chronomode.

"Mr. Bei doesn't mention his plugs," Petra said, feeling a little sick. "Guess he wasn't the only one that got riddled with arrows."

"It's what the job requires. If you have the aptitude, it's excellent work."

"It can't be worth it."

"Nothing is worth what we give it," said Simone. She dropped her copy of the paper on Petra's desk. "You need to practice your running stitch at home. The curve on that back seam looks like a six-year-old made it."

Tibi cornered Petra at the Threaders' Guild meeting. Tibi worked at Mansion, which outfitted Vagabonders with a lot more pomp and circumstance than Simone's two-man shop.

Tibi had a dead butterfly pinned to her dress, and when she hugged Petra it left a dusting of pale green on Petra's shoulder.

"Petra! Lord, I was JUST thinking about you! I passed Chronomode the other day and thought, Poor Petra, it's SUCH a prison in there. Holding up?" Tibi turned to a tall young tailor beside her. "Michael, darling, Petra works for Carew over at Chronomode."

The tailor raised his eyebrows. "There's a nightmare. How long have you hung in there, a week?"

Five years and counting. "Sure," Petra said.

"No, for AGES," Tibi corrected. "I don't know how she makes it, I really don't, it's just so HORRIBLE." Tibi wrapped one arm around the tailor and cast a pitying glance at Petra. "I was there for a week, I made the Guild send me somewhere else a week later, it was just inhuman. What is it LIKE, working there for SO long without anyone getting you out of there?"

"Oh, who knows," said Petra. "What's it like getting investigated for sending people back to medieval France with machine-sewn clothes?"

Tibi frowned. "The company settled that."

Petra smiled at Tibi, then at the tailor. "I'm Petra."

"Michael," he said, and frowned at her hand when they shook.

"Those are just calluses from the needles," Petra said. "Don't mind them."

"Ms. O'Rourke's kimono is ready for you to look at," Petra said, bringing the mannequin to Simone's desk.

"No need," said Simone, her eyes on her computer screen, "you don't have enough imagination to invent mistakes."

Petra hoped that was praise; suspected otherwise.

A moment later Simone slammed a hand on her desk. "Damn it all, look at this. The hair ornament I need is a reproduction. Because naturally a 20th-century reproduction is indistinguishable from an 18th-century enamel original. The people of 1743 Kyoto will never notice.

"Are they hiring antiques dealers out of primary school these days?" Simone asked the computer, and left through the door to the shop, heels clicking.

Petra smoothed the front of the kimono. It was heavy grey silk, painted with cherry blossoms and chrysanthemums. Petra had added butterflies, purple and blue and gold.

The light in the shop was still on; Petra saw it just as she was leaving.

Careless, she thought as she crossed the workshop. Simone would have killed me.

She had one hand on the door when the sound of a footstep stopped her. Were they being robbed? She thought about the Danish Bronze-age brooches hidden behind the counter in their velvet wrappers.

Petra grabbed a fabric weight in her fist and opened the door a crack.

Simone stood before the fitting mirror, holding a length of bright yellow silk against her shoulders. It washed her out (she'd never let a client touch the stuff), but her reflection was smiling.

She hung it from her collarbones like a Roman; draped it across her shoulder like the pallav of a sari; bustled it around her waist. The bright gold slid through her fingers as if she was dancing with it.

Simone gathered the fabric against her in two hands, closed her eyes at the feel of it against her face.

Petra closed the door and went out the back way, eyes fixed on the wings at her feet.

When she came around the front of the shop, the light was still on in the window, and Simone stood like a doll wrapped in a wide yellow ribbon, imagining a past she'd never see.

Petra turned for home.

Disease Control hadn't made the rounds yet, and the darkness was a swarm of wings, purple and blue and gold.

DRESS CODE

SANDRA McDONALD

Here's a tip if you're hoping to be bumped up to First Class: no butt cracks. No sagging sweatpants, scuffed trainers, or rubber sandals that show off your gnarled toenails. Dress like a slob and you'll stay crammed back in Economy, along with all the other passengers who couldn't be bothered to iron their shirts. When we're overbooked and need to upgrade a passenger, I'm choosing the man in a well-cut suit with a crisp shirt, smart tie and leather shoes. A silk pocket square of any color or pattern makes my knees go weak; a waistcoat will make me swoon.

"You should have been a fashion designer, Colleen," says my friend Linda, whenever we work together. "You spend every flight obsessing about men's clothes."

Not true. During short hauls, we're too busy to do much other than solve problems and serve drinks. Being an air hostess is sometimes no more glamorous than being a barmaid back home in Dublin. On long hauls over the Atlantic, however, hours of boredom may lead to speculation, fantasizing, and envy. Sometimes I'll compliment a passenger, flatter his taste, and pick up the names of exclusive tailors in Paris, London, or Milan. I tell them the information is for my boyfriend—as if I had one, or that he could ever get buzzed past the front door, but that's not really the point.

Meanwhile I spend every flight in a white polyester blouse,

green polyester jacket and green polyester slacks. All that green makes me look airsick. The only reason I work for this airline is that all the others in the European Union make female attendants wear skirts, and I won't.

"Auntie Colleen doesn't like frills," is how my sister explains it.

No frills, no lace, no perfume, no fancy haircuts; just me, with my short dark hair and absolutely minimum makeup (stupid regulations) and the lowest heels I can get away with. Transcontinental flights are hard on the body enough without shoes that pinch your toes or heels.

Like tonight, for instance. We're thirty thousand miles over the ocean and four hours from Boston. Most of my First Class passengers are asleep but 5B keeps ringing his bell: another soda water please, a ballpoint pen please, do I have another pillow? If I have to get up one more time—

The plane bounces on turbulence. Pain cramps through my uterus. I grab the edges of my folding seat and bow over a little.

"Are you okay?" Linda asks.

"Fine," I lie. "It's that time of the month."

In the lavatory, I try to will the pain away. But you can't deny Sorrow when she comes riding on the winds with her red eyes weeping. Someone on this plane is about to die or lose a loved one. Maybe 3A, immaculate in pinstripe Yves St. Laurent, will suffer a stroke. Maybe 5B will meet his fate in traffic, regardless of his H. Huntsman tweed sports coat. Maybe Sorrow is coming for the woman in Economy who tried to sneak herself past the curtain to the first class lavatory, or for the American soldier a few rows behind her.

Another cramp cuts through me. Sorrow swirls around the fuselage, snakes writhing in her hair. Her tears rattle the hull like hail. We bounce again. The fasten seatbelt indicator chimes and lights up.

I begin to sing a lament. A soft, lilting tune meant to soothe Sorrow. Sleeping passengers might hear it in their dreams, but most won't notice a single note. Not unless they carry the blood of the Great Houses. She's coming for one of them or one of their kin.

Hunched over on the toilet lid, I sing and sing.

I'm twenty-four years old and I'm a banshee. Unlicensed, unsanctioned. Illegal.

Luckily no one on this flight is likely to report me to the Queen of the Fairies for a code violation.

When Sorrow departs and I step back outside, Linda's flipping through the pages of a magazine. The first class passengers are all asleep or absorbed in their computers. I peek past the curtain to Economy, and most of them are dozing as well.

The American soldier is awake, though. He's a muscled fellow with a square jaw and short dark hair. He's gripping the aisle armrest as if he wants to rip it off, and his gaze is fixed out the window at the wing. Later, when I'm in the jetway and passengers are disembarking, I can see the nametag sewn on his jacket: O'Neill. One of the greatest houses in all of Irish history.

Chances are, I was singing for him. But he'll never know, and our paths will never cross again. Small shame, that. He's handsome indeed, and he wears his uniform well: steel-tipped boots, a well-fitted top, a cap snug on his head. A girl like me could use an outfit like that. Maybe it's not too late for me to join the army.

A week later, I'm sleeping off a late flight in my tiny apartment in Dublin when my phone buzzes: *See Maeve.*

Two simple words, but better than an entire pot of coffee for waking me up. After a hot shower, I pull on a blue and gray sweater vest and pressed trousers and waterproof boots. November in Dublin's not a kind season, so I add a gray trenchcoat as well.

"Still you dress like a boy," says Loman when I let myself into the office not far from O'Connell Bridge.

"And still you sound like a tea kettle crawled up your sinuses," I retort. Loman's a leprechaun, but you wouldn't know it unless you had the Sight. Otherwise he's just another short man with a prim mustache and poor taste in off-the-rack suits.

"And your so very pleasant disposition, also unchanged," he sniffs. "Don't drip on the carpet."

The office resembles a tiny accounting firm stranded in time, with typewriters and carbon paper and a rotary phone. The faded newspapers on the table still talk about the Troubles. But it's not as if someone's likely to stumble by and notice; you have to have fey blood in you just to find the front door. Maeve's inner office is barely big enough for a desk, a filing cabinet, and a window that overlooks the Liffey River.

And for Maeve herself, six feet and six inches tall, with fiery red hair and bright white teeth. She looks my age, but she's looked that way since I was a little girl squirming on my mother's knee. I ignore women's fashion as much as possible but let's just say that A-line skirt doesn't flatter her hips at all.

"Colleen," she says, and invites me into a hug.

Keep in mind that she's not human, our Maeve. Hugging her is like trying to wrap your arms around an enormous oak, something rough and ancient and thrumming with life. You have to be careful not to scrape your skin on the bark. When we sit down, divided by her messy desk, I feel like she squeezed a year or two out of my life.

But she wouldn't do that without a warning. Usually.

"How's Air Killarney these days?" she asks. "Still serving the cheap whiskey?"

"Surely you've never been on a plane in your life, móraí," I reply, using the Gaelic word for grandmother.

Her eyes twinkle even though her mouth frowns. "But I hear stories, child. In particular, I hear a story that someone was singing a lament for the House O'Neill on Air Killarney flight 112 just a week ago."

"I don't know how you could possibly hear such a thing," I reply.

She pushes a piece of paper across the desk. It's a printout from Craigslist Dublin, in the "Missed Connections" section:

AK112 November 14 I heard a banshee sing. When we landed I found out my father had died. I know what I heard. Must talk to you. Please contact.

Beneath it was a phone number and email address for someone named John O'Neill.

"No one believes in banshees these days," I say, pushing the paper back. "He's just going to get crank calls and nasty messages."

Maeve folds her hands primly. "You sang. You know you're not supposed to and you did it anyway."

It's too hot in this little office, and too quiet. The loudest sound is the hissing of the steam radiator. Loman's probably pressed up to the door, eavesdropping on every word. I don't fidget, though, and I don't flinch. No matter how much I want to.

"No one can deny Sorrow, and you'd never ask me to," I tell her. "Turn your back on the wind and you're turning your back on shamrocks and potatoes and turf fires."

"Could you possibly be more cliché?" she chides.

"But it's the truth! Sorrow calls and we answer."

"Officially licensed banshees answer," Maeve says, her face gone steely. "In specific places and times. Don't you remember anything from your studies? 'Banshees may answer the call of Sorrow in forests, vales, crossroads, fields, bogs, marshes, and winding roads.' Not in a Boeing 747 zooming over the Atlantic Ocean!"

To be accurate, Air Killarney's long haul planes are all Airbus 330s. I don't think she cares.

Maeve sits back. "You've put us in a very awkward position."

"What position? We just ignore him."

"No banshee can ignore a summoning by an O'Neill," she replies. "It's in the oldest codes."

The phone rings in the outer office. The Great War of 1839 severely diminished the fairy race but their descendants, now bound by bureaucracy and regulations, still squabble. Queen Maeve is the one to call on to solve problems, arbitrate disagreements, and keep the peace. She also tracks down fairy folk who've gone missing or silent, and tries to keep our existence as secret as possible.

I tell her, "No officially approved banshee can ignore a summoning by an O'Neill. I'm not licensed, therefore I'm not required. Send Monnie. She'll do it."

"Your sister can't go jaunting off to America to solve a problem you created," she replies.

"Someone else, then," I say. "Someone who's *licensed*."

I don't dwell on it, really I don't, but it's one thing to be told you've got a great talent and quite another to be denied the chance to use it because you won't follow a silly rule or two.

Maeve's expression turns crafty. "Go and meet this O'Neill, and when you come back you can tell us all about it on Wren Day."

I haven't been invited to a fairy holiday gathering for four years now. It's not that I miss the carousing and the singing and the food, but it would be nice to dance with my cousins again, the earth tingling beneath our bare feet.

She pushes the paper back across the desk. "Meet him, find out what he wants, and politely decline it. And by all things sacred, no more lamenting on airplanes. At least wait until you get to baggage claim."

I don't have much choice here, so I pocket the information.

"Wear something nice!" Loman calls out, a parting zing. "You can't look like a boy in front of a Great House."

Just for that, I plan to wear the manliest things I own when I meet this John O'Neill.

Three days later I'm back in America. I telephone O'Neill from one of the last remaining payphones in Logan Airport and reach a voicemail. Around me, passengers scoop up their luggage and hurry outside into the blustery cold wind.

"If you're looking for the girl who sang on Flight 112, call me back right now," I say. "I won't be here long."

I figure he might need some proof that I'm not a prankster or crazy woman, so I sing a few notes and hang up.

The crew van has already left without me, meaning I'll have to take the bus to the hotel. I've been awake for about eighteen hours. To kill time I silently note every single fashion faux pas around me, including ill-fitting pants, clashing ties, soiled jackets, and cheap brown shoes. Honestly, some men should not be let out of their houses.

The phone rings. O'Neill sounds convinced, if a little cautious, as he says, "Thank you for calling me. Where are you?"

"The airport," I reply. "Just passing through."

"I'm in Marblehead. This time of day, it's about forty minutes away. Will you wait for me?"

"I can't meet you now," I tell him. Certainly not in my Air Killarney uniform, and not when I'm so dead tired that my eyeballs feel swollen. "How about four o'clock? There's a pub in Revere called The Broken Mug. Near City Hall. Meet me there."

"How will I know you?"

"I'll be the only one with a silver comb in my hair," I say.

Seven hours later, after a shamefully small amount of sleep, I put on black slacks and a reasonably feminine dark red blouse. This is the only blouse I own. Actually, Monnie owns it, but she let me borrow it. All personal vows aside, it's probably best to blend in when I meet O'Neill. Hair as short as mine is easy to recognize, so I conjure a simple glamour to make it seem long and curly. I don't have a coat but the cab ride is mercifully short and the pub is warm. It's the kind of place long past its glory, if it ever had a glory to begin with, but the ale is good and the patrons mind their own business.

John O'Neill arrives at four o'clock sharp, wearing new black jeans, a blue sweater from Nautica, black boots and a vintage black leather coat. He's even more handsome than I remember. In the brief moment it takes for him to scan the pub and spy me, I can pretend that he's here for me, Colleen, and not some supernatural creature he heard on a midnight flight over the ocean.

I like men for more than just their clothes, after all.

As promised I'm wearing a silver comb in my hair. Traditional calling card of all banshees. He approaches my table carefully.

"You're here," he says.

"As agreed," I say. "Sit down."

He slides off his coat before he sits. Nice square shoulders, long arms, fingers that look deft enough to both fire a weapon and cradle a baby. He smells like woodsmoke.

"What do I call you?" John asks.

I want to tell him just to hear the syllables roll off his tongue. But some things are best unsaid. "It doesn't matter, Mr. O'Neill. We won't be meeting again."

He's staring at me in a way that's bordering on rude. I hope the glamour isn't flickering, or that I haven't somehow messed it up.

"How did you know my father was dying? We were over the middle of the ocean and he was here, at Mass General. Heart attack."

"That doesn't matter either." It's not as if Maeve told me to spill any banshee secrets, after all. "It's what we do. Sing a lament."

A muscle twitches along his jaw. "I've lost men in battle and you've never sung for them."

77

"They weren't your blood, and I wasn't in the neighborhood." I drink from the coffee in front of me. Straight coffee, nothing with a kick, because I'm flying in four hours. "I'm sorry for your father."

"Don't be. He wasn't—well, he was old. He was from here, Boston. My mother came from Galway. They married late and they had me late and now it's too late to say most of what I wanted—" Abruptly he stands up again. "Will you wait here while I get a drink?"

It's no hardship to watch him go to the bar and order a Guinness. Those jeans fit his backside quite well. He isn't wearing a wedding ring but surely he has a girlfriend somewhere, a woman who'd be wise not to let him out of her sight for too long. When he sits down again he says, "My mother told me all banshees are haggard old crones, toothless and gray haired. I'm glad she's wrong."

"Trick of the light," I say lightly. "I'm as cronish and ugly as they come."

"No, you're beautiful," he says, and then ducks his gaze. "I haven't been able to get your song out of my head."

Banshees don't enchant men. It's not our job. For a moment I worry that somehow I cast a spell or built the glamour too strongly.

Maeve will not be happy if I accidentally use fey magic to snare a human lover.

"Mr. O'Neill, why is it you had to speak to me so urgently?" I ask.

He lifts his head and eyes me squarely. "To find out if I was losing my mind. I'm on emergency leave from Iraq. I tried to get here before he died, but it was too late. When I go back, I have to know that my brain's not cracked or fried. Not that it matters to the U.S. Army . . . "

Despite myself, I touch his hand. His skin is warm but there's Sorrow inside him, swollen and raw. His father might have been a good man, or maybe not, but it's a rare son who can bury his father without cost.

"Your brain is fine, Mr. O'Neill. You won't hear me again."

"Never?" he asks.

I steel my resolve. "Our paths aren't likely to cross again. Honest truth, no denying it. I'm leaving tonight and won't be back this way soon. You're going back to Iraq. "

"Is there a way I can reach you? A cell phone, a post office box?"

The door opens to let in three men in the middle of a sports argument. They're loud, boisterous types, good-humored until they drink too much, bad-humored afterward. Just like many of my passengers. They remind me that I have to get back to the hotel, get myself in uniform, eat dinner, catch the van, and fly back across the Atlantic tonight.

"It's not in our best interests," I tell him.

"I think you're wrong," he said, again with that direct stare. "I think it would be completely in my interest to see you again."

It's been awhile since anyone flirted with me. But it's not me he's flirting with. It's a woman with long hair in a red blouse.

"I have to go," I tell him. "My condolences, again, on your father."

Out on the sidewalk, I see that he rode here on a motorcycle.

If ever Sorrow had reason to wail, it's because of men and their motorcycles. "Can I give you a ride somewhere?" he asks.

Banshees can lie just like anyone else. "No, my ride is coming."

He passes me his leather coat. "You'll freeze to death in the meantime. Take this."

His hands brush my shoulders as he helps pull it on. I think, under slightly different circumstances, he might try to kiss my cheek. And I'd let him. But the rawness is still in him, and it stings.

He goes his way and I go mine.

At the hotel I realized I don't have any way to return his jacket. Worse, still, he left his cell phone in the inside pocket. A nice silver gadget, one with all the latest apps. I call the number from the Craigslist ad but it goes to voicemail. I can't just leave it, so I take it with me on the flight and back in Dublin leave it in a kitchen drawer. The leather jacket, I wear to market. It smells like an American soldier and it looks good on me.

It's my luck to work on Thanksgiving. It's also my luck to catch the flu and spend the week afterward sick in bed, because being a banshee doesn't save you from tiny little bacteria of doom. And it's my luck that I'm just getting out of the shower, barely feeling well again, when my neighbor Mr. Hubbard comes knocking to borrow sugar again.

Except that the man on my door is not Mr. Hubbard at all.

"Sorry." John O'Neill eyes my oversized men's bathrobe and spiky wet hair. "Bad time?"

Dark circles stain the skin under his eyes, and he's got the sour smell of a man who's been cooped up recently on an airplane. He's wearing rumpled civilian clothes.

"How did you find me?" I ask.

"You have my phone. It has a GPS function."

"Did you plan that?" I ask angrily. "Lend me your jacket just so you could track it across the world?"

"No. I didn't plan it. But it was lucky for me that you turned it on while you were here," he says. "You cut your hair. It looks good."

Surely he's kidding. Very few men like short hair on a woman. They think we're lesbians or man-haters. But he seems sincere.

"Can I come in?" He holds up a paper bag. "I brought bagels. With nutella. I don't like nutella, but I thought maybe you would."

So, yes, I'm angry he came looking for me, but let's be frank. My doorstep hasn't seen this fine a man since the bathroom flooded and the landlord sent Thomas the plumber. Shabby clothes but a chiseled jaw and lovely biceps, that Thomas.

"It's a mess inside," I warn him.

"I live in a barracks with a dozen unwashed men. When they throw their underwear aside, sometimes it sticks to the wall."

I grimace. He grimaces, too, and says, "Sorry, I've been awake for twenty hours."

"Just to come see me?"

"It's my mother," he says. "She's dying."

Once inside, seated at my breakfast table, he tells the whole tale. He'd barely been settled back with his unit in Iraq before the Red Cross delivered another message. His mother has fallen ill and is not expected to survive much longer. He's the only child, no close relatives to speak of, and she needs him. Also, she asked for him to bring home the "girl who sang" for his father.

"I know it's an imposition," he says. "But it's a dying woman's wish and I'd be in your debt."

It's hard to look him in the eye. "I'm sorry about your mother, but I'm not allowed. I'm not properly qualified. It's a special thing that requires a special person. But I can find you one . . . "

"I don't need anyone else," he says. "You're qualified enough. You sang for him and you can sing for her. For me, when she goes. I won't have anyone left."

"I'm not licensed, Mr. O'Neill. I don't have permission. I didn't pass the exam. I didn't even take it."

He looks puzzled. "Why not?"

Some things are better shown than told. "Come this way, and please ignore my terrible housekeeping."

On the mantel in my living room wall is a portrait of my mother in her official garb. Her black gown flows like liquid off her shoulders. Her hair blows backward in the wind. A vintage photo of my grandmother, taken on the moors, is propped next to it. Her wool gown is steel gray, and she wears a frilly shawl.

"To be a banshee you have to look the part," I tell him. "I don't even own a single dress."

John scratches his head. "They don't pay you enough at the airline?"

"It's not about money." I drag him into my bedroom. "There. That's my closet. That's what I like and that's what I wear."

For a long moment he stares at the pleated trousers and pants, the pinstripe shirts and wool sports coats, the half-zip sweaters and sweater vests. Boxes of men's shoes and boots are stacked on the shelves and ties hang neatly on a rack.

"You wear your boyfriend's clothes?" he asks.

I cross my arms over my chest. "They're mine. Next, ask me if I'm a lesbian. Because that's what they call women who don't like to wear frills and lace and dresses barely to the thigh, right?"

John reaches out and runs his fingers along a linen jacket.

I wait for him to make some scathing comment.

He says, "You have great taste. Now, what will it take to get you packed and on a plane for Boston?"

"You said I can't say no to an O'Neill," I tell Maeve. "So here we are."

Maeve's standing at her office door, which is barely cracked open. Through it, she's eyeing John O'Neill sitting by the coat rack. I left him with Loman, who squeaked like a mouse when I brought a human through the front door. Maeve says, "Handsome one, isn't he?"

This is not what I want to hear. "Will you please tell him you forbid me from going to America and singing for his dying mother?"

Maeve swings open the door. "Mr. O'Neill! Such a pleasure to meet you in person."

John quickly stands up. "Thank you. Miss . . . "

"Call me Maeve." She shakes his hand robustly. "Your mother is from Galway, is she? What of her mother before her, and your great-grandmother?"

"I think they were all from Galway, too."

"It suffered terrible damage during the Oídhche na Gaoithe Móire," Maeve said.

He looks perplexed. "I don't speak Gaelic, ma'am."

"Night of the Big Wind," I put in. "It was a big storm. Damaged a lot of the country."

Historians and meteorologists know it as a devastating windstorm that wrecked houses, sank fishing boats, and brought a large storm surge to many low-lying villages. It also just happened to be the culmination of a century-long Fairy War that scattered the survivors and left a bitter taste for decades. It's not like Maeve to drop casual refeences to it in conversation, regardless of where John's great-grandmother might come from.

"I'm sadly uneducated in Irish history or customs," John tells Maeve. I don't think he's used to looking up to a woman taller than he is. "All I know is that Colleen says she needs your permission to attend to my mother's passing."

"Nonsense!" Maeve exclaims, to my utter shock. "I'm merely a consultant. I would never interfere with such a decision. Our Colleen is her own person, quite independent. As you can tell from her choice of attire."

His gaze focuses on me. "I think she looks great."

I blush.

"Go with my blessing," Maeve says, patting my head. "Send us a message to let us know you arrived safely. And my deepest sympathy to you, Mr. O'Neill, on your losses."

Which is how John and I end up as passengers on a British Airways flight to Boston three hours later. Nothing was available in First Class or Business, so we're jammed in Economy. John generously gives me the window and sits in the aisle next to a college student who sticks ear buds into his ears and plays computer games for six solid hours.

"Tell me about your clothes," John says, just as it seems like we'll be stuck on this plane forever. "When did you decide you hated dresses?"

I try not to sound defensive. "The minute my mother put me in one. Every day after school I'd rip off my uniform skirt and get into trousers. Girl's clothes just don't make sense. They're flimsy and frilly and make you look silly."

"I guess I should ditch my lace underwear," he says, his expression dry.

I gape at him. "You're not."

He smiles. "No. But I had a friend in boot camp who did. Big secret. Who cares?"

"Plenty of people."

"Let them worry about other things, like war and death." His smile fades then. He peers past me through the window at the flawless blue sky. "Do you know . . . is she dying? My mother?"

I squeeze his hand. "I don't sense anything."

He sits back in his seat. "She can't leave. Not yet."

Death doesn't work that way, but we both know that already.

Finally the flight ends with a town car and chauffer waiting for us in Boston. The car takes us north along the winding coastline. John is an army sergeant on a limited income but his parents' house in Marblehead is a white and gray mansion overlooking the ocean. It's getting to be dusk but the whitecaps on the ocean are clear, as is the smell of salt and seaweed.

"My father made his fortune in commercial fishing long before I was born," John says when he helps me out of the car. "I never even saw any of his boats."

A housekeeper greets us, followed by a male nurse in a blue uniform. I expected Mrs. O'Neill to be in a hospital but she obviously afford top-notch care here at home. She's up in a second-floor bedroom, sequestered behind white double doors, and John excuses himself to see to her.

My guest room is full of fine furniture and a view of the Atlantic Ocean, black and fathomless. The housekeeper says dinner will be ready soon. In the bathroom I freshen up and see that Loman has sent me a text message: *M wants to know how people can possibly endure air travel.*

As usual, he spells and punctuates everything perfectly.

I type back: *most of them get drunk.*

John knocks and opens the door. He's freshly showered and wearing clean clothes. "Mother wants me to sit with her. I think she's afraid she'll go tonight. Please eat, and feel free to ask Martha if you need anything."

There's no sense of Sorrow on the wind, no signs that she'll be wailing and crying in the dark. But some people know she's coming even before a banshee sings a lament.

"Don't worry about me," I say.

So I eat supper alone in the dining room. The house is very quiet. The housekeeper, Martha, says that Mrs. O'Neill asked for all family pictures to be put away, which explains the squares on the walls that don't match the rest of the paint. Afterward I walk the grounds, protected from the cold by my thick wool coat, and lean on a wall to watch the ocean crash on rocks below. A light shines steadily from Mrs. O'Neill's bedroom. Once or twice I think I see John's silhouette move behind the curtain. A deathwatch is a sad and lonely business, and he's endured so much loss: his men in battle, his father to the grips of time.

"How is it, to be around Death so much?" I'd once asked my mother, when I was much younger.

She'd brushed my bangs from my forehead and said, "What's it like to be around autumn and winter after the sweet summer?"

It's hard to get a straight answer out of a banshee.

Still there's no Sorrow here. Only the wind and sea spray, and my face turning numb in the cold. Back inside, I shed the coat and study myself in the mirror. Trousers, an Oxford shirt, loafers. I think about what my mother and sister would wear at a time like this and call the housekeeper.

"I'm sorry to bother you," I say, "but my luggage got mixed up. Is there . . . a blouse or something I can borrow?"

Martha eyes my body critically. "Wait here."

After several minutes she comes back with a shopping bag filled with neatly folded clothes. "You're about the same size as Mrs. O'Neill once was. She meant to donate these. Here, try this."

From the slacks and skirts she extracts a purple and black printed blouse with three-quarter length sleeves and beaded cuffs. It's flowing and pretty and completely unlike anything I would ever wear, but at least I don't have to ditch my black trousers.

"Looks lovely," Martha says, once I've changed. Her approval nearly sends me back into my oxford shirt. But this isn't about me, so I go down the hall and knock on Mrs. O'Neill's large doors. When John opens the door, I can see his eyes are red.

I say, "I wanted to say my respects before retiring. And I don't want you to be alone."

He glances backward. "I don't know . . . she doesn't want visitors."

Mrs. O'Neill's weak but clear voice says, "Let her in, John."

Her room is bigger than my apartment. The only light comes from a tall white lamp on the bedside table. John's mother is propped up against a sea of blue silk pillows in a four poster bed carved of oak. Above her is a painting of a tall ship, the kind that once carried Irish emigrants away from the famines to the promise of America.

But it's not the painting that makes me gasp, or the obvious luxury of the bedding, or even the familiar smell of heather from a pot of warm oil.

Instead it's Mrs. O'Neill herself—tiny, withered, her gray hair hanging long to her waist. To humans she appears quite normal. Anyone with the Sight would see the seaweed twined in her hand and silver scales covering her hands.

"John," I say. "You didn't tell me your mother was a merrow."

"A what?" John asks.

"He doesn't know," Mrs. O'Neill says. "Sit down, little Banshee. Tell me of Ireland, which I've missed these many years."

A merrow is what Americans might call a mermaid. Under the sea is where they live, and in the days before the Fairy Wars they were mortal enemies of the banshees for reasons lost to history. I don't think she's very dangerous—she seems too frail—but she's very old and there's power in old things.

There's a knock on the door that John just closed. I expect Martha the housekeeper, but instead it's a quite impossible sight: Maeve and Loman, looking disheveled from their first-ever transatlantic airplane flight.

Triumphantly Maeve says, "I knew it!"

"You're not dying," Maeve tells Mrs. O'Neill, some minutes later, from the chair beside the elderly woman's bed.

"I'm surely dying," Mrs. O'Neill says. "You can't feel like I do and not be dying."

Maeve tosses back her hair. "You're grieving, and that's a different kind of dying. But there's no Sorrow on the wind, is there, Colleen?"

"Not at all," I say.

Mrs. O'Neill sniffs delicately into a lace handkerchief. "I know what I know. But it's nice that you came all this way to say goodbye."

John asks, "Can someone please explain what's going on?"

Loman consults the small brown notebook he always keeps in his pocket. "Your mother went missing after the Night of the Big Wind in 1839 and was presumed dead, as many were. You are the product of her marriage to a mortal named John Jacob O'Neill, recently deceased—"

"Yes, he knows that," I say, interrupting. John doesn't need to be reminded about his own father. "But how did you know?"

"You can smell it," Maeve says. "He smells like the son

of a merrow and an O'Neill. I decided to come investigate immediately."

"I smell like a what?" John asks.

I sniff. "I can't smell anything."

"When you're as old as I am, you smell everything." Maeve turns back to Mrs. O'Neill. "Now then, the war was a terrible thing and many fine fairies died on both sides, but it's time to reconcile. What you need is a turf fire and some boiled potatoes and a leprechaun to sing you a song."

"Could you possibly be more cliché?" I mutter.

Loman puts away his notebook. "As a matter of fact, I sing quite well."

Maeve pats Mrs. O'Neill's knee. "We need merrows back in Ireland. Women who know the ways of the ocean and can teach the younger generations. They know nothing these days, the children. Come with me and we'll toast you on Wren Day."

John asks, "What's a Wren Day?"

"The men wear wrens on their head," Loman said. "Paper ones, these days. Not the dead ones. I know several wren songs, if you'd like."

Mrs. O'Neill waves her handkerchief again. "I'm too old for such a trip."

"You're no older than me," Maeve says. "Put aside that glamour you're wearing, pick out a nice dress, and let's have some supper. What they serve on airplanes isn't fit for pigs."

John takes his mother's hand. "If what they're saying is true, Mother, then please do whatever you can not to die. I can't lose you."

Mrs. O'Neill sighs. Her eyes water a bit. But she takes her

hand from John's, folds her fingers together, and bows her head. The smell of heather fades, replaced by salt and sea and a gust of wind from nowhere. Before our eyes, the illusion of an old woman dissolves to a young woman with beautiful brown hair and a smooth pale face.

"Ah, quite nice," Maeve says.

John steps backward from the bed. I bump up beside him, trying to look reassuring. This must be a bit overwhelming. But once things settle down, I hope to explain everything to him—banshees and fairy wars, merrows and men with wrens on their heads. He's a human but he's also half merrow, and this is his heritage as much as ours.

Mrs. O'Neill gazes plaintively at Maeve. "But I still miss my husband."

Maeve holds out her hand to help her rise. "As you will for a long, long time. But he would want you to live, and so does your son, and so do we all."

The merrow stands up. Her legs are strong and smooth now, her gait steady as she crosses the dark green carpet. She reaches up on tiptoes and kisses John's cheek. "My brave, strong son. I have so many things to tell you, so many stories to share."

"As do I," I promise him.

He pats his mother's cheek in wonder, then turns to me and gives me a sweet, warm kiss. My toes curl and my heart speeds up and hello, here's a man I hope to get to know much, much better as soon as possible.

"Tell me everything," he murmurs.

Maeve heads for the door with Loman right behind her. "First we eat."

Mrs. O'Neill doesn't move. She's gazing at me with sharp merrow eyes and keen disapproval. Jealousy over her son, I guess. I square my shoulders, prepared to withstand any objection or withering comment.

Instead she asks, "Is that my blouse?"

THE ANADEM

SHARON MOCK

"I have a question to ask of you," the nobleman said.

The man before me was either young or ageless, I couldn't tell which. Rosewood velvet and perfumed hair and not a care for social convention. He hadn't even granted me the courtesy of his name. If he'd come for a commission, he was making a bad start of it.

I nodded for him to continue, and begrudged him even that much of a response.

"Is this your work?" He held out his hand, manicured and unadorned. In his palm rested a brooch in the shape of a dobsonfly. I didn't recognize it, but it certainly looked like something I might have made.

I put on my glasses and took the brooch from his hand. There was the atelier's mark, underneath the pin. Student work, and old enough to be mine. The juxtaposition of coarse steel body and long opal wings, so witty to a youth, so obvious to one who's learned better. A hairline fracture ran the length of one wing, probably from the inlay being cut too thin. I'd use enamel now, if I were foolish enough to make an ornament out of such an ugly beast.

Any jeweler in the city could have told him who had made this piece. But I had too much pride to lay claim to it. "I don't remember it," I said, holding it out to him. "But it certainly could be."

He didn't take the brooch. He stared down at me patiently, as though he were waiting for me to notice something.

I looked closer. The workmanship was reasonable, the subject matter anything but. I'd clearly had some point to make, probably something about the tyranny of ornament, the contrast between delicate wings and vicious pincers. They shouldn't have let good opal go to such waste. Its patterns matched an insect wing so closely, it should have gone to a nice gold dragonfly, something a fashionable woman would actually wear.

It took me that long to realize what I was supposed to see. Opal didn't come in patterns like that straight out of the ground. The stone had changed—or something had changed it.

The dobsonfly rested warm in my hand. Too warm, like a living thing, and lighter than steel. And as I watched, its slender, rigid mandibles twitched.

I looked up at the man, and he smiled. Not young, then. Not young at all.

"I would like to offer you a commission, my lady," the sorcerer said.

The portrait of my commission's recipient sat on my workbench to inspire me. Delicate, fashionably pretty, though I suspected a fair bit of her beauty came off with the cosmetics. I had been her age, when I had first come here to study. I'd not had her advantages, but I considered that a blessing. They'd make a matched pair, the two of them, like a set of earrings.

For all I knew the woman was a sorceress in her own right, the gift an offering to her power. But I doubted it. A headpiece—I knew little about matters of magic, but even I could guess at its intention. Something to control the mind, to make the wearer docile and obedient.

This is why an artisan never takes commissions from a sorcerer. Magic draws great power from creative energy, manipulates it to mirror the artist's will. The workshop floor was filled with cautionary tales. What had possessed me to think myself above them? I should have refused the commission. My patron might not have allowed me, of course, but at least I'd have my pride.

I refused to be paralyzed by thoughts of my patron's intentions for my work. The sorcerer had given me free rein and I used it to my fullest, the image of his supposed fiancée gazing always down at me. I set aside all other commissions, neglected the daily business of my shop. The sorcerer's payment would cover months without sales. Each day I wove gold into threads, threads into links, links into chains. I carved, I pounded, I laid down acid and paste. A month's solid work, a month's solid concentration. My patron would accept no less. And whatever else I might do, I intended not to disappoint him.

My hands trembled in my pockets as I led him to the finished piece. A spider's web of gold and platinum filament, decorated with skeletal leaves and enameled feathers. Moonstones carved into the shape of snowdrops dangled from its edge.

He examined my work for a long time, not saying a word. He knew what it meant. He had to have known. *How dare you. How dare you use my work for your slavery.* If I caused him offense, I'd receive no more than I deserved.

But when he turned to me, he was not angry. If I hadn't known better, I would have said he was in awe.

He did not invite me to the wedding, thank the gods. For all I knew, there was never a wedding at all.

Having completed my mysterious commission, I set myself to replenishing my shop's inventory. Bizarre images came out in those first weeks, creatures of the sea and of the air, of shadow and of fairy tale. No spiders, no insects of any sort, though I was tempted more than once. I kept thinking of that poor misbegotten dobsonfly. A creature dedicated to bloodshed, without question. Would I have made it if I had known what it would become?

Then, late one night, there came a banging on the door of the shop. I woke up in terror, certain for a moment that the sorcerer had come to murder me in my sleep. But if that was what he wished, he'd have no need of noise. I looked out my window, saw nothing in the street. If he had used my work to commit some especially deviant crime, the guard might arrest me as an accessory. At least then my retirement would be marked by a satisfying scandal.

I pulled a cape around my nightgown and made my way downstairs. A young woman stood at my door. She was dressed much the same way as I was, except for the bejeweled web she wore on her head. I knew her face, of course, though I'd returned her portrait several weeks before.

What had I done?

It would do no good to show my alarm and distress. The poor girl was scared enough as it was. "Come in," I told the sorcerer's bride. "There's a fire in the kitchen. And here, let me get that thing off your head."

We waited together for the sorcerer to come. There was no question that he would, only how long it would take him, and what he would do when he got here.

The girl told me her story while we waited. The only daughter of a family of sorcery now much reduced, brokered into marriage with a man half a continent away, whom nobody knew except through letters. He had not lied to me, at least, though at this point it was small comfort. "Do you want to stay with him?" I asked her. She didn't answer. I don't think she realized she had any other option.

Dawn came, and he still had not arrived. I dressed hastily, dismissed my salesmen for the day. I gave no explanations, they demanded none. And as the city bells rang in the day, so the doorbell rang as well. His attention to etiquette surprised me, given how careless he had been before.

Even as I opened the door the sorcerer was bowing to me. "I am—most impressed, my lady. Astounded, one might say. But still, there is business we must conclude."

He was the expert in the ways of magic. He had the advantage of me still.

I nodded and led him to the kitchen.

"I first came across your work nearly thirty years ago," he said. He looked like he should have been no more than an infant, but I had no idea of his true age. "Such a curious thing, so plain, so close to life. I swore I saw it move in the case."

"The dobsonfly."

"I thought of making my introductions then. But your reputation was rising so quickly, even as an apprentice—"

"Student," I corrected him. *Apprentice* was a magical word. It had nothing to do with me.

He nodded with cold grace. "I knew my attention would interrupt your career. I had no intention of making you my creature."

I looked over at his fiancée or wife or whatever she was. She sat by the fire, back turned to us, pretending not to listen.

"I knew," he continued, "that in time my patronage would be a story no more or less remarkable than any of the others you'd collect around yourself. Even then, it took me a while before I had a reason to commission you. But the results, I must say—" He picked up the headdress from where it lay in a careless pile on the table. The leaves and stones rang like bells as they dangled from his hand. "Did you know what you were doing?"

"I'm not a sorcerer," I pointed out. "I had some idea of your intent. I thought perhaps I could subvert it, if I was honest enough. I never thought—" I left the sentence unfinished. I had no language for what I had managed to do.

"You must hate me very much."

"I hate that—thing. I hate what it was meant to do. I'm not so stupid as to hate you."

He looked down at the chains in his hand and smiled. "And yet it's the most beautiful piece you've done."

"How much of my work have you collected?"

He only smiled at me, and did not answer.

He took the headdress with him, and his bride. Perhaps I could have stopped him if I'd tried. But that would have taken a level of arrogance even I couldn't manage. I had turned his magic against him; that didn't mean I could repeat the results at will, even if I wanted to.

In what I think was his idea of honor, he left the dobsonfly brooch with me. I had no idea what he had done with it in the thirty years since I had created it in naive, bitter frustration. Such a vicious, ugly insect. How could I have been so reckless as to create such a thing?

I picked it up off the table. It was still warm, still light, still far closer to life than an object of metal and stone should have been. I stroked its long opal wings, far more beautiful than those of its living kin.

I'd use enamel next time, definitely.

THE FIRST WITCH OF DAMANSARA

ZEN CHO

Vivian's late grandmother was a witch—which is just a way of saying she was a woman of unusual insight. Vivian, in contrast, had a mind like a hi-tech blender. She was sharp and purposeful, but she did not understand magic.

This used to be a problem. Magic ran in the family. Even her mother's second cousin who was adopted did small spells on the side. She sold these from a stall in Kota Bharu. Her main wares were various types of fruit fried in batter, but if you bought five pisang or cempedak goreng, she threw in a jampi for free.

These embarrassing relatives became less of a problem after Vivian left Malaysia. In the modern Western country where she lived, the public toilets were clean, the newspapers were allowed to be as rude to the government as they liked, and nobody believed in magic except people in whom nobody believed. Even with a cooking appliance mind, Vivian understood that magic requires belief to thrive.

She called home rarely, and visited even less often. She was twenty-eight, engaged to a rational man, and employed as an accountant.

Vivian's Nai Nai would have said that she was attempting to deploy enchantments of her own—the fiancé, the ordinary hobbies and the sensible office job were so many sigils to ward off chaos. It was not an ineffective magic. It worked—for a while.

There was just one moment, after she heard the news, when Vivian experienced a surge of unfilial exasperation.

"They could have call me on Skype," she said. "Call my handphone some more! What a waste of money."

"What's wrong?" said the fiancé. He plays the prince in this story: beautiful, supportive, and cast in an appropriately self-effacing role—just off-screen, on a white horse.

"My grandmother's passed away," said Vivian. "I'm supposed to go back."

Vivian was not a woman to hold a grudge. When she turned up at KLIA in harem trousers and a tank top it was not through malice aforethought, but because she had simply forgotten.

Her parents embraced her with sportsmanlike enthusiasm, but when this was done her mother pulled back and plucked at her tank top.

"Girl, what's this? You know Nai Nai won't like it."

Nai Nai had lived by a code of rigorous propriety. She had disapproved of wearing black or navy blue at Chinese New Year, of white at weddings, and of spaghetti straps at all times. When they went out for dinner, even at the local restaurant where they sat outdoors and were accosted by stray cats requesting snacks, her grandchildren were required to change out of their ratty pasar malam T-shirts and faded shorts. She drew a delicate but significant distinction between flip-flops and sandals, singlets and strapless tops, soft cotton shorts and denim.

"Can see your bra," whispered Ma. "It's not so nice."

"That kind of pants," her dad said dubiously. "Don't know what Nai Nai will think of it."

"Nai Nai won't see them what," said Vivian, but this offended her parents. They sat in mutinous silence throughout the drive home.

Their terrace house was swarming with pregnant cats and black dogs.

"Only six dogs," said Vivian's mother when Vivian pointed this out. "Because got five cats. Your sister thought it's a good idea to have more dogs than cats."

"But why do we have so many cats?" said Vivian. "I thought you don't like to have animals in the house."

"Nai Nai collected the cats," said Vivian's sister. "She started before she passed away. Pregnant cats only."

"Wei Yi," said Vivian. "How are you?"

"I'm OK. Vivian," said Wei Yi. Her eyes glittered.

She'd stopped calling Vivian jie jie some time after Vivian left home. Vivian minded this less than the way she said "Vivian" as though it were a bad word.

But after all, Vivian reminded herself, Wei Yi was seventeen. She was practically legally required to be an arsehole.

"Why did Nai Nai want the pregnant cats?" Vivian tried to make her voice pleasant.

"Hai, don't need to talk so much," said their mother hastily. "Lin—Vivian so tired. Vivian, you go and change first, then we go for dinner. Papa will start complaining soon if not."

It was during an outing to a prayer goods store, while Vivian's mother was busy buying joss sticks, that her mother's friend turned to Vivian and said,

"So a lot of things to do in your house now ah?"

Vivian was shy to say she knew nothing about what preparations were afoot. As her mother's eldest it would only have been right for her to have been her mother's first support in sorting out the funeral arrangements.

"No, we are having a very simple funeral," said Vivian. "Nai Nai didn't believe in religion so much."

This was not a lie. The brutal fact was that Nai Nai had been an atheist with animist leanings, in common with most witches. Vivian's mother preferred not to let this be known, less out of a concern that her mother would be outed as a witch, than because of the stale leftover fear that she would be considered a Communist.

"But what about the dog cat all that?" said Auntie Wendy. "Did it work? Did your sister manage to keep her in the coffin?"

Vivian's mind whirred to a stop. Then it started up again, buzzing louder than ever.

Ma was righteously indignant when Vivian reproached her.

"You live so long overseas, why you need to know?" said Ma. "Don't worry. Yi Yi is handling it. Probably Nai Nai was not serious anyway."

"Not serious about what?"

"Hai, these old people have their ideas," said Ma. "Nai Nai live in KL so long, she still want to go home. Not that I don't want to please her. If it was anything else . . . but even if she doesn't have pride for herself, I am her daughter. I have pride for her!"

"Nai Nai wanted to be buried in China?" said Vivian, puzzled.

"China what China! Your Nai Nai is from Penang lah," said Ma. "Your Yeh Yeh is also buried in Bukit Tambun there. But even if he's my father, the way he treat my mother, I don't think they should be buried together."

Vivian began to understand. "But Ma, if she said she wanted to be with him—"

"It's not what she wants! It's just her idea of propriety," said Ma. "She thinks woman must always stay by the husband no matter what. I don't believe that! Nai Nai will be buried here and when her children pass on we will be buried with her. It's more comfortable for her, right? To have her loved ones around her?"

"But if Nai Nai didn't think so?"

Ma's painted eyebrows drew together.

"Nai Nai is a very stubborn woman," she said.

Wei Yi was being especially teenaged that week. She went around with lightning frizzing her hair and stormclouds rumbling about her ears. Her clothes stood away from her body, stiff with electricity. The cats hissed and the dogs whined when she passed.

When she saw the paper offerings their mother had bought for Nai Nai, she threw a massive tantrum.

"What's this?" she said, picking up a paper polo shirt. "Where got Nai Nai wear this kind of thing?"

Ma looked embarrassed.

"The shop only had that," she said. "Don't be angry, girl. I bought some bag and shoe also. But you know Nai Nai was never the dressy kind."

"That's because she like to *keep* all her nice clothes," said Wei Yi. She cast a look of burning contempt on the paper handbag, printed in heedless disregard of intellectual property rights with the Gucci logo. "Looks like the pasar malam bag. And this slippers is like old man slippers. Nai Nai could put two of her feet in one slipper!"

"Like that she's less likely to hop away," Ma said thoughtlessly.

"Is that what you call respecting your mother?" shouted Wei Yi. "Hah, you wait until it's your turn! I'll know how to treat you then."

"Wei Yi, how can you talk to Ma like that?" said Vivian.

"You shut up your face!" Wei Yi snapped. She flounced out of the room.

"She never even see the house yet," sighed Ma. She had bought an elaborate palace fashioned out of gilt-edged pink paper, with embellished roofs and shuttered windows, and two dolls dressed in Tang dynasty attire prancing on a balcony. "Got two servants some more."

"She shouldn't talk to you like that," said Vivian.

She hadn't noticed any change in Ma's appearance before, but now the soft wrinkly skin under her chin and the pale brown spots on her arms reminded Vivian that she was getting old. Old people should be cared for.

She touched her mother on the arm. "I'll go scold her. Never mind, Ma. Girls this age are always one kind."

Ma smiled at Vivian.

"You were OK," she said. She tucked a lock of Vivian's hair behind her ear.

Old people should be grateful for affection. The sudden disturbing thought occurred to Vivian that no one had liked Nai Nai very much because she'd never submitted to being looked after.

Wei Yi was trying to free the dogs. She stood by the gate, holding it open and gesturing with one hand at the great outdoors.

"Go! Blackie, Guinness, Ah Hei, Si Hitam, Jackie, Bobby! Go, go!"

The dogs didn't seem that interested in the great outdoors. Ah Hei took a couple of tentative steps towards the gate, looked back at Wei Yi, changed her mind and sat down again.

"Jackie and Bobby?" said Vivian.

Wei Yi shot her a glare. "I ran out of ideas." The *so what?* was unspoken, but it didn't need to be said.

"Why these stupid dogs don't want to go," Wei Yi muttered. "When you open the gate to drive in or out, they go running everywhere. When you want them to chau, they don't want."

"They can tell you won't let them back in again," said Vivian.

She remembered when Wei Yi had been cute—as a little girl, with those pure single-lidded eyes and the doll-like lacquered bowl of hair. When had she turned into this creature? Hair at sevens and eights, the uneven fringe falling into malevolent eyes. Inappropriately tight Bermuda shorts worn below an unflatteringly loose plaid shirt.

At seven Wei Yi had been a being perfect in herself. At seventeen there was nothing that wasn't wrong about the way she moved in the world.

Vivian had been planning to tell her sister off, but the memory of that lovely child softened her voice. "Why you don't want the dogs anymore?"

"I want Nai Nai to win." Wei Yi slammed the gate shut.

"What, by having nice clothes when she's passed away?" said Vivian. "Winning or losing, doesn't matter for Nai Nai anymore. What does it matter if she wears a polo shirt in the afterlife?"

Wei Yi's face crumpled. She clutched her fists in agony. The words broke from her in a roar.

"You're so stupid! You don't know anything!" She kicked the gate to relieve her feelings. "Nai Nai's brain works more than yours and she's dead! Do you even belong to this family?"

This was why Vivian had left. Magic lent itself to temperament.

"Maybe not," said Vivian.

When Vivian was angry she did it with the same single-minded energy she did everything else. This was why she decided to go wedding dress shopping in the week of her grandmother's funeral.

There were numerous practical justifications, actually. She went through them in her head as she drove past bridal studios where faceless mannequins struck poses in clouds of tulle.

"Cheaper to get it here than overseas. Not like I'm helping much at home what. Not like I was so close to Nai Nai."

She stared mournfully at herself in the mirror, weighted down by satin and rhinestones. Did she want a veil? Did she like lace? Ball gown or mermaid shape?

She'd imagined her wedding dress as being white and long. She hadn't expected there to be so many permutations on a theme. She felt pinned in place by the choices available to her.

The shop assistant could tell her heart wasn't in it.

"Some ladies like other colour better," said the shop assistant.

"You want to try? We have blue, pink, peach, yellow—very nice colour, very feminine."

"I thought usually white?"

"Some ladies don't like white because—you know—" the shop assistant lowered her voice, but she was too superstitious to say it outright. "It's related to a not so nice subject."

The words clanged in Vivian's ears. Briefly light-headed, she clutched at the back of a chair for balance. Her hands were freezing. In the mirror the white dress looked like a shroud. Her face hovering above it was the face of a mourner, or a ghost.

"Now that I've tried it, I'm not sure I like Western gown so much," said Vivian, speaking with difficulty.

"We have cheongsam or qun kua," said the shop assistant. "Very nice, very traditional. Miss is so slim, will suit the cheongsam."

The jolt of red brocade was a relief. Vivian took a dress with gold trimmings, the highest of high collars and an even higher slit along the sides. Dragons and phoenixes writhed along the fabric. It was as red as a blare of trumpets, as red as the pop of fireworks.

This fresh chilli red had never suited her. In it she looked paler than ever, washed out by the vibrant shade. But the colour was a protective charm. It laid monsters to rest. It shut out hungry ghosts. It frightened shadows back into the corners where they belonged.

Vivian crept home with her spoils. That night she slept and did not dream of anything.

The next morning she regretted the purchase. Her fiancé would think it was ridiculous. She couldn't wear a cheongsam down the aisle of an Anglican church. She would take it back to the boutique and return it. After all the white satin mermaid dress had suited her. The sweetheart neckline was so much more flattering than a mandarin collar.

She shoved the cheongsam in a bag and tried to sneak out, but Wei Yi was sitting on the floor of the laundry room, in the way of her exit. She was surrounded by webs of filigreed red paper.

"What's this?" said Vivian.

"It's called paper cutting," said Wei Yi, not looking up. "You never see before meh?"

On the floor the paper cuttings unfurled. Some were disasters: a mutilated fish floated past like tumbleweed; a pair of flirtatious girls had been torn apart by an overly enthusiastic slash. But some of the pieces were astounding.

"Kwan Yin," said Vivian.

The folds in the goddess's robes had been rendered with extraordinary delicacy. Her eyes were gentle, her face double-chinned. Her halo was a red moon circled by ornate clouds.

"It's for Nai Nai," said Wei Yi. "Maybe Kwan Yin will have mercy on her even though she's so blasphemous."

"Shouldn't talk like that about the dead," said Vivian.

Wei Yi rolled her eyes, but the effort of her craft seemed to absorbing all her evil energies. Her response was mild: "It's not disrespectful if it's true."

Her devotion touched Vivian. Surely not many seventeen-year-olds would spend so much time on so laborious a task. The sleet of impermanent art piled around her must have taken hours to produce.

"Did Nai Nai teach you how to do that?" Vivian said, trying to get back on friendlier ground.

Wei Yi's face spasmed.

"Nai Nai was a rubber tapper with seven children," she said. "She can't even read! You think what, she was so free she can do all these hobbies, is it? I learnt it from YouTube lah!"

She crumpled the paper she was working on and flung it down on the floor to join the flickering red mass.

"Oh, whatever!" said Vivian in the fullness of her heart.

She bought the whitest, fluffiest, sheeniest, most beaded dress she could find in the boutique. It was strapless and low-backed to boot. Nai Nai would have hated it.

That night Vivian dreamt of her grandmother.

Nai Nai had climbed out of her coffin where she had been lying in the living room. She was wearing a kebaya, with a white baju and a batik sarong wrapped around her hips. No modern creation this—the blouse was fastened not with buttons but with kerongsang, ornate gold brooches studded with pearls and rhinestones.

Nai Nai was struggling with the kerongsang. In her dream Vivian reached out to help her.

"I can do!" said Nai Nai crossly. "Don't so sibuk." She batted at the kerongsang with the slim brown hands that had been so deft in life.

"What's the matter? You want to take it off for what?" said Vivian in Hokkien.

"It's too nice to wear outside," Nai Nai complained. "When I was alive I used safety pins and it was enough. All this hassle just because I am like this. I didn't save Yeh Yeh's pension so you can spend on a carcass!"

"Why do you want to go outside?" Vivian took the bony arm. "Nai Nai, come, let's go back to sleep. It's so late already. Everybody is sleeping."

Nai Nai was a tiny old lady with a dandelion fluff of white hair standing out from her head. She looked nothing like the spotty, tubby, furiously awkward Wei Yi, but her expression suddenly showed Vivian what her sister would look like when she was old. The contemptuous exasperation was exactly the same.

"If it's not late, how can I go outside?" she said. "I have a long way to go. Hai!" She flung up her hands. "After they bury me, ask the priest to give you back the kerongsang."

She started hopping towards the door, her arms held rod-straight out in front of her. The sight was comic and horrible.

This was the secret the family had been hiding from Vivian. Nai Nai had become a kuang shi.

"Nai Nai," choked Vivian. "Please rest. You're so old already, you can't run around so much."

"Don't answer back!" shouted Nai Nai from the foyer. "Come and open the door for Nai Nai! Yeh Yeh will be angry. He cannot stand when people are late."

Vivian envisioned Nai Nai hopping out of the house—past the neighbourhood park with its rustling bushes and creaking swings, past the neighbours' Myvis and Peroduas, through the toll while the attendant slumbered. She saw Nai Nai hopping along the curves of the Titiwangsa Mountains, her halo of hair white against the bleeding red of the hills where the forests had peeled away to show the limestone. She saw Nai Nai passing oil palm plantations, their leaves dark glossy green under the brassy glare of sunshine—sleepy water buffalo flicking their tails in wide hot fields—rows of new white terrace houses standing in empty rows on bare hillsides. Up the long North-South Expressway, to her final home.

"Nai Nai," said Vivian. Don't leave us, she wanted to say.

"Complain, complain!" Nai Nai was slapping at the doorknob with her useless stiff hands.

"You can't go all that way," said Vivian. She had an inspiration. "Your sarong will come undone."

Whoever had laid Nai Nai out had dressed her like a true nyonya. The sarong was wound around her hips and tucked in at the waist, with no fastenings to hold it up.

"At my age, who cares," said Nai Nai, but this had clearly given her pause.

"Come back to sleep," coaxed Vivian. "I'll tell Mummy. Bukit Tambun, right? I'll sort it out for you."

Nai Nai gave her a sharp look. "Can talk so sweetly but what does she do? Grandmother is being buried and she goes to buy a wedding dress!"

Vivian winced.

"The dress is not nice also," said Nai Nai. "What happened to the first dress? That was nice. Red is a happy colour."

"I know Nai Nai feels it's pantang, but—"

"Pantang what pantang," snapped Nai Nai. Like all witches, she hated to be accused of superstition. "White is a boring colour! Ah, when I got married everybody wanted to celebrate. We had two hundred guests and they all had chicken to eat. I looked so beautiful in my photo. And Yeh Yeh . . . "

Nai Nai sank into reminiscence.

"What about Yeh Yeh?" prompted Vivian.

"Yeh Yeh looked the same as always. Like a useless playboy," said Nai Nai. "He could only look nice and court girls."

"Then you want to be buried with him for what?"

"That's different," said Nai Nai. "Whether I'm a good wife doesn't have anything to do with what he was like."

As if galvanised by Vivian's resistance, she turned and made to hit the door again.

"If you listen to me, I'll take the dress back to the shop," said Vivian, driven by desperation.

Nai Nai paused. "You'll buy the pretty cheongsam?"

"If you want also I'll wear the kua," said Vivian recklessly.

She tried not to imagine what her fiancé would say when he saw the loose red jacket and long skirt, embroidered in gold and silver with bug-eyed dragons and insectoid phoenixes. And the three-quarter bell sleeves, all the better to show the wealth of the family in the gold bracelets stacked on the bride's wrists! How that would impress her future in-laws.

To her relief, Nai Nai said, "No lah! So old-fashioned. Cheongsam is nicer."

She started hopping back towards the living room.

Vivian trailed behind, feeling somehow as if she had been outmaneouvred.

"Nai Nai, do you really want to be buried in Penang?"

Nai Nai peered up with suspicion in her reddened eyes as Vivian helped her back into the coffin.

"You want to change your mind, is it?"

"No, no, I'll get the cheongsam. It'll be in my room by tomorrow, I promise."

Nai Nai smiled.

"You know why I wanted you all to call me Nai Nai?" she said before Vivian closed the coffin. "Even though Hokkien people call their grandmother Ah Ma?"

Vivian paused with her hand on the lid.

"In the movies, Nai Nai is always bad!"

Vivian woke up with her grandmother's growly cackle in her ears.

Wei Yi was in the middle of a meltdown when Vivian came downstairs for breakfast. Ma bristled with relief:

"Ah, your sister is here. She'll talk to you."

Wei Yi was sitting enthroned in incandescence, clutching a bread knife. A charred hunk of what used to be kaya toast sat on her plate. The *Star* newspaper next to it was crisping at the edges.

Vivian began to sweat. She thought about turning on the ceiling fan, but that might stoke the flames.

She pulled out a chair and picked up the jar of kaya as if nothing was happening. "What's up?"

Wei Yi turned hot coal eyes on Vivian.

"She doesn't want to kill the dogs wor," said Ma. "Angry already."

"So? Who ask you to kill the dogs in the first place?" said Vivian.

"Stupid," said Wei Yi. Her face was very pale, but her lips had

115

the dull orange glow of heated metal. Fire breathed in her hair. A layer of ash lay on the crown of her head.

"Because of Nai Nai," Ma explained. "Wei Yi heard the blood of a black dog is good for Nai Nai's . . . condition."

"It's not right," said Wei Yi. "It's better for Nai Nai if—but you won't understand one."

Vivian spread a layer of kaya on her piece of bread before she answered. Her hands were shaking, but her voice was steady when she spoke.

"I think Ma is right. There's no need to kill any dogs. Nai Nai is not serious about being a kuang shi. She's just using it as an emotional blackmail." She paused for reflection. "And I think she's enjoying it also lah. You know Nai Nai was always very active. She likes to be up and about."

Wei Yi dropped her butter knife.

"Eh, how you know?" said Ma.

"She talked to me in my dream last night because she didn't like the wedding dress I bought," said Vivian.

Ma's eyes widened. "You went to buy your wedding dress when Nai Nai just pass away?"

"You saw Nai Nai?" cried Wei Yi. "What did she say?"

"She likes cheongsam better, and she wants to be buried in Penang," said Vivian. "So I'm going to buy cheongsam. Ma, should think about sending her back to Penang. When she got nothing to complain about she will settle down."

"Why she didn't talk to me?" said Wei Yi. Beads of molten metal ran down her face, leaving silver trails. "I do so many jampi and she never talk to me! It's not fair!"

Ma was torn between an urge to scold Vivian and the necessity of comforting Wei Yi. "Girl, don't cry—Vivian, so disrespectful, I'm surprise Nai Nai never scold you—"

"Yi Yi," said Vivian. "She didn't talk to you because in Nai Nai's eyes you are perfect already." As she said this, she realised it was true.

Wei Yi—awkward, furious, and objectionable in every way—was Nai Nai's ideal grandchild. There was no need to monitor or reprimand such a perfect heir. The surprise was that Nai Nai even thought it necessary to rise from the grave to order Vivian around, rather than just leaving the job to the next witch.

Of course, Nai Nai probably hadn't had the chance to train Wei Yi in the standards expected of a wedding in Nai Nai's family. The finer points of bridal fashion would certainly escape Wei Yi.

"Nai Nai only came back to scold people," said Vivian. "She doesn't need to scold you for anything."

The unnatural metallic sheen of Wei Yi's face went away. Her hair and eyes dimmed. Her mouth trembled. Vivian expected a roar. Instead Wei Yi shoved her kaya toast away and laid her head on the table.

"I miss Nai Nai," she sobbed.

Ma got up and touched Vivian on the shoulder.

"I have to go buy thing," she whispered. "You cheer up your sister."

Wei Yi's skin was still hot when Vivian put her arm around her, but as Vivian held her Wei Yi's temperature declined, until she merely felt feverish. Her tears went from scalding to lukewarm.

"Nai Nai, Nai Nai," she wailed in that screechy show-off way Vivian had always hated. When they were growing up Vivian had not believed in Wei Yi's tears—they seemed no more than a show, put on to impress the grown-ups.

Vivian now realised that the grief was as real as the volume deliberate. Wei Yi did not cry like that simply because she was sad, but because she wanted someone to listen to her.

In the old days it had been a parent or a teacher's attention that she had sought. These howls were aimed directly at the all-too-responsive ears of their late grandmother.

"Wei Yi," said Vivian. "I've thought of what you can do for Nai Nai."

For once Wei Yi did not put Vivian's ideas to scorn. She seemed to have gone up in her sister's estimation for having seen Nai Nai's importunate spectre.

Vivian had a feeling Nai Nai's witchery had gone into Wei Yi's paper cutting skills. YouTube couldn't explain the unreal speed with which she did it.

Vivian tried picking up Wei Yi's scissors and dropped them, yelping.

"What the—!" It had felt like an electric shock.

Wei Yi grabbed the scissors. "These are no good. I give you other ones to use."

Vivian got the task of cutting out the sarong—a large rectangular piece of paper to which Wei Yi would add the batik motifs later. When she was done Wei Yi took a look and pursed her lips. The last time Vivian had felt this small was when she failed her first driving test two minutes after getting into the car.

"OK ah?"

"Not bad," said Wei Yi unconvincingly. "Eh, you go help Ma do her whatever thing lah. I'll work on this first."

A couple of hours later she barged into Vivian's room. "Why you're here? Why you take so long? Come and see!"

Vivian got up sheepishly. "I thought you need some time to finish mah."

"Nonsense. Nai Nai going to be buried tomorrow, where got time to dilly-dally?" Wei Yi grasped her hand.

The paper dress was laid in crisp folds on the dining table. Wei Yi's scissors had rendered the delicate lace of the kebaya blouse with marvellous skill. Peacocks with uplifted wings and princely crowns draped their tails along the hems, strutted up the lapels, and curled coyly around the ends of the sleeves. The paper was chiffon-thin. A breath set it fluttering.

The skirt was made from a thicker, heavier cream paper. Wei Yi had cut blowsy peonies into the front and a contrasting grid pattern on the reverse. Vivian touched it in wonder, feeling the nubby texture of the paper under her fingertips.

"Do you think Nai Nai will like it?" said Wei Yi.

Vivian had to be honest. "The top is a bit see-through, no?"

"She'll have a singlet to wear underneath," said Wei Yi. "I left that for you to do. Very simple one. Just cut along the line only."

This was kindness, Wei Yi style.

"It's beautiful, Yi Yi," said Vivian. She felt awkward—they were not a family given to compliments—but once she'd started it was easy to go on. "It's so nice. Nai Nai will love it."

"Ah, don't need to say so much lah," Wei Yi scoffed. "OK enough already. I still haven't done shoe yet."

They burnt the beautiful cream kebaya as an offering to Nai Nai. It didn't go alone—Wei Yi had created four other outfits, working through the night. Samfu for everyday wear; an old-fashioned loose, long-sleeved cheongsam ("Nicer for older lady. Nai Nai is not a Shanghai cabaret singer"); a sarong for sleeping in; and a Punjabi suit of all things.

"Nai Nai used to like wearing it," said Wei Yi when Vivian expressed surprise. "Comfortable mah. Nai Nai likes this simple kind of thing to wear for every day."

"Four is not a good number," said Vivian. "Maybe should make extra sarong?"

"You forgot the kebaya. That's five," Wei Yi retorted. "Anyway she die already. What is there to be pantang about?"

They threw in the more usual hell gold and paper mansion into the bonfire as well. The doll servants didn't burn well, but melted dramatically and stuck afterwards.

Since they were doing the bonfire outside the house, on the public road, this concerned Vivian. She chipped doubtfully away at the mess of plastic.

"Don't worry," said Ma. "The servants have gone to Nai Nai already."

"I'm not worried about that," said Vivian. "I'm worried about MPPJ." She couldn't imagine the local authorities would be particularly pleased about the extra work they'd made for them.

"They're used to it lah," said Ma, dismissing the civil service with a wave of the hand.

They even burnt the fake Gucci bag and the polo shirt in the end.

"Nai Nai will find some use for it," said Wei Yi. "Maybe turn out she like that kind of style also."

She could afford to be magnanimous. Making the kebaya had relieved something in Wei Yi's heart. As she'd stood watch over the flames to make sure the demons didn't get their offerings to Nai Nai, there had been a serenity in her face.

As they moved back to the house, Vivian put her arm around her sister, wincing at the snap and hiss when her skin touched Wei Yi's. It felt like a static shock, only intensified by several orders of magnitude.

"OK?"

Wei Yi was fizzling with magic, but her eyes were calm and dark and altogether human.

"OK," replied the Witch of Damansara.

In Vivian's dream a moth came fluttering into the room. It alighted at the end of her bed and turned into Nai Nai.

Nai Nai was wearing a green-and-white striped cotton sarong, tucked and knotted under her arms as if she were going to bed soon. Her hair smelled of Johnson & Johnson baby shampoo. Her face was white with beduk sejuk—powder moistened and spread over the face as a cooling paste.

"Tell your mother the house is very beautiful," said Nai Nai. "The servants have already run away and got married, but it's not so bad. In hell it's not so dusty. Nothing to clean also."

"Nai Nai—"

"Ah Yi is very clever now, har?" said Nai Nai. "The demons

looked at my nice things but when they saw her they immediately run away."

Vivian experienced a pang. She didn't say anything, but perhaps the dead understood these things. Or perhaps it was just that Nai Nai, with 65 years of mothering behind her, did not need to be told. She reached out and patted Vivian's hand.

"You are always so guai," said Nai Nai. "I'm not so worried about you."

This was a new idea to Vivian. She was unused to thinking of herself—magicless, intransigent—as the good kid in the family.

"But I went overseas," she said stupidly.

"You're always so clever to work hard. You don't make your mother and father worried," said Nai Nai. "Ah Yi ah . . . . " Nai Nai shook her head. "So stubborn! So naughty! If I don't take care sekali she burn down the house. That girl doesn't use her head. But she become a bit guai already. When she's older she won't be so free, won't have time to cause so much problems."

Vivian did not point out that age did not seem to have stopped Nai Nai. This would have been disrespectful. Instead she said, "Nai Nai, were you really a vampire? Or were you just pretending to turn into a kuang shi?"

"Hai, you think so fun to pretend to be a kuang shi?" said Nai Nai indignantly. "When you are old, you will find out how suffering it is. You think I have time to watch all the Hong Kong movies and learn how to be a vampire?"

So that was how she did it. The pale vampirish skin had probably been beduk sejuk as well. How Nai Nai obtained beduk sejuk in the afterlife was a question better left unasked. Vivian had questions of more immediate interest.

"If you stayed because you're worried about Wei Yi, can I return the cheongsam to the shop?"

Nai Nai bridled. "Oh, like that ah? Not proud of your culture, is it? If you want to wear the white dress, like a ghost, so ugly—"

"Ma wore a white dress on her wedding day. Everyone does it."

"Nai Nai give you my beduk sejuk and red lipstick lah. Then you can pretend to be kuang shi also!"

"I'll get another cheongsam," said Vivian. "Not that I don't want to wear cheongsam. I just don't like this one so much. It's too expensive."

"How much?"

Vivian told her.

"Wah, so much ah," said Nai Nai. "Like that you should just get it tailored. Don't need to buy from shop. Tailored is cheaper and nicer some more. The seamstress's phone number is in Nai Nai's old phonebook. Madam Teoh."

"I'll look," Vivian promised.

Nai Nai got up, stretching. "Must go now. Scared the demons will don't know do what if I leave the house so long. You must look after your sister, OK?"

Vivian, doubtful about how any attempt to look after Wei Yi was likely to be received, said, "Ah."

"Nai Nai already gave Ah Yi her legacy, but I'll give you yours now," said Nai Nai. "You're a good girl, Ah Lin. Nai Nai didn't have chance to talk to you so much when you were small. But I'm proud of you. Make sure the seamstress doesn't overcharge. If you tell Madam Teoh you're my granddaughter she'll give you discount."

"Thank you, Nai Nai," said Vivian, but she spoke to an empty room. The curtains flapped in Nai Nai's wake.

On the floor lay a pile of clothes. Moonlight-sheer chiffon, brown batik, maroon silk, and floral print cotton, and on top of this, glowing turquoise even in the pale light of the moon, the most gilded, spangled, intricately embroidered Punjabi suit Vivian had ever seen.

THE FAERY HANDBAG

KELLY LINK

I used to go to thrift stores with my friends. We'd take the train into Boston, and go to The Garment District, which is this huge vintage clothing warehouse. Everything is arranged by color, and somehow that makes all of the clothes beautiful. It's kind of like if you went through the wardrobe in the Narnia books, only instead of finding Aslan and the White Witch and horrible Eustace, you found this magic clothing world—instead of talking animals, there were feather boas and wedding dresses and bowling shoes, and paisley shirts and Doc Martens and everything hung up on racks so that first you have black dresses, all together, like the world's largest indoor funeral, and then blue dresses—all the blues you can imagine—and then red dresses and so on. Pink-reds and orangey reds and purple-reds and exit-light reds and candy reds. Sometimes I would close my eyes and Natasha and Natalie and Jake would drag me over to a rack, and rub a dress against my hand. "Guess what color this is."

We had this theory that you could learn how to tell, just by feeling, what color something was. For example, if you're sitting on a lawn, you can tell what color green the grass is, with your eyes closed, depending on how silky-rubbery it feels. With clothing, stretchy velvet stuff always feels red when your eyes are closed, even if it's not red. Natasha was always best at guessing colors, but Natasha is also best at cheating at games and not getting caught.

One time we were looking through kid's t-shirts and we found a Muppets t-shirt that had belonged to Natalie in third grade. We knew it belonged to her, because it still had her name inside, where her mother had written it in permanent marker, when Natalie went to summer camp. Jake bought it back for her, because he was the only one who had money that weekend. He was the only one who had a job.

Maybe you're wondering what a guy like Jake is doing in The Garment District with a bunch of girls. The thing about Jake is that he always has a good time, no matter what he's doing. He likes everything, and he likes everyone, but he likes me best of all. Wherever he is now, I bet he's having a great time and wondering when I'm going to show up. I'm always running late. But he knows that.

We had this theory that things have life cycles, the way that people do. The life cycle of wedding dresses and feather boas and t-shirts and shoes and handbags involves the Garment District. If clothes are good, or even if they're bad in an interesting way, the Garment District is where they go when they die. You can tell that they're dead, because of the way that they smell. When you buy them, and wash them, and start wearing them again, and they start to smell like you, that's when they reincarnate. But the point is, if you're looking for a particular thing, you just have to keep looking for it. You have to look hard.

Down in the basement at the Garment Factory they sell clothing and beat-up suitcases and teacups by the pound. You can get eight pounds worth of prom dresses–a slinky black dress, a poufy lavender dress, a swirly pink dress, a silvery, starry lamé dress so fine you could pass it through a key ring—for eight dollars. I go there every week, hunting for Grandmother Zofia's faery handbag.

The faery handbag: It's huge and black and kind of hairy. Even when your eyes are closed, it feels black. As black as black ever gets, like if you touch it, your hand might get stuck in it, like tar or black quicksand or when you stretch out your hand at night, to turn on a light, but all you feel is darkness.

Fairies live inside it. I know what that sounds like, but it's true.

Grandmother Zofia said it was a family heirloom. She said that it was over two hundred years old. She said that when she died, I had to look after it. Be its guardian. She said that it would be my responsibility.

I said that it didn't look that old, and that they didn't have handbags two hundred years ago, but that just made her cross. She said, "So then tell me, Genevieve, darling, where do you think old ladies used to put their reading glasses and their heart medicine and their knitting needles?"

I know that no one is going to believe any of this. That's okay. If I thought you would, then I couldn't tell you. Promise me that you won't believe a word. That's what Zofia used to say to me when she told me stories. At the funeral, my mother said, half-laughing and half-crying, that her mother was the world's best liar. I think she thought maybe Zofia wasn't really dead. But I went up to Zofia's coffin, and I looked her right in the eyes. They were closed. The funeral parlor had made her up with blue eyeshadow, and blue eyeliner. She looked like she was going to be a news anchor on Fox television, instead of dead. It was creepy and it made me even sadder than I already was. But I didn't let that distract me.

"Okay, Zofia," I whispered. "I know you're dead, but this is important. You know exactly how important this is. Where's the handbag? What did you do with it? How do I find it? What am I supposed to do now?"

Of course she didn't say a word. She just lay there, this little smile on her face, as if she thought the whole thing—death, blue eyeshadow, Jake, the handbag, faeries, Scrabble, Baldeziwurlekistan, all of it—was a joke. She always did have a weird sense of humor. That's why she and Jake got along so well.

I grew up in a house next door to the house where my mother lived when she was a little girl. Her mother, Zofia Swink, my grandmother, babysat me while my mother and father were at work.

Zofia never looked like a grandmother. She had long black hair which she wore up in little, braided, spiky towers and plaits. She had large blue eyes. She was taller than my father. She looked like a spy or ballerina or a lady pirate or a rock star. She acted like one too. For example, she never drove anywhere. She rode a bike. It drove my mother crazy. "Why can't you act your age?" she'd say, and Zofia would just laugh.

Zofia and I played Scrabble all the time. Zofia always won, even though her English wasn't all that great, because we'd decided that she was allowed to use Baldeziwurleki vocabulary. Baldeziwurlekistan is where Zofia was born, over two hundred years ago. That's what Zofia said. (My grandmother claimed to be over two hundred years old. Or maybe even older. Sometimes she claimed that she'd even met Ghenghis Khan. He was much shorter than her. I probably don't have time to tell that story.) Baldeziwurlekistan is also an incredibly valuable word in

Scrabble points, even though it doesn't exactly fit on the board. Zofia put it down the first time we played. I was feeling pretty good because I'd gotten forty-one points for "zippery" on my turn.

Zofia kept rearranging her letters on her tray. Then she looked over at me, as if daring me to stop her, and put down "eziwurlekistan", after "bald." She used "delicious," "zippery," "wishes," "kismet", and "needle," and made "to" into "toe." "Baldeziwurlekistan" went all the way across the board and then trailed off down the righthand side.

I started laughing.

"I used up all my letters," Zofia said. She licked her pencil and started adding up points.

"That's not a word," I said. "Baldeziwurlekistan is not a word. Besides, you can't do that. You can't put an eighteen letter word on a board that's fifteen squares across."

"Why not? It's a country," Zofia said. "It's where I was born, little darling."

"Challenge," I said. I went and got the dictionary and looked it up. "There's no such place."

"Of course there isn't nowadays," Zofia said. "It wasn't a very big place, even when it was a place. But you've heard of Samarkand, and Uzbekistan and the Silk Road and Ghenghis Khan. Haven't I told you about meeting Ghenghis Khan?"

I looked up Samarkand. "Okay," I said. "Samarkand is a real place. A real word. But Baldeziwurlekistan isn't."

"They call it something else now," Zofia said. "But I think it's important to remember where we come from. I think it's only fair that I get to use Baldeziwurleki words. Your English is

129

so much better than me. Promise me something, mouthful of dumpling, a small, small thing. You'll remember its real name. Baldeziwurlekistan. Now when I add it up, I get three hundred and sixty-eight points. Could that be right?"

If you called the faery handbag by its right name, it would be something like "orzipanikanikcz," which means the "bag of skin where the world lives," only Zofia never spelled that word the same way twice. She said you had to spell it a little differently each time. You never wanted to spell it exactly the right way, because that would be dangerous.

I called it the faery handbag because I put "faery" down on the Scrabble board once. Zofia said that you spelled it with an "i," not an "e." She looked it up in the dictionary, and lost a turn.

Zofia said that in Baldeziwurlekistan they used a board and tiles for divination, prognostication, and sometimes even just for fun. She said it was a little like playing Scrabble. That's probably why she turned out to be so good at Scrabble. The Baldeziwurlekistanians used their tiles and board to communicate with the people who lived under the hill. The people who lived under the hill knew the future. The Baldeziwurlekistanians gave them fermented milk and honey, and the young women of the village used to go and lie out on the hill and sleep under the stars. Apparently the people under the hill were pretty cute. The important thing was that you never went down into the hill and spent the night there, no matter how cute the guy from under the hill was. If you did, even if you only spent a single night under the hill, when you came out again a hundred years might have passed. "Remember that," Zofia said to me. "It doesn't matter how cute a guy is. If he wants you to come back to his place, it isn't a good idea. It's okay to fool around, but don't spend the night."

Every once in a while, a woman from under the hill would marry a man from the village, even though it never ended well. The problem was that the women under the hill were terrible cooks. They couldn't get used to the way time worked in the village, which meant that supper always got burnt, or else it wasn't cooked long enough. But they couldn't stand to be criticized. It hurt their feelings. If their village husband complained, or even if he looked like he wanted to complain, that was it. The woman from under the hill went back to her home, and even if her husband went and begged and pleaded and apologized, it might be three years or thirty years or a few generations before she came back out.

Even the best, happiest marriages between the Baldeziwurle-kistanians and the people under the hill fell apart when the children got old enough to complain about dinner. But everyone in the village had some hill blood in them.

"It's in you," Zofia said, and kissed me on the nose. "Passed down from my grandmother and her mother. It's why we're so beautiful."

When Zofia was nineteen, the shaman-priestess in her village threw the tiles and discovered that something bad was going to happen. A raiding party was coming. There was no point in fighting them. They would burn down everyone's houses and take the young men and women for slaves. And it was even worse than that. There was going to be an earthquake as well, which was bad news because usually, when raiders showed up, the village went down under the hill for a night and when they came out again the raiders would have been gone for months or decades or even a hundred years. But this earthquake was going to split the hill right open.

The people under the hill were in trouble. Their home would be destroyed, and they would be doomed to roam the face of the earth, weeping and lamenting their fate until the sun blew out and the sky cracked and the seas boiled and the people dried up and turned to dust and blew away. So the shaman-priestess went and divined some more, and the people under the hill told her to kill a black dog and skin it and use the skin to make a purse big enough to hold a chicken, an egg, and a cooking pot. So she did, and then the people under the hill made the inside of the purse big enough to hold all of the village and all of the people under the hill and mountains and forests and seas and rivers and lakes and orchards and a sky and stars and spirits and fabulous monsters and sirens and dragons and dryads and mermaids and beasties and all the little gods that the Baldeziwurlekistanians and the people under the hill worshipped.

"Your purse is made out of dog skin?" I said. "That's disgusting!"

"Little dear pet," Zofia said, looking wistful. "Dog is delicious. To Baldeziwurlekistanians, dog is a delicacy."

Before the raiding party arrived, the village packed up all of their belongings and moved into the handbag. The clasp was made out of bone. If you opened it one way, then it was just a purse big enough to hold a chicken and an egg and a clay cooking pot, or else a pair of reading glasses and a library book and a pillbox. If you opened the clasp another way, then you found yourself in a little boat floating at the mouth of a river. On either side of you was forest, where the Baldeziwurlekistanian villagers and the people under the hill made their new settlement.

If you opened the handbag the wrong way, though, you found yourself in a dark land that smelled like blood. That's where the guardian of the purse (the dog whose skin had been been sewn into a purse) lived. The guardian had no skin. Its howl made blood come out of your ears and nose. It tore apart anyone who turned the clasp in the opposite direction and opened the purse in the wrong way.

"Here is the wrong way to open the handbag," Zofia said. She twisted the clasp, showing me how she did it. She opened the mouth of the purse, but not very wide and held it up to me. "Go ahead, darling, and listen for a second."

I put my head near the handbag, but not too near. I didn't hear anything. "I don't hear anything," I said.

"The poor dog is probably asleep," Zofia said. "Even nightmares have to sleep now and then."

After he got expelled, everybody at school called Jake Houdini instead of Jake. Everybody except for me. I'll explain why, but you have to be patient. It's hard work telling everything in the right order.

Jake is smarter and also taller than most of our teachers. Not quite as tall as me. We've known each other since third grade. Jake has always been in love with me. He says he was in love with me even before third grade, even before we ever met. It took me a while to fall in love with Jake.

In third grade, Jake knew everything already, except how to make friends. He used to follow me around all day long. It made me so mad that I kicked him in the knee. When that didn't work,

I threw his backpack out of the window of the school bus. That didn't work either, but the next year Jake took some tests and the school decided that he could skip fourth and fifth grade. Even I felt sorry for Jake then. Sixth grade didn't work out. When the sixth graders wouldn't stop flushing his head down the toilet, he went out and caught a skunk and set it loose in the boy's locker room.

The school was going to suspend him for the rest of the year, but instead Jake took two years off while his mother home-schooled him. He learned Latin and Hebrew and Greek, how to write sestinas, how to make sushi, how to play bridge, and even how to knit. He learned fencing and ballroom dancing. He worked in a soup kitchen and made a Super Eight movie about Civil War reenactors who play extreme croquet in full costume instead of firing off cannons. He started learning how to play guitar. He even wrote a novel. I've never read it—he says it was awful.

When he came back two years later, because his mother had cancer for the first time, the school put him back with our year, in seventh grade. He was still way too smart, but he was finally smart enough to figure out how to fit in. Plus he was good at soccer and he was really cute. Did I mention that he played guitar? Every girl in school had a crush on Jake, but he used to come home after school with me and play Scrabble with Zofia and ask her about Baldeziwurlekistan.

Jake's mom was named Cynthia. She collected ceramic frogs and knock-knock jokes. When we were in ninth grade, she had cancer again. When she died, Jake smashed all of her frogs. That was the first funeral I ever went to. A few months later, Jake's father asked Jake's fencing teacher out on a date. They got married right after the school expelled Jake for his AP project on Houdini. That was the first wedding I ever went to. Jake and I stole a bottle of wine and drank it, and I threw up in the swimming pool at the country club. Jake threw up all over my shoes.

So, anyway, the village and the people under the hill lived happily every after for a few weeks in the handbag, which they had tied around a rock in a dry well which the people under the hill had determined would survive the earthquake. But some of the Baldeziwurlekistanians wanted to come out again and see what was going on in the world. Zofia was one of them. It had been summer when they went into the bag, but when they came out again, and climbed out of the well, snow was falling and their village was ruins and crumbly old rubble. They walked through the snow, Zofia carrying the handbag, until they came to another village, one that they'd never seen before. Everyone in that village was packing up their belongings and leaving, which gave Zofia and her friends a bad feeling. It seemed to be just the same as when they went into the handbag.

They followed the refugees, who seemed to know where they were going, and finally everyone came to a city. Zofia had never seen such a place. There were trains and electric lights and movie theaters, and there were people shooting each other. Bombs were falling. A war going on. Most of the villagers decided to climb right back inside the handbag, but Zofia volunteered to stay in the world and look after the handbag. She had fallen in love with movies and silk stockings and with a young man, a Russian deserter.

Zofia and the Russian deserter married and had many

adventures and finally came to America, where my mother was born. Now and then Zofia would consult the tiles and talk to the people who lived in the handbag and they would tell her how best to avoid trouble and how she and her husband could make some money. Every now and then one of the Baldeziwurlekistanians, or one of the people from under the hill came out of the handbag and wanted to go grocery shopping, or to a movie or an amusement park to ride on roller coasters, or to the library.

The more advice Zofia gave her husband, the more money they made. Her husband became curious about Zofia's handbag, because he could see that there was something odd about it, but Zofia told him to mind his own business. He began to spy on Zofia, and saw that strange men and women were coming in and out of the house. He became convinced that either Zofia was a spy for the Communists, or maybe that she was having affairs. They fought and he drank more and more, and finally he threw away her divination tiles. "Russians make bad husbands," Zofia told me. Finally, one night while Zofia was sleeping, her husband opened the bone clasp and climbed inside the handbag.

"I thought he'd left me," Zofia said. "For almost twenty years I thought he'd left me and your mother and taken off for California. Not that I minded. I was tired of being married and cooking dinners and cleaning house for someone else. It's better to cook what I want to eat, and clean up when I decide to clean up. It was harder on your mother, not having a father. That was the part that I minded most.

"Then it turned out that he hadn't run away after all. He'd spent one night in the handbag and then come out again twenty years later, exactly as handsome as I remembered, and enough time had passed that I had forgiven him all the quarrels. We made up and it was all very romantic and then when we had another fight the next morning, he went and kissed your mother, who had slept right through his visit, on the cheek, and then he climbed right back inside the handbag. I didn't see him again for another twenty years. The last time he showed up, we went to see 'Star Wars' and he liked it so much that he went back inside the handbag to tell everyone else about it. In a couple of years they'll all show up and want to see it on video and all of the sequels too."

"Tell them not to bother with the prequels," I said.

The thing about Zofia and libraries is that she's always losing library books. She says that she hasn't lost them, and in fact that they aren't even overdue, really. It's just that even one week inside the faery handbag is a lot longer in library-world time. So what is she supposed to do about it? The librarians all hate Zofia. She's banned from using any of the branches in our area. When I was eight, she got me to go to the library for her and check out a bunch of biographies and science books and some Georgette Heyer romance novels. My mother was livid when she found out, but it was too late. Zofia had already misplaced most of them.

It's really hard to write about somebody as if they're really dead. I still think Zofia must be sitting in her living room, in her house, watching some old horror movie, dropping popcorn into her handbag. She's waiting for me to come over and play Scrabble.

Nobody is ever going to return those library books now.

My mother used to come home from work and roll her eyes. "Have you been telling them your fairy stories?" she'd say. "Genevieve, your grandmother is a horrible liar."

Zofia would fold up the Scrabble board and shrug at me and Jake. "I'm a wonderful liar," she'd say. "I'm the best liar in the world. Promise me you won't believe a single word."

But she wouldn't tell the story of the faery handbag to Jake. Only the old Baldeziwurlekistanian folktales and fairytales about the people under the hill. She told him about how she and her husband made it all the way across Europe, hiding in haystacks and in barns, and how once, when her husband went off to find food, a farmer found her hiding in his chicken coop and tried to rape her. But she opened up the faery handbag in the way she showed me, and the dog came out and ate the farmer and all his chickens too.

She was teaching Jake and me how to curse in Baldeziwurleki. I also know how to say I love you, but I'm not going to ever say it to anyone again, except to Jake, when I find him.

When I was eight, I believed everything Zofia told me. By the time I was thirteen, I didn't believe a single word. When I was fifteen, I saw a man come out of her house and get on Zofia's three-speed bicycle and ride down the street. His clothes looked funny. He was a lot younger than my mother and father, and even though I'd never seen him before, he was familiar. I followed him on my bike, all the way to the grocery store. I waited just past the checkout lanes while he bought peanut butter, Jack Daniels, half a dozen instant cameras, and at least sixty packs of Reeses Peanut Butter Cups, three bags of Hershey's kisses, a handful of Milky Way bars and other stuff from the rack of checkout candy. While the checkout clerk was helping him bag up all of that chocolate, he looked up and saw me. "Genevieve?" he said. "That's your name, right?"

I turned and ran out of the store. He grabbed up the bags and ran after me. I don't even think he got his change back. I was still running away, and then one of the straps on my flip flops popped out of the sole, the way they do, and that made me really angry so I just stopped. I turned around.

"Who are you?" I said.

But I already knew. He looked like he could have been my mom's younger brother. He was really cute. I could see why Zofia had fallen in love with him.

His name was Rustan. Zofia told my parents that he was an expert in Baldeziwurlekistanian folklore who would be staying with her for a few days. She brought him over for dinner. Jake was there too, and I could tell that Jake knew something was up. Everybody except my dad knew something was going on.

"You mean Baldeziwurlekistan is a real place?" my mother asked Rustan. "My mother is telling the truth?"

I could see that Rustan was having a hard time with that one. He obviously wanted to say that his wife was a horrible liar, but then where would he be? Then he couldn't be the person that he was supposed to be.

There were probably a lot of things that he wanted to say. What he said was, "This is really good pizza."

Rustan took a lot of pictures at dinner. The next day I went with him to get the pictures developed. He'd brought back some film with him, with pictures he'd taken inside the faery handbag, but those didn't come out well. Maybe the film was too old. We got doubles of the pictures from dinner so that I could have some too. There's a great picture of Jake, sitting outside on the porch. He's laughing, and he has his hand up to his mouth, like he's going to catch the laugh. I have that picture up on my computer, and also up on my wall over my bed.

I bought a Cadbury Cream Egg for Rustan. Then we shook hands and he kissed me once on each cheek. "Give one of those kisses to your mother," he said, and I thought about how the next time I saw him, I might be Zofia's age, and he would only be a few days older. The next time I saw him, Zofia would be dead. Jake and I might have kids. That was too weird.

I know Rustan tried to get Zofia to go with him, to live in the handbag, but she wouldn't.

"It makes me dizzy in there," she used to tell me. "And they don't have movie theaters. And I have to look after your mother and you. Maybe when you're old enough to look after the handbag, I'll poke my head inside, just long enough for a little visit."

I didn't fall in love with Jake because he was smart. I'm pretty smart myself. I know that smart doesn't mean nice, or even mean that you have a lot of common sense. Look at all the trouble smart people get themselves into.

I didn't fall in love with Jake because he could make maki rolls and had a black belt in fencing, or whatever it is that you get if you're good in fencing. I didn't fall in love with Jake because he plays guitar. He's a better soccer player than he is a guitar player.

Those were the reasons why I went out on a date with Jake. That, and because he asked me. He asked if I wanted to go see a movie, and I asked if I could bring my grandmother and Natalie and Natasha. He said sure and so all five of us sat and watched "Bring It On" and every once in a while Zofia dropped a couple of milk duds or some popcorn into her purse. I don't know if she was feeding the dog, or if she'd opened the purse the right way, and was throwing food at her husband.

I fell in love with Jake because he told stupid knock-knock jokes to Natalie, and told Natasha that he liked her jeans. I fell in love with Jake when he took me and Zofia home. He walked her up to her front door and then he walked me up to mine. I fell in love with Jake when he didn't try to kiss me. The thing is, I was nervous about the whole kissing thing. Most guys think that they're better at it than they really are. Not that I think I'm a real genius at kissing either, but I don't think kissing should be a competitive sport. It isn't tennis.

Natalie and Natasha and I used to practice kissing with each other. Not that we like each other that way, but just for practice. We got pretty good at it. We could see why kissing was supposed to be fun.

But Jake didn't try to kiss me. Instead he just gave me this really big hug. He put his face in my hair and he sighed. We stood there like that, and then finally I said, "What are you doing?"

"I just wanted to smell your hair," he said.

"Oh," I said. That made me feel weird, but in a good way. I put my nose up to his hair, which is brown and curly, and I smelled it. We stood there and smelled each other's hair, and I felt so good. I felt so happy.

Jake said into my hair, "Do you know that actor John Cusack?"

I said, "Yeah. One of Zofia's favorite movies is 'Better Off Dead.' We watch it all the time."

"So he likes to go up to women and smell their armpits."

"Gross!" I said. "That's such a lie! What are you doing now? That tickles."

"I'm smelling your ear," Jake said.

Jake's hair smelled like iced tea with honey in it, after all the ice has melted.

Kissing Jake is like kissing Natalie or Natasha, except that it isn't just for fun. It feels like something there isn't a word for in Scrabble.

The deal with Houdini is that Jake got interested in him during Advanced Placement American History. He and I were both put in tenth grade history. We were doing biography projects. I was studying Joseph McCarthy. My grandmother had all sorts of stories about McCarthy. She hated him for what he did to Hollywood.

Jake didn't turn in his project–instead he told everyone in our AP class except for Mr. Streep (we call him Meryl) to meet him at the gym on Saturday. When we showed up, Jake reenacted one of Houdini's escapes with a laundry bag, handcuffs, a gym locker, bicycle chains, and the school's swimming pool. It took him three and a half minutes to get free, and this guy named Roger took a bunch of photos and then put the photos online. One of the photos ended up in the *Boston Globe*, and Jake got expelled. The really ironic thing was that while his mom was in the hospital, Jake had applied to M.I.T. He did it for his mom. He thought that way she'd have to stay alive. She was so excited about M.I.T. A couple of days after he'd been expelled, right after the wedding, while his dad and the fencing instructor were in Bermuda, he got an acceptance letter in the mail and a phone call from this guy in the admissions office who explained why they had to withdraw the acceptance.

My mother wanted to know why I let Jake wrap himself up in bicycle chains and then watched while Peter and Michael pushed him into the deep end of the school pool. I said that Jake had a backup plan. Ten more seconds and we were all going to jump into the pool and open the locker and get him out of there. I was crying when I said that. Even before he got in the locker, I knew how stupid Jake was being. Afterwards, he promised me that he'd never do anything like that again.

That was when I told him about Zofia's husband, Rustan, and about Zofia's handbag. How stupid am I?

So I guess you can figure out what happened next. The problem is that Jake believed me about the handbag. We spent a lot of time over at Zofia's, playing Scrabble. Zofia never let the faery handbag out of her sight. She even took it with her when she went to the bathroom. I think she even slept with it under her pillow.

I didn't tell her that I'd said anything to Jake. I wouldn't ever have told anybody else about it. Not Natasha. Not even Natalie, who is the most responsible person in all of the world. Now, of course, if the handbag turns up and Jake still hasn't come back, I'll have to tell Natalie. Somebody has to keep an eye on the stupid thing while I go find Jake.

What worries me is that maybe one of the Baldeziwurlekistanians or one of the people under the hill or maybe even Rustan popped out of the handbag to run an errand and got worried when Zofia wasn't there. Maybe they'll come looking for her and bring it back. Maybe they know I'm supposed to look after it now. Or maybe they took it and hid it somewhere. Maybe someone turned it in at the lost-and-found at the library and that stupid librarian called the F.B.I. Maybe scientists at the Pentagon are examining the handbag right now. Testing it. If Jake comes out, they'll think he's a spy or a superweapon or an alien or something. They're not going to just let him go.

Everyone thinks Jake ran away, except for my mother, who is convinced that he was trying out another Houdini escape and is probably lying at the bottom of a lake somewhere. She hasn't said that to me, but I can see her thinking it. She keeps making cookies for me.

What happened is that Jake said, "Can I see that for just a second?"

He said it so casually that I think he caught Zofia off guard. She was reaching into the purse for her wallet. We were standing in the lobby of the movie theater on a Monday morning. Jake was behind the snack counter. He'd gotten a job there. He was wearing this stupid red paper hat and some kind of apron-bib thing. He was supposed to ask us if we wanted to supersize our drinks.

He reached over the counter and took Zofia's handbag right out of her hand. He closed it and then he opened it again. I think he opened it the right way. I don't think he ended up in the dark place. He said to me and Zofia, "I'll be right back." And then he wasn't there anymore. It was just me and Zofia and the handbag, lying there on the counter where he'd dropped it.

If I'd been fast enough, I think I could have followed him. But Zofia had been guardian of the faery handbag for a lot longer. She snatched the bag back and glared at me. "He's a very bad boy," she said. She was absolutely furious. "You're better off without him, Genevieve, I think."

"Give me the handbag," I said. "I have to go get him."

"It isn't a toy, Genevieve," she said. "It isn't a game. This isn't Scrabble. He comes back when he comes back. If he comes back."

"Give me the handbag," I said. "Or I'll take it from you."

She held the handbag up high over her head, so that I couldn't reach it. I hate people who are taller than me. "What are you going to do now," Zofia said. "Are you going to knock me down? Are you going to steal the handbag? Are you going to go away and leave me here to explain to your parents where you've gone? Are you going to say goodbye to your friends? When you come out again, they will have gone to college. They'll have jobs and babies and houses and they won't even recognize you. Your mother will be an old woman and I will be dead."

"I don't care," I said. I sat down on the sticky red carpet in the lobby and started to cry. Someone wearing a little metal name tag came over and asked if we were okay. His name was Missy. Or maybe he was wearing someone else's tag.

"We're fine," Zofia said. "My granddaughter has the flu."

She took my hand and pulled me up. She put her arm around me and we walked out of the theater. We never even got to see the stupid movie. We never even got to see another movie together. I don't ever want to go see another movie. The problem is, I don't want to see unhappy endings. And I don't know if I believe in the happy ones.

"I have a plan," Zofia said. "I will go find Jake. You will stay here and look after the handbag."

145

"You won't come back either," I said. I cried even harder. "Or if you do, I'll be like a hundred years old and Jake will still be sixteen."

"Everything will be okay," Zofia said. I wish I could tell you how beautiful she looked right then. It didn't matter if she was lying or if she actually knew that everything was going to be okay. The important thing was how she looked when she said it. She said, with absolute certainty, or maybe with all the skill of a very skillful liar, "My plan will work. First we go to the library, though. One of the people under the hill just brought back an Agatha Christie mystery, and I need to return it."

"We're going to the library?" I said. "Why don't we just go home and play Scrabble for a while." You probably think I was just being sarcastic here, and I was being sarcastic. But Zofia gave me a sharp look. She knew that if I was being sarcastic that my brain was working again. She knew that I knew she was stalling for time. She knew that I was coming up with my own plan, which was a lot like Zofia's plan, except that I was the one who went into the handbag. *How* was the part I was working on.

"We could do that," she said. "Remember, when you don't know what to do, it never hurts to play Scrabble. It's like reading the I Ching or tea leaves."

"Can we please just hurry?" I said.

Zofia just looked at me. "Genevieve, we have plenty of time. If you're going to look after the handbag, you have to remember that. You have to be patient. Can you be patient?"

"I can try," I told her. I'm trying, Zofia. I'm trying really hard. But it isn't fair. Jake is off having adventures and talking to talking animals, and who knows, learning how to fly and some beautiful three thousand year old girl from under the hill is teaching him how to speak fluent Baldeziwurleki. I bet she lives in a house that runs around on chicken legs, and she tells Jake that she'd love to hear him play something on the guitar. Maybe you'll kiss her, Jake, because she's put a spell on you. But whatever you do, don't go up into her house. Don't fall asleep in her bed. Come back soon, Jake, and bring the handbag with you.

I hate those movies, those books, where some guy gets to go off and have adventures and meanwhile the girl has to stay home and wait. I'm a feminist. I subscribe to Bust magazine, and I watch Buffy reruns. I don't believe in that kind of shit.

We hadn't been in the library for five minutes before Zofia picked up a biography of Carl Sagan and dropped it in her purse. She was definitely stalling for time. She was trying to come up with a plan that would counteract the plan that she knew I was planning. I wondered what she thought I was planning. It was probably much better than anything I'd come up with.

"Don't do that!" I said.

"Don't worry," Zofia said. "Nobody was watching."

"I don't care if nobody saw! What if Jake's sitting there in the boat, or what if he was coming back and you just dropped it on his head!"

"It doesn't work that way," Zofia said. Then she said, "It would serve him right, anyway."

That was when the librarian came up to us. She had a nametag on as well. I was so sick of people and their stupid nametags. I'm not even going to tell you what her name was. "I saw that," the librarian said.

"Saw what?" Zofia said. She smiled down at the librarian,

like she was Queen of the Library, and the librarian were a petitioner.

The librarian stared hard at her. "I know you," she said, almost sounding awed, like she was a weekend birdwatcher who had just seen Bigfoot. "We have your picture on the office wall. You're Ms. Swinks. You aren't allowed to check out books here."

"That's ridiculous," Zofia said. She was at least two feet taller than the librarian. I felt a bit sorry for the librarian. After all, Zofia had just stolen a seven-day book. She probably wouldn't return it for a hundred years. My mother has always made it clear that it's my job to protect other people from Zofia. I guess I was Zofia's guardian before I became the guardian of the handbag.

The librarian reached up and grabbed Zofia's handbag. She was small but she was strong. She jerked the handbag and Zofia stumbled and fell back against a work desk. I couldn't believe it. Everyone except for me was getting a look at Zofia's handbag. What kind of guardian was I going to be?

"Genevieve," Zofia said. She held my hand very tightly, and I looked at her. She looked wobbly and pale. She said, "I feel very bad about all of this. Tell your mother I said so."

Then she said one last thing, but I think it was in Baldeziwurleki.

The librarian said, "I saw you put a book in here. Right here." She opened the handbag and peered inside. Out of the handbag came a long, lonely, ferocious, utterly hopeless scream of rage. I don't ever want to hear that noise again. Everyone in the library looked up. The librarian made a choking noise and threw Zofia's handbag away from her. A little trickle of blood came out of her nose and a drop fell on the floor. What I thought at first was that it was just plain luck that the handbag was closed when it landed. Later on I was trying to figure out what Zofia said. My Baldeziwurleki isn't very good, but I think she was saying something like "Figures. Stupid librarian. I have to go take care of that damn dog." So maybe that's what happened. Maybe Zofia sent part of herself in there with the skinless dog. Maybe she fought it and won and closed the handbag. Maybe she made friends with it. I mean, she used to feed it popcorn at the movies. Maybe she's still in there.

What happened in the library was Zofia sighed a little and closed her eyes. I helped her sit down in a chair, but I don't think she was really there any more. I rode with her in the ambulance, when the ambulance finally showed up, and I swear I didn't even think about the handbag until my mother showed up. I didn't say a word. I just left her there in the hospital with Zofia, who was on a respirator, and I ran all the way back to the library. But it was closed. So I ran all the way back again, to the hospital, but you already know what happened, right? Zofia died. I hate writing that. My tall, funny, beautiful, book-stealing, Scrabble-playing, story-telling grandmother died.

But you never met her. You're probably wondering about the handbag. What happened to it. I put up signs all over town, like Zofia's handbag was some kind of lost dog, but nobody ever called.

So that's the story so far. Not that I expect you to believe any of it. Last night Natalie and Natasha came over and we played Scrabble. They don't really like Scrabble, but they feel like it's their job to cheer me up. I won. After they went home, I flipped all the tiles upside-down and then I started picking them up in groups of seven. I tried to ask a question, but it was hard to pick just one. The words I got weren't so great either, so I decided that they weren't English words. They were Baldeziwurleki words.

Once I decided that, everything became perfectly clear. First I put down "kirif" which means "happy news", and then I got a "b," an "o," an "l," an "e," a "f," another "i," an "s," and a "z." So then I could make "kirif" into "bolekirifisz," which could mean "the happy result of a combination of diligent effort and patience."

I would find the faery handbag. The tiles said so. I would work the clasp and go into the handbag and have my own adventures and would rescue Jake. Hardly any time would have gone by before we came back out of the handbag. Maybe I'd even make friends with that poor dog and get to say goodbye, for real, to Zofia. Rustan would show up again and be really sorry that he'd missed Zofia's funeral and this time he would be brave enough to tell my mother the whole story. He would tell her that he was her father. Not that she would believe him. Not that you should believe this story. Promise me that you won't believe a word.

THE TRUTH OR SOMETHING BEAUTIFUL

SHIRIN DUBBIN

Every emotion can be mimicked in fabric. Pride is liquid gold lamé, fit to perfection, begging to be seen and to be praised. Hatred finds its twin in fur, intemperate, born of blood and sacrifice. Death.

I've been stripped bare in this moment, made numb, with nothing to hold on to except my brother's hand. Strange. I'm not sure how often losing is synonymous with death or winning constitutes a kind of murder, but I understand. My brother's gunmetal tipped nails gouge the flesh between my fingers and we face off with our rivals, the House of Chantico.

This is how a fashion house dies.

Tonight should've been our comeback, the return of Nommos. All facets fell into place brilliantly, our fall collection, the buzzing of the press, and the venue. The Russian Gardens, a storied location, lauded, and equally difficult to book. Unfortunately, securing the venue required sex with the caretaker. Not fun, but he hadn't been horrible. Although he'd seemed convinced my *kumquat* held a magic button within its folds and he'd kept pressing, apparently in hopes of inducing instant orgasm.

We do sacrifice for fashion, don't we?

Yet the benefits outweighed the drawbacks. I'd been vindicated when I peeked around the flats, flanking the runway, and found a standing room audience who looked amazing. My brother, Anwar, and I had timed our show to the rising of the full moon and our crew had lit the gardens to emulate moon glow—everyone looked good in this lighting. Especially our key guests, the fashion-nobles, front row, stage right. Seated there were all those who mattered, from Wintour to Mallis.

Winter to malice might've been more appropriate, but I hadn't known it then. Every facet had fallen into place so seamlessly the businesswoman in me should've intuited something wrong. I'd known my brother created a seminal collection and giddiness had obfuscated sensibility.

In the years after my aunt, the most famous designer in the history of Nommos, had disappeared or been kidnapped or been killed, we didn't know which, we only knew her absence had diminished us, we'd produced several less than stellar seasons since.

My brother and I hadn't understood the reasons until we fell. Our failure came in trying to imitate our aunt's designs, her sense of style. We'd destroyed our house as plainly as fools dismantle logic. Surrogates do not innovate; of course our attempts came to lesser effect than her triumphs. She'd been ahead of her time and time had moved on.

With this collection we'd woken up, me on the business end. Anwar had stepped out in his own creative direction and it was ingenious. Petals of fabric made to emulate flowers, shades of the garden, paired with luxurious coats of tapestry and fur, contrasted with a bit of edge—leather in matching pale hues and a hint of hardware in zippers and buckles. Glorious. We both knew it.

At the end of the show I'd blown past the producer, blinded by my anticipation. My brother wouldn't have noticed the foreboding looks surrounding us either. He's not observant, too often distracted by the pretty things and the prospect of our resurrection glittered most seductively.

The moment we hit the runaway I cast my gaze right. Nervous energy bordered on palpitations and constricted within my throat. The faces on the front row should have told me where we stood, how far we'd re-risen . . . but there were no faces as indication.

The front row stood empty. It still is.

Those who make the fashion have deserted us, walked out. Worse, they'd left their swag bags beneath their chairs, not even to be enticed by iPads, imported chocolate, or Swarovski crystal bracelets. We'd been snubbed.

And here we stand, stripped bare. My brother collapses, jerking me to one side, his nails digging deeper into my flesh. I don't look at him. I can't. Acid waves of shame emanate from his clenched fingers and eat away at me. Pain lends only a small diversion. There are cold gazes on us. Our enemies have arrived.

The gardens are empty other than the three Chanticos. None of them stands taller than five-feet-eight-inches but they are stunning, dark haired, nearly oxblood eyed, with skin so warm a glow it seems gold dusted, and auras so chilling few choose to stand closer to them than an arm could reach. They are as gorgeous as we are, with our dark skin and Donatello hewed features, but beauty does not rest pleasingly on them. It is sharp and rapacious in their grasps.

Santiago Chantico inclines his head, his expression an echo of his victory. Their family reigns from the end of our runway. We merely stand on it. They own this fantasy we'd built to save our house as surely as they own this era in fashion.

"What happened, Lu?" my brother whispers, his attention trapped by the Chanticos. He tries to pull me down beside him but I won't bend.

"I don't know."

"Luciana, I don't understand what this means." He gestures to the emptiness around us and then to our lifelong counterparts, our opponents in a two-hundred-year-old feud.

"They've beaten us, Anwar. We're done."

An alert buzzes my phone. I lift it out of the pocket hidden within my dress. The latest news scrolls across the touch screen, generated by the keyword Nommos.

The Internet proclaims: The House of Nommos Frets and Dies On the Runway.

There is value in deception, in the way our rivalry doesn't appear to have changed, even now as Santiago and I stand on opposite sides of vintage clothing racks and stare one another down. There are differences, though. I no longer believe I am his equal. It isn't something I think about but the curve of my spine knows, for the first time it holds a bend.

Santiago despises me. Always has. Had we known each other as children I image bloody noses and clandestine pushes out of tree houses as the result. His contempt is immutable as leather, it may be dyed or take on a patina but the core remains that of the animal. Beyond his hate, this beast, this Chantico, has gotten angry with me. His eyes don't ridicule the way they once did and there is the slightest twitch to his jaw.

I have no idea what caused his fury but I adore it. My gaze drops to the racks and I finger a string of black beads. When I look back at Santiago it's with a sneer from my arsenal of nasty expressions—a flash of showmanship for anyone watching. It's something my family is very good at, being lovely while sneering.

Let the public believe in this ghost of the Nommos vs. Chantico rivalry. If it isn't new it isn't newsworthy and our feud is a classic. As long as the perception of it remains the same I'll be saved the humiliation of fashion journalists seeking fresh takes and forcing me to relive Nommos' fall.

My brother is bad press enough.

A solid weight strikes the back of my knee and I drop, grasping for the racks before I'm caught around the ribcage. Santiago is at my back, his forearm compressing around me.

"Tell me you haven't forgotten, Nommos." His tone is calm. Not even a whisper of breath disturbs my skin. But I feel his anger. He'd never touch me for any other reason. "Tell me you haven't forgotten the 1920s when my grandmother CeCi's little black dress-suit made your house an afterthought."

Murmurs begin to volley around us. If I don't free myself our families will make the pages again. I push up and away but Santiago holds me. "Say you remember the 50s Nommos pencil skirt and the way it drove our house mad. Or us striking back at you, after a decade, with super short metallic cocktail dresses."

Yes. These skirmishes were as familiar to me as my parents' faces. I'd been raised on these history lessons.

Remembering to maintain my sneer, I grasped his forearm in both hands and jerked. His muscles didn't flex beneath my fingers and he didn't let go. Instead he laughed. "Later, your aunt Soma triumphed with the women's tuxedo," he says. "It was unconscionable Nommos had created such an iconic look and it burned at me . . . until the night we took you down." The skin of his cheek presses, cold, against my ear. "Tell me you remember."

The fall of my house at Chantico's hands is not a memory. It is my wakeup call and my lullaby. Two turns of the seasons have passed since that night: Pre-Spring, Spring, Resort, Pre-Fall, and Fall. Then repeat. And I haven't left that runway.

Our last collection had been inspired; there could be no argument. How were my brother and I to know that earlier in the day the House of Chantico had beaten us to it?

Where we'd reinvented, their collection deconstructed pre-1917 Russian Revolution fashion, resulting in sensation causing silhouettes. In the finale they'd featured authentic evening gowns cut into jackets and frock coats worthy of rockstars. This was their skill, to take the trends of other eras and hurl them one step past the now into futuristic looks the rest of us could only follow. Chantico is what *Imitation of Christ* had aspired to. In that battle the former had ripped out the throats of the latter, just as they'd preempted our fatal collection and done it better.

Better?

It seems ridiculous anyone could out-innovate The House of Nommos. Yet history says Chantico did. Louder than history, the memory of the audience's departure continues to spit our failure in my and my brother's face.

The rejection. The shame. The guilt of bringing down my

family's legacy is ground glass in my intestines. The pain continuously works itself through my body.

Tell him what? I can't speak. I've lost the part of myself who wore fierce in the form of flowing dresses and seven-inch boots. My latest wardrobe is structured and hard lined, built around men's suiting fabrics—tweed and wool crepes. I masquerade in the armor of the businessman now, when before I'd been strong on the inside.

The rapid fire clicks of a camera sound and I slump against Santiago. He hisses and lets me go. I don't feel it when I fall but I hear his knee-high motorcycle boots strike the floor as he leaves me behind.

Out at the curb my driver opens the door. I hand my purchases off to him as I slide into the car, ignoring the twinge of fresh bruises. Once the black shields of my Jackie-O sunglasses are patted into place I feel better. Best to forget the losses, disregard the press coverage I know is coming, and let it all go. At the traffic light a man in leg warmers pirouettes into the crosswalk. If his mind and body are still connected it is from a distance of light years. Best not to let myself go that far.

I turn away. Despite my effort to disconnect the dancing man reminds me of my brother. This could easily be Anwar. I smooth my hand over the twin buns at the nape of my neck and exhale. Diana Vreeland once said, "There is a glory to madness that only madmen know." My brother must be living a glorious life. I can tell by the way he bites his thumb when agitated or by his insistence on going clubbing in only underwear, tailored in peek-a-boo folds of silk chiffon.

Yet Anwar's resolve to remain in the press is not the worse thing he's done. Six months ago he moved out of the family manor to live across town with his lover. Until then I hadn't realized how well our home reflects emptiness back at a person.

Inside the manor's grand foyer I kick off my shoes, I can't stand the echoes that bounce off the marble when I walk. One housekeeper or another takes the dresses I will never wear and I take the stairs, stripping as I ascend to the second floor. Santiago's smell has dogged me since I left the vintage shop. These clothes must come off. His scent is as metallic as his skin, coppery and overwhelming. A chill licks across my neck but when I spin on the stair I am alone, only me, memories of Santiago's anger, and perhaps a haunting of my brother's madness.

All the things—the statues, paintings, and family portraits—that used to give me comfort surround me, but the manor has become more a vault than a home. Lately there is a stillness here, indistinguishable from darkness.

It seems I am the last in our fashion line. The old guard are all dead, the auntie seamstresses, and the fabric sourcing uncles. My parents have gone as well. The few remaining cousins aren't interested. They've built social networks and hotels, opened chains of bakeries or become film stars. The family business is old hat and they're far too fashionable for it.

My aunt Soma wouldn't have allowed this. She'd have designed a must-have collection, been invited to appear on Project Runway, and Nommos would live on. Strange how I didn't appreciate her until after she'd disappeared. My traitorous adoration had trained on another fashion-noble, yet Soma Nommos had been the one to innovate the *women's tuxedo* in 1975, two months after turning fifteen. Another of my regrets lies in not learning all I could from her.

The curtains in my rooms are open, and the sunset descends behind the twin mansion across the street. Both are gothic revivals, stone with arched windows and turrets, but I prefer our reddish facade to the Chantico's tan one. Our homes have stood in perpetual face-off since grandpapa decided to build across from our rivals and, as a bonus, obstruct their view. He'd hoped to annoy them. It worked. Their fall collection that season flopped like live bait on the runway.

Ground glass continues to twist in my guts. As prevention against it I walk to the bed and slip on the slim cuffed trousers and blouse laid there. Draped in my own scent again, I flip back the duvet to expose a keypad. The series of numbers I encode is long but soon enough the drawer to the safe beneath the bed slides open.

Aunt Soma's last sketchbook crowns the stack of things I cherish. I settle onto the floor, using the bed as a backrest, and take her sketches from the drawer. My fingers sift through, trace her pen strokes. Occasionally, I lift the pages and breathe them in. Setting the sketchbook aside I pick up my second treasure out, a signed copy of C'est CeCi, the autobiography of CeCi EnChant.

I'd robbed Auntie Soma of my adoration and given it to this woman instead. The beauty of her profile, her signature sapphire ring, and the fact she is still synonymous with style, eighty-nine years later, are my drugs. I am a traitor in this but if I could I would run Nommos in the same manner she did her own house. I would create something as singular as her little black suit-dress. If I could I would be the modern Cecilia Chantico.

A second chill bites into my spine and, scanning the room, I warm it by massaging my neck. I'm alone in the still and darkness.

The last of the things I keep hidden is the most shameful, my own sketches, designs I'd been too small or too afraid to bring to my brother. A looping Luciana crosses the pages and mocks my lack of pride. The designs here are edgy, unexpected. I don't know whether or not we could've succeeded with them. I hadn't tried. And these phantoms of what I haven't done haunt me more then the specter of our failure.

"Luciana," the voice says, drawing the "ana" out into a taunt. My flesh chills. The voice is old and knowing, vaguely familiar. I don't turn around, but I wonder if I've died and Hades calls. Before I can ask who dares to invade my home Galen Chantico appears between my bent knees. He grips me by the shoulders and we are gone.

What has depth or what is shallow are matters of perception. Fashion is often labeled the latter and although I don't see it as a contribution to this belief, I have chosen the ensemble I am to be buried in.

Galen Chantico drags me down the path on one side of his family's manor and deposits me in their courtyard. I try to rise but he mashes me back to my knees. With the method of my death becoming ever more apparent, I wish I'd also picked an outfit for the police to find my body in. Of course, if mine is the same end as my aunt Soma's I will not be found, so it doesn't matter.

Dirt and moisture seep into my palms and knees. When I push back, resting my backside on crossed ankles, there's nowhere to wipe the grime off my hands. My fingers curl into fists. I'm tired of being manhandled by Chanticos. Let them put a final end to our battle tonight. I won't carry this impotent hate anymore. Everything is an annoyance, the dirt, the scent of jasmine in their garden; even the sound of their water feature makes me want to dig out their eyes with chopsticks.

Adriana Chantico arrives on the same path Galen took to bring me here. She carries a man draped in a fur cloak and wearing gladiator sandals. His bare ass peek-a-boos with each of her footfalls. It's my brother, but I'm more surprised by how the five-foot-five-inch woman carries my six-foot twin with no effort at all.

She deposits Anwar beside me. Her smile is wicked. Her skin luminous, as though internally lit.

Anwar scrambles backward. Then, seeing me, dives to throw his arms around my neck. "This is how a house dies. Yes, Lu?" he says with enough bravado to make me proud.

"Yes." I kiss his cheek. "I'm glad I'm going with you."

"Well, hell," he says, examining his manicure before biting his thumb. "We arrived together. We might as well *do-si-do*."

A glow at the edge of my vision draws my attention away from our dysfunctional I-love-yous. Headed by Santiago, the three Chanticos step down from the paved patio behind their house as a unit. Galen sits down and rests an elbow over his knee. Adriana throws out her arms in a stretch and perches on the side of a lawn chair. Santiago glares.

A gasp escapes my brother. I know the feeling. The Chanticos have changed and they're putting on a grand show in vintage fashions from every era. Authentic fashions. My eye can't be fooled. The looks are worthy of ovation, but they aren't the reason I can't close my mouth. Beyond the clothes, the Chanticos' aspects have transformed. Their rapacious features are smoother, better defined, unnatural, and the three gleam, metallic gold, with shimmering oxblood eyes.

"I thought about giving a speech," Santiago says, "but I can show you better than I could tell you."

A fourth figure, an impossible one, exits the house and takes a seat beside Galen.

Anwar whispers to me. "Clearly, I'm acting out and you've had me committed. Right, Lu? Otherwise, I think you should. I cannot be looking at a young Oscar Chantico right now."

"But you are looking at him," I say.

This is what I know; fifty years ago our grandpapa and Oscar Chantico took up the family feud with such skill their strategies against one another are taught as a course at Pratt. When Oscar retired to Mauritius, and never returned, grandpapa mourned him. Both men were supposed to be dead now. I know my grandfather is. Yet I know Oscar Chantico is not, and the word gorgeous will need to be expanded to define him.

I'm not dense. I don't need another example to tell me what the Chanticos are, but she walks out onto the second floor balcony. Her light is seductive and I close my eyes as her glow falls on me. The hair is longer. The ensemble—an exquisite lamé tuxedo with nothing beneath—wouldn't have been worn in the 20s. The face, however, and the sapphire are eternally hers. My brother slumps against my shoulder. I think he fainted. Opening my eyes to check I find CeCi's gaze on me, unreadable yet too golden to be called cold.

My awe is galling.

"Look at her," she says. "This Nommos probably thinks we're vampires."

Santiago glances at the balcony and down to me. "Certainly my rival has more imagination than that."

A delicate shrug in response. "It's not like what we are hasn't been featured in movies, to one extent or some other."

"Given," Santiago says to her. For me he expounds. "We are the children of an Aztec blood god, one of treasures, pleasure and pain—"

"Vengeance and sacrifice." CeCi laughs. Damn me, I love the sound, and I wonder what kind of madness it is that I find comfort in being murdered by my idol, the blood goddess.

Santiago covers his face. His grimace seems self-directed but after a moment his shoulders square. As he approaches he is clearly resolute.

"I cannot do this without you," he says.

What? I scan his face to make sense of his words.

"By 'you' I mean the House of Nommos. I cannot run Chantico without you."

My hand unwittingly grips Anwar's relaxed form. To Santiago I give my finest sneer. He approves because he smiles. "Who would push us? Who would turn our hearts to jealousy, give life meaning, make us burn?"

He slaps me. My head whips to the side with the force. I turn back to him slowly, not bothering to wipe the blood away. "But you won."

"Winning is nothing. It is a byproduct of superiority," Santiago says. "How could we claim to be the best if we aren't constantly challenged by you?"

Anwar should be awake for this. Santiago Chantico has admitted we are their equals, the measure against which they prove themselves. And it's about time.

He slaps me again. I'm too pleased to feel it.

"We are so cold, Nommos. Only blood sacrifice and our hatred of you warms us." His lips curl. Both his canines and incisors are daggers of bone. "How could you give up? Don't you remember our glorious battles?"

I'd standup if I were that stupid. Instead I shrug. "I wasn't alive for most of it."

Santiago taps a finger against his mouth and the others chuckle. CeCi calls out, "But you know our histories because of me. Don't you, Nommos? You adore me, you live for fashion, and you love your family line. Without doubts this impasse troubles you as much as it does us."

I adore her a little less for taunting me, but she's right.

A silent exchange takes place between Santiago and CeCi before he looks back at me. "We cannot allow your house to die. Therefore we'll give you time. Among other gifts."

Galen rises and goes into the house.

White noise fills my head and I realize I'm afraid. "I don't want your gifts," I say.

Living forever isn't something I crave. It's not the blood that scares me. The risk of failing over and over again, without end, is something one lifetime makes bearable. Beyond that I couldn't account for my sanity.

The third Chantico returns with a woman in his arms. Her body is a testimony of cuts, old and new, some scarred over, others barely healed. Santiago makes room and Galen lays her down in front of me.

I hate them, these Chanticos. I let them see it in my eyes, and embrace her, my sobs muffled by her hair. Auntie Soma. She's alive and she paid for it.

"I regret taking her from you," Santiago says. "I will make up for it."

I'm tempted to believe him. He lost a great opponent when he took Soma down. "The blood transforms," he says, "and for the first fifty years or so you'll be able to spawn." Adriana pretends to retch. Santiago nods and continues. "Some of your seed will bear the gift and some will not, but it is enough to begin again. To become strong and challenge us again."

With glances at each of his siblings or kin—I don't know what to call them—Santiago lifts his pointer finger. The nail grows and thickens, taking on the shape of a leaf blade. With it he slices a long gouge into his tongue. A drop of blood falls from the tip of the nail and flowers on the cuff of his white shirt.

Fascination overtakes my fear. He kisses Soma first and drops her to move on to my brother. After tossing Anwar away, Santiago curses, slicing his tongue again. His fingers dig into my scalp when he lifts me. His mouth seals over mine. The blood pours down my throat. It is poison, a cold venomous deluge. Santiago lets me fall. Convulsions wrack my body and I think I bite through my tongue, but there is too much hurt coming from too many places to be sure. They tricked us with all the talk of immortality and the need for our rivalry. Nothing hurts this badly without killing you. I twitch, face down in the courtyard, and accept death.

The beast, Santiago, spits and it lands centimeters from my face. I'm as disgusted as he is, so I close my eyes to it all.

Flame is the first thing I see. It is my own fireplace in the sitting room of Nommos Manor. To my left my brother sleeps, flung across a couch. His skin is now dark bronze with golden highlights, like mine. Behind me, my aunt is propped in a chair. Her scars heal over while I watch and her skin takes on the same glow as ours.

I'm the only one Santiago chose to leave sprawled on the floor. *Game on, sir.* I stagger to the stairs; confident my family will rise when they're ready. In my rooms, I shake the buns from my hair and set the mass loose. A blue glint catches my eye. CeCi's sapphire rests on my second finger, as though I'm affianced to immortality. Yes.

After a shower I put on the patterned Pucci halter dress I found on my last visit to the vintage shop. The pink ruffles, from bodice to hemline, compliment my glow and I admire the ring again. The Chanticos meant it to remind they'd ultimately won and I'd forever chase their lead. That isn't how I see it. For me, the ring is a symbol of my succession to CeCi's throne. The Chanticos will rue my deathless state and we'll duel with every collection, leaving blood on the runway.

I'm colder than I've ever been and I burn with need. Mine is not a transformation into monster. I am choosing to become a predator—a gleaming, well-heeled beast—because once you understand the world is yours, it's easy to do whatever you want with it.

Touching my tongue to sharpened teeth, I wonder when my family will take first blood. I imagine it will be difficult but we'll do it. We've always sacrificed for fashion.

Chanticos, beware.

WAIFS

DIE BOOTH

The girl in this photograph, her name is Marie Bochert. You know this because across the white panel at the bottom of the square image, that name is written. It doesn't seem likely that Marie wrote it herself. This hand is sure and forward-slanting, the pressure so confident that the pen point has engraved the paper with its en-guarde "t." Marie looks softer than that. Marie looks more the 2B type, with her white, heart-shaped face and her pink, heart-shaped lips. Her dark hair hanging and her broad cheekbones, this is what you see in this picture. Her disheartened eyes, scolding you for noticing them first, for not seeing what is important.

"She's pretty."

"She's certainly *pretty*."

The woman turned the photograph over in her golden hands and regarded the square, black back as if expecting there to be additional information written there. She turned back to the image side and shuffled again through the handful of casting Polaroids, pursing and smoothing her lipstick mouth against her teeth, pursing and smoothing, deep in thought. She continued to the man at her side, "Marie Bochert. But is she *now*?"

The man shook a pen between two fingers until it became a fan-shaped blur. He looked at his hands, at the table top, not up. "What's she done? Magazines—any catwalk?"

"London, spring collection, Holly Fulton: the silk jersey monochrome print."

"Oh yes, I remember." The man did not sound as if he remembered. He dropped his pen on the desk and pressed his fingertips to his eyelids. "I remember her more than the collection."

The woman nodded. She slipped the glossy image labelled *Marie Bochert* to the back of a second pile. "We can't use her. She takes attention away from the designs."

"Agreed. Who's next?"

"We have . . . Andrea Pollici."

The man took the next offered image and peered. "Ah yes, much better—much, much better. Not so *loud*."

Marie checked behind her, looking towards the now-open door where an assistant was beckoning curtly. Behind him, a girl cast like a shadow against the apple-white wall. With effort not to make a sound, Marie inched back the plastic chair she was perched on and stood, scuttling to the exit with a parting glance unnoticed by the agents.

First shelf: nothing. Second shelf: nothing appealing either. Marie picked out sardines canned in chilli tomato sauce and peeled back the ring-pull lid to eat them from the can in delicate forkfuls. When Marie felt hungry, all she could think of was couture. Ruffles like cream and icing-precise piping, a red-wine fall of satin splashing across the catwalk, biscuit-base separates in oat-textured tweed. She wasn't trying to diet, it was just her calling. Fashion was her nourishment, her entertainment, her everything. The thing was: Marie Bochert really, *really* loved clothes.

When she'd finished school with quiet grades, Marie had told people she wanted to be a fashion designer. Her friends applauded her, her teachers hid smiles, and her parents raised their voices after dinner in favour of *real work*. Design *was* real work. It was hard. Marie struggled through "Fashion Portfolio" in a foundation-level wash of muddy ink sketches and pricked fingers. *You're so pretty though*, people told her, *you could be a model*. She worked weekends in retail, ringing up sales of high-street versions of the clothes she should have been creating. It supplemented her parents' payments of fees but it didn't stem their complaints. On the other side of the counter, plain teens gawped at her one-track poise. Boys worked hard designing creative ways to ask for her telephone number. When her foundation year finished, Marie applied for an Honours Degree in Fashion Design and Development, even though *research methods* and *concept initiation* baffled and bored her; she just needed her ideas made real. But her grades were mundane and her portfolio muddled, no clear marketable path defined. The samples she produced seemed somehow never to sit right. *Maybe not the ideal career path for you*, the interviewers suggested gently, *perhaps consider retail management?* They said, *you're very pretty*.

"Perhaps I could be a model," Marie agreed.

When you model, you bring alive someone else's vision. That was one way to look at it; another was, in Marie's experience, that models were little more than animated clothes hangers. She was "so pretty," but she was so little often right. She wasn't expressive enough, or else she pulled the wrong faces. She put her feet out of line. She was too obtrusive. Really, she was none of these things—or rather, *all* models are these things. Marie was as good at showcasing clothes as any of her peers. And what clothes!

Suedette fringes like peach skin on budget-brand festival frocks, the popcorn bobble of autumn/winter's kitsch Yuletide knitwear. Marie pouted for the cameras and blanked for the runway and worked her way up wishing for high-end designer gowns.

The lettuce-crisp of starched satin between her fingers; an edging of filigree lace, stiff as spun-sugar.

"No, all wrong."

Marie let her mind wash clear and fixated on the feeling of the satin rosettes beneath her palms. "Go again," the photographer's voice instructed her. She lifted her chin, set her hands at a jauntier angle on her blossomed hips. The studio with its sheeted walls and hidden kitchenette might as well have existed to someone else; she was transported. "No good, no good." Marie's exhale of breath was not impatience, it was dismay. *Never good enough.* "No—not the dress, the dress is perfect: her. Her hair is wrong. Yes I know this was what we discussed, but I see it now." As two stylists descended to pluck at her, Marie tried very hard to disappear.

Marie tried very hard indeed. More than that; she worked very hard. Standing around wearing an ever-changing array of delicious clothing that is rotated like dishes on a kaiten sushi-go-round takes not only talent but also practiced skill. It's a matter of stamina and patience: these outfits will not wear themselves, and Marie had both patience and stamina in bellyfuls. She could stand still as a sculpture; walk with long, gliding strides whilst appearing to not be moving her feet. She could rival a Volto mask for expression when she tried.

"Oh, sorry, I didn't see you there."

Marie smiled slightly at the woman who, squinting, continued, "Are you *meant* to be here?" She gestured around her at the pieces prepared for display and Marie nodded a noncommittal nod.

"I'm modelling the collection tomorrow."

"Right. Sorry, why do you need to be in here right now?"

She must have been an assistant to somebody, or more likely an organiser. Marie said, "Do you know who'll be wearing which outfit?" and the woman looked at her as if she'd asked if there was any chance of borrowing a couple.

"Which are you interested in, in particular?"

"That dress." She got the sarcasm OK, but then Marie was used to being talked down to. The dress wasn't hanging, like most of the other pieces, wrapped in plastic on the racks of freestanding rails; it was displayed on a form. In the chilly fluoro lights leaking in from the adjoining corridor the dress looked alive, draped in potential. Its contoured velvet held the shadows, deep red as dead meat. The diaphanous puff of stuff at the shoulders shimmered in the dim light like a fine, hanging mist of blood.

The woman shuddered. The whole room was suddenly as cold as a walk-in freezer. She said, haltingly, "It looks about your size. Don't hold your breath though."

Then with an aggravated head-jerk of a gesture, she ushered Marie from the room. Marie had wanted to stay and looked longingly back at the dress, snug in the darkness. As the door closed on it, it seemed to be waiting. The woman turned off each light in turn as they walked down the corridors towards the exit, the building tipping dark like dominoes behind them. When they were almost at the foyer, Marie hung back and the woman kept going. She gave one confused-looking glance behind her, her hand poised on the last light-switch and then she shook her head and Marie heard the pop of the last light and the blind rattle of keys.

Marie held her breath and hoped. She prayed to the ghosts of Versace and McQueen. When the door clicked shut and the beeps of the burglar alarm ceased—its red eye blinking blindly at her passing—she crept back along the corridor and let herself into the dressing room. In the tailored dark the walls seemed to breathe. She sensed the dress like a watching thing. When she found it and laid her hands on it, it was warm.

"Two minutes, OK—two minutes."

"Where's makeup? Get me Rob over here now."

"Andrea, then Meena, then . . . OK, Andrea then Stefanie *then* Meena."

"Who's in the red Gespenst gown?"

"Marie."

"Where is she?"

"I'm here."

It started as a ripple that became a wave as every head turned to gape in awe at Marie in the red dress. A terrible, breath-stealing dress of saturated scarlet like a heart turned inside out; like its architect's heart torn out and presented, glinting with gory beads of glass. The room fell quiet, all eyes on the train of the gown that dragged with the graceful measure of a peacock's tail, out behind the screens towards the runway, so heavy and fluid that it might have left behind a wipe of blood on the Lino. With a clatter somebody dropped a tin box of pins that chimed in the silence but still the people weren't distracted; they couldn't look away. As the last few inches of embellished mousseline disappeared from view the watchers sagged.

From beyond the screens, there came a collective gasp of audience breath. They cowered before the majesty of the creation in front of them, the perfect expression of heart as art. There was nobody wearing the gown. It was filled in form but no figure, the force inside rippling its curves and swishing its train, but all that the audience saw was its raw radiance, the triumph of the dress made animate by the one who brought it to life.

The girl in this photograph, her name is—wait a minute. You thought there was a face there but you're just seeing what you expect to see. Shaking the paper the image seems to fade out like this Polaroid is still developing—evolving—even though the glossy surface is dry to the touch. There's no woman in this photograph, you fool: it's a dress on a form, a soufflé of a dress with a cascading skirt of champagne-coloured chiffon like whipped, folded cream. Signed across the bottom in ballpoint, *Marie Bochert*—that must be the creator, the one who brought this dress to life. And what a beautiful dress it is.

WHERE SHADOWS MEET LIGHT

RACHEL SWIRSKY

Princess Diana's ghost emerges at night. There are other ghosts, presumably, but she doesn't see them. She only sees the living.

At first she haunted Charles and Harry and William, but eventually it grew too painful to think about her life. She even grew tired of the longtime pleasure she'd taken from blowing into Elizabeth's ear while she slept, making the old woman's dreams as disturbed and uncomfortable as she had made Diana's life.

She went overseas to America where she'd once visited the White House and danced with John Travolta in a midnight blue velvet gown that sold at auction for a hundred thousand pounds. This time, she traveled between ordinary houses, some white and others beige and mint and yellow. It was easy to find people she could haunt there, people who owned memorabilia with her face on it, but whose distance from the British Isles meant they didn't know every detail of her reported life, giving her enough room to dwell and still keep her secrets.

After all these years, the memorabilia remained strange. Coins commemorating her marriage to Charles. Serving bowls and sugar jugs and butter dishes. Rhinestone-rimmed plates. Dolls with plastic distortions of her smile, signed photographs, mint tins, magazine clippings. One family even owned Princess Diana paper dolls with all her famous dresses carefully cut out in miniature, abandoned in the toy box of some grown child who no longer played at being royalty.

In a Florida condominium, she came upon a man whose dearest wish was to be her. She felt his desire hot in his mind when she drew forth from the shadows in his bedroom while he slept. It burned clearly through his dreams, a fervent call: to be Diana.

She lingered.

At first she assumed he was one of those men who want to be women, but after a few nights, she realized she was wrong. He wanted froth and silk and glamour, things that were feminine, but not necessarily female.

He wanted the kind of dazzle that drew the heir to the throne. He wanted to wear spangled red silk chiffon and emerald georgette and white lace embroidered with silk flowers and sequins. He wanted photographers to capture his every angle. He wanted crowds to sigh when he crossed to the other side of the street. He wanted a wedding with thirty-five hundred guests and seven hundred and fifty million more people watching. He even owned the paper dolls—not cut out, but displayed in a cabinet above the dishes, along with a hundred other images of Diana's face.

Diana couldn't observe him during the day—in the morning, she evaporated with the sunlight—but Jeffrey was a restless sleeper. When he woke at night, Diana followed him through the dark hallways as he paced the house. He was a fragile-looking man with white hair interspersed among the blond. He wore black silk pajamas with red and gold faux-Chinese embroidery, the jacket done up with frogging. White tabi socks warmed his feet. He was too chic for slippers.

Jeffrey sat at the wicker table in the atrium and rested his head in his hands, staring morosely at the shadows that the palm fronds cast on the wall. Diana settled behind him, integrating with the shadows he cast on the chair, imagining she was tangible enough to comfort him.

She'd comforted homeless children, landmine victims, lepers. She'd shaken hands with an AIDS patient, skin on skin, even when her advisers told her to wear rubber gloves. Now there was no skin on skin, no way to pat Jeffrey's shoulder and say in the language of touch, *whatever's wrong, you'll be all right.*

His sad blue eyes looked dusky beneath his pale brows. Easy lines folded around his frown, but she'd seen other lines shape themselves around his smile, suggesting that he spent most of his life doing one or the other. His face was easy to decipher, but his mind was a mystery—everything but the core of need that called her name.

Why do you want to be me? she wanted to ask. Don't you see what happened when I was me?

After dark one night, Jeffrey's husband came home late with a box wrapped in glittering paper. "Ooh!" Jeffrey exclaimed, coming to accept it. "Ray! You shouldn't have!" Something in his high-pitched excitement sounded false, but Diana couldn't discern what.

"Happy birthday," Ray said, extending the box. Jeffrey pushed his hands away with a gesture that was a touch too hard to be playful.

"Sit," said Jeffrey, pointing to the couch. "I'll make drinks."

Ray settled, shifting a bamboo-print cushion out of his way. Diana wasn't sure whether he was actually older than Jeffrey, but he looked older, fine wrinkles etching the bags under his eyes. He looked a little fat and a little tired in a pull-over and grey wool slacks. The latter were wrinkled, black and blue ink stains marring the pockets.

Bustling behind the curve of the bar, Jeffrey was immaculate in white pants and a crisply ironed button-down patterned with navy diamonds. He held the bottle almost horizontally as he poured. He looked up at Ray over the stream of alcohol and flashed him a strained smile.

He returned with two shot glasses, one with ice and one without. He handed the first to Ray and stood aside while he drank. He held out his hand for the empty glass.

"Let me get you another one."

"I'm good," said Ray, pushing past him to set the glass on a coaster. "Open, open."

The edges of Jeffrey's smile vanished. He set his full glass next to Ray's empty one and took the present. Beneath the glittering green paper, there was a plum velvet box. Inside the velvet box, there were two tickets.

"To the national tour of *Forty-Second Street*," said Ray. "Front row, center. Look at the date."

Stiffly, Jeffrey held up one of the tickets to the light. "Day after tomorrow."

"You can turn forty-nine at *Forty-Second Street*."

"Clever," murmured Jeffrey, staring at the ticket. He turned it back and forth in the light, glossy paper shining, and then replaced it beside its twin. He traded the box for his drink and knocked it back.

Ray frowned. "I thought you liked *Forty-Second Street*."

"I do."

"Would you rather go to another show? The college is doing *Secret Garden.*"

"I like *Forty-Second Street.*"

"I don't get what's wrong."

Jeffrey ran his fingers through his hair, ruining his careful styling. When he looked up at Ray again, he was smiling gently. "I'm just tired."

Diana watched while they sat, chatting, for another hour. Ray detailed an office farce centering on conflicting operating systems while Jeffrey poured himself another shot and then a third. Afterward, they ate stir-fried vegetables over brown rice, Jeffrey keeping their glasses full of citrus wine.

Was that how other peoples' marriages fell apart? Marriages that were between two people, without involving press and protocol and a mother-in-law who wields a sceptre?

Afterward, Jeffrey went into the bathroom for a long time. Diana hid in the wall, listening to him weep. When he emerged at last, he went into the bedroom, checking to make sure Ray was asleep before he slipped between the sheets.

Diana had come because she was intrigued by his desire. Now she found herself drawn by his sadness.

Voyeurism diverted her from the griefs of her own life. These had only magnified after death. Sometimes she thought ghosts weren't whole souls, only the saddest pieces.

People had asked so much of her. She'd tried to give them what they wanted. She prayed, and paced, and purged. Still there were always more needy hands, more photographers, more commemorative plates rimmed with rhinestones.

The next night, Jeffrey feigned illness and went to bed early, switching off the lamp to lie in pitch dark. He pretended to be asleep when Ray came in, lying still while he changed into his pajamas and slipped into bed.

The second night, they dressed in single-breasted black wool tuxedos with handkerchiefs in the pockets. Jeffrey sighed over Ray, who continued to look disheveled no matter how many times Jeffrey straightened his jacket.

They rode to the theater in a limousine. Diana coalesced in the leather seats. Ray poured champagne. They clinked, twining their arms to sip from each other's glasses.

At first Jeffrey looked anxious, but soon the bubbly began working. He laughed loudly and kept extending his empty glass.

"What the hell," said Ray, opening a second bottle. "This is what we got a chauffeur for."

Jeffrey was flushed when they arrived. Ray stopped to tip the driver while Jeffrey grinned at the crowd of smokers grabbing their last cigarettes before the performance. They went through gold-edged doors into the sweeping lobby where more theatergoers lingered, most dressed as if attending church, in floral-print dresses and polo shirts and slacks. Heads turned at tuxedos.

Ray took his arm and led Jeffrey, regally, down to the usher who took their ticket.

Inside the theater, Jeffrey squeezed Ray's hand as his eyes darted between gold cornices. They made their way down a row of red velvet seats, Diana hiding in the shadows between arm rests. The theater thrummed with voices. Ray flipped through his program, glossy sheets rustling. Jeffrey sat on the edge of his seat, staring at the curtain.

The theater went dark. The audience fell silent as the overture began, brasses taking up a merry beat.

"Happy forty-nine," Ray whispered in Jeffrey's ear. Jeffrey batted him away, leaning toward the music.

Silently, Diana counted years. Yes, she'd have been forty-nine, too. Her ethereal form thrummed with jealousy.

The play began. Diana watched Jeffrey's face instead of the show. His enraptured expression was more compelling than any performance Diana remembered. Still tipsy, he leaned in at the dramatic moments, laughing more loudly than he should when someone told a joke, and gasping when something went wrong. He tapped his hand silently against his armrest in time with the dancers' heels clicking across the stage. He applauded with all his strength, almost propelling himself out of his seat.

When Diana's curiosity grew overpowering, she flickered into the shadows cast by the actors to watch the show up close. It seemed ordinary—ersatz glitz on over-worked actors, bright paint on well-worn sets.

Afterward, as Jeffrey and Ray stood outside waiting for the limo to return, their tuxedo jackets draped over their arms, Jeffrey began to weep. Passersby turned to look, without interrupting their strides.

Ray took Jeffrey by the shoulders and turned him so they faced each other squarely. "What is it?" he asked. "Can you tell me?"

"I just wish I," Jeffrey began. A sob caught in his throat. "I could have been, if I'd been someone else, I could have—" He stopped, sobs coming harder.

"The world just wasn't made for you," Ray said, wrapping his arms around his husband.

The world had made Diana think it was made for her once. Seven hundred and fifty million people watched her walk down the aisle in her puff ball meringue dress with its romantically ruffled neckline and twenty-five foot train. She'd been adorned by lace and sequins, hand-stitched embroidery and ten thousand pearls.

The night before, she'd been crying, too. Was the world made for anyone?

She followed them back into the shadows of their room. They switched on their bedside lamps and she swam under the bed to respect their privacy.

It sounded like love.

When the lamps were off again, Diana lifted back into the shadowed drapery of their quilt. Ray was asleep. Jeffrey stared at the ceiling, his eyes dry, his face sallow.

"I'm happy," he whispered into the nothing.

You should be, Diana couldn't say.

"I have a good life. A good house. Good health. A good husband. I'm lucky and loved."

You are, Diana couldn't say.

"I'm forty-nine years old."

Diana could not say that she would never be forty-nine years old.

"I'm never going to be the duck that turns into the swan. My foot will never fit the slipper. It's never going to be all lights and cameras. It's never going to be all action. No one is ever going to care who I am. It's never going to happen. Not for me."

It had happened for her. The swan, the dress, the lights, and oh yes, the cameras. It wasn't what she wanted. It wasn't what anyone wanted, not really.

She wished she could trade him—a forty-ninth birthday and a husband who wasn't Charles—it seemed appealing. But then would she want that either? A life of wanting to be wanted and never being seen? Of desiring glamour and receiving anonymity?

A little of each then. If only they could mingle, the way shadows bleed into one another, the way ghosts bleed into shadows.

But he is neither ghost nor shadow. Not yet.

He stares at the ceiling. His eyelids drift down. A blink, and then a second. He will fall asleep soon.

Diana swims away.

CAPTURING IMAGES

MARIA V. SNYDER

Monday

Evelyn's brain cells had declared war inside her skull. The right side of her brain attacked the left with mortars and heavy artillery, while the left responded with bombs and gunfire. Why did she order that *third* Long Island Ice Tea? Because she had already drunk two and logic and reason had left her to photocopy their asses.

Memories of last night's party pulsed. Had she really bragged to the publisher of *Vackra* magazine that she could transform anyone from ugly to beautiful? And then make a bet with the woman? God, she hoped not.

And who was the idiot who had scheduled a party on a Sunday night? She rested her forehead on her desk as more brain cells died. The doorbell to her studio dinged. Without checking the security camera, she buzzed the door open. Evelyn rolled her head to the side and watched Vincenza, her make-up artist, through a curtain of blond hair. The tall Italian woman sported the latest European fashions. Even her nickname—Vee was trendy.

Vee spotted her. "What happened?"

"Too much alcohol, not enough sense."

"I knew I should have stayed last night." She tsked. "Not to worry. I'll make you a tonic." Vincenza bustled off making way too much noise with her heels.

Another painful ding sounded and Evelyn's assistant—a bundle of energy contained in human form—arrived. The girl was too young and too inexperienced, but she was whip smart.

"What stinks?" Olivia asked.

"Vodka, gin, tequila, rum, and triple sec fumes, courtesy of our boss lady," Vee said.

"Oh." She crinkled her nose. "Do you want me to cancel your appointments?"

"No. We're doing the cover for *Glam More*." It had taken Evelyn two months to find an open date with the model and the magazine's deadline was looming.

Another time limit popped unbidden into her mind. *Produce a beautiful photo for me in one week. If you can not, then you are mine.* Camilla D. Quinton's liquid voice sounded in her head. Maybe Camilla would forget all about the bet. She snorted. Not Camilla, otherwise known as the Demon Queen. She had not only earned that reputation, but embraced it.

The only reason Evelyn had gone to that party was to meet her. One of Camilla's rare public appearances, and Evelyn had hoped to impress the woman and be offered a cover shoot for *Vackra*. But Camilla's notorious resistance to using freelancers remained, preferring to do everything in house.

Evelyn raised her head, causing another brain cell salvo. "I'll need my Nikon with the fifty millimeter lens, the white backdrop, and two strobes," she said to Olivia.

As the girl hurried to set up the equipment, Vee pressed a hot mug of . . . "What the hell is this? It smells like rancid cottage cheese."

"Drink it, you'll feel better."

She cringed at the taste, but kept sipping until Vee appeared satisfied. The model for the photo shoot arrived in a fit of tears over her blotchy skin. Vee whisked the girl back to the dressing room. It didn't matter how horrible the model's skin tone, hair, or shape was, with Vee and Evelyn's expertise, her photo would show a gorgeous young woman.

Evelyn admitted to a certain amount of confidence. After all, she had the best reputation in the business, and it hadn't occurred overnight. She committed years, sacrificed her social life, and worked hard. Seven years later, she owned a studio and loft in the heart of Manhattan. Still, she shouldn't have made that boast. Yet a part of her felt equal to the challenge.

Vee returned with a now radiant model. Feeling steadier, Evelyn picked up her camera. The familiar weight of the Nikon in her hand was like a caffeine fix. Dismissing her worries about the party, Evelyn concentrated on her work.

After her last Monday client left, Evelyn uploaded the day's photos to her computer. Taking pictures was only the first half of the job. She scanned the shots and didn't look up when Olivia chirped a good bye or when Vee admonished her not to work too late before leaving.

Pulling up the *Glam More* job, Evelyn picked the best pose and clicked on the photo's histogram. Then she proceeded to turn the pretty model into a goddess.

When a low cough sounded, she jumped from her seat. Her heart banged in her chest as she stifled a scream.

"Pardon me," a man said. "I didn't mean to startle you." He stood near the door.

How the hell did he get in? Evelyn's New Yorker instincts kicked in, and she assessed him to determine the level of threat. Well dressed, well groomed, clean shoes. Not a vagrant. No jacket and short sleeves despite the chilly October air. No obvious weapons. Designer clothes.

She met his amused gaze and was stunned. His features were perfectly proportioned, eyes a deep sapphire blue, pale skin without a single flaw, and thick black hair that reached the base of his neck. The best looking guy she has seen before make-up and Photoshop. The best looking guy *ever*.

Evelyn raked a hand through her messy hair. "If you want a portfolio, you need to make an appointment."

"Camilla sent me." He gave her a wry smile. "I'm your . . . test subject."

A rollercoaster of emotions rolled through her. Relief—he was gorgeous. Suspicion—what game was the Demon Queen playing? She had expected Camilla to send a hag. Surprised—that Camilla would act so soon.

Evelyn shrugged. This would be easy. "Call my assistant tomorrow and we'll set up a time."

"It has to be tonight," he said.

"I can't, I've a deadline."

"Should I tell her you concede?"

That word sent a rush of memories. Concede meant closing her studio and working solely for the Demon Queen. Fear shot through her. "She said I had a week."

He nodded. "Yes. A week to produce a photo or to get your affairs in order."

That made it sound as if she had a terminal disease. He had

an odd formal way of speaking as if he'd be more comfortable wearing a fedora and suit than the gray slacks and black polo shirt. However, with his athletic build, he'd look good in a T-shirt and off the rack jeans.

"All right. Give me a minute." She considered calling Olivia and Vee, but the man didn't need make-up. She'd adjust for his pale skin, and shoot in black and white.

As she set up her equipment, she watched him from the corner of her eye. Unlike most models, he didn't check his appearance in the mirrors.

Instead, he studied her framed photos. Not the ones filled with covers, but the ones from Iraq. The stark images of war that she had taken on her last "vacation" had been tucked out of way. All the major magazines had rejected the photos, claiming the images were too disturbing.

Yet he didn't flinch from them. Perhaps he had more depth than the other male models she'd photographed. He was a little older than them—closer to her age of thirty. Maybe they'd have something in common. Oh, who was she kidding? He probably dated gorgeous women barely out of high school.

"I'm ready, Mr . . . ?"

He extended a hand. "Grayson Windsor. But everyone calls me Gray."

She shook his hand. His cold fingers grasped hers a little longer than proper. But he let go and stood before the white background.

"Stand on the X and face me," she instructed.

He smirked when she aimed her camera at him. Her opinion of him dropped a few notches. Oh well. Camilla wanted beautiful, and even smirking Gray met that requirement. Evelyn snapped a few shots to test the lighting, aperture, and shutter speed, then brought up the pictures to view.

Odd. His clothes and shoes showed up, but not his face and arms. She frowned, tried a few more shots, netting the same results. To the camera, it appeared as if he were invisible. Aiming at her desk, she took another set. The pictures were fine. Evelyn tried her Canon and then her Olympus. Same thing.

"Are you ready to admit defeat?" Gray asked from right behind her.

She yelped. "There must be something wrong."

"There's nothing wrong with your equipment. Please, allow me to show you." He gestured to the mirrors.

Curious, she followed him. He stood in front of them. His reflection matched her pictures of him. Just his clothes. To prove his point he removed his shirt. Gaping, she glanced between the pants and shoes in the mirror to his muscular torso. Impossible. She could *see* him.

Now he gave her a full smile, revealing straight teeth and fangs. She stepped back as fear coiled around her heart.

He stayed close, grabbing her upper arm. "Nothing can take a picture of us. Our souls have already been taken. You will not win the bet with our queen."

This was way too much for Evelyn's sputtering brain. She focused on one. "Us? You mean there are more of you?"

"Many more. A whole nest of nasties."

Her heart rate jumped.

"Don't worry." He stroked her throat with his free hand. His icy fingers sent tremors through her muscles. "I'm not allowed to drink from this lovely neck. My queen wishes for you to be healthy. She desires only your photographic genius."

"Your queen? Camilla?" Her voice squeaked.

"Yes. Her nickname is more accurate than anyone can imagine."

"Or believe."

"There is that. But pictures don't lie, Miss Mitchell. You know that."

"Actually, pictures lie all the time."

"No they don't. *You* change them with your computer. Except, I suspect your war photos haven't been altered."

"That wouldn't be right."

"I agree. Now according to the terms of your bet, you're to pack up your studio, fire your staff, put your studio up for sale, and be available for our queen next week. She will provide everything else. And don't bother the police. That will just anger us. You really don't want to do that."

His words felt like a death sentence. Evelyn had worked so hard to be independent.

Gray released her. "I'll return each evening to check on your progress." He headed toward the door.

"Wait. Can I try to take your picture again?"

"How you decide to spend your last week is up to you. However in one week's time you *will* be the queen's property regardless." He left.

Evelyn sank to the floor as the whole encounter with Gray replayed in her mind. Disbelief warred with panic. She debated calling her lawyer, her mother or calling the police despite his threat. *Would any of them believe her?* Anger at Camilla flipped with fear that she'd send more of her . . . vampires to harm her if she didn't comply. God, she was so screwed. Or was she?

Snapping out of her shock, Evelyn jumped to her feet. She checked the pictures—still the same, but she wrote a list of techniques she could try in order to capture Gray's image. After all, she could see him. It was just a matter of finding the right combination of lighting and equipment.

Tuesday

When Olivia arrived the next morning, Evelyn told her to cancel all her appointments for the week.

"What should I tell them?" the girl asked her.

"Tell them I'm sick."

Too new to question her boss, Olivia nodded and rushed to her desk. Vee, however had been working with her for the last six years. She peered at Evelyn through thick mascara-laden eyelashes when Evelyn gave her the rest of the week off.

"What's going on?" Vee waved a hand at the mess of cameras heaped on the table. "This isn't you." She picked up an old camera, and gasped in mock horror. "This has *four* megapixels."

Evelyn decided not to tell her friend about the bet. "It's a . . . special retro project. A real challenge and . . . very important for my career." *And my life.*

Vee arched a slender eyebrow. "You're not photographing cadavers again?"

She stifled a cough. Were vampires cadavers? "I haven't done that since grad school." Back when she had needed money she'd worked for a funeral home, photographing the deceased for grieving family members. She also photographed birthday parties, worked in a one-hour photo lab, and tutored freshmen.

Vee gestured to her war photos. "Then what do you call those?"

The conversation with Gray replayed in Evelyn's mind. "The truth."

"This isn't about some man is it?"

She stared at Vee. "Why would you think that? I haven't had a date in over a year."

"Exactly. Desperate people do desperate things."

"I'm not desperate. I just haven't found a kindred soul yet."

"Hard to find one when you don't leave your studio," Vee said.

"I went out on Sunday night and look what happened."

"A hangover isn't the end of the world." But after another uncomfortable scrutiny, Vee agreed to take the week off. "Call me if you need me for *any* reason. Okay?"

"Okay." She relaxed.

Evelyn spent the remainder of the day prepping for Gray. Olivia broke her concentration when she announced that she had finally rescheduled all of Evelyn's appointments.

"Do you need me tomorrow?" Olivia asked.

Just in case tonight's efforts failed, Evelyn told her to come back in the morning. Disappointed, Olivia schlepped out without saying good-bye.

Unaffected by the dramatics, Evelyn returned to her work, skipping supper in order to be ready.

Once again Gray arrived without warning or sound. Surprise mixed with instant fear. She only had his word he wouldn't kill her. This time he wore tight black jeans, cowboy boots with silver buckles, and a white T-shirt with a design of black wings spread across his chest.

Proud that her voice didn't warble, she asked, "Something wrong with the door bell?"

Smirking, he glanced at the security video screen. "I'm camera shy."

She considered. "It must be difficult to avoid them. They're all over the place, and everyone has a camera on their cell phone." Another connection popped into her mind. "Is that why Camilla avoids the public?" And probably why the light had been so dim at the party.

His smirk faded. "It helps that we are creatures of the night, but it does limit our . . . social life."

An image of him hunting a hapless person to feed on popped into her head.

"It's not what you think," he said as if he could read her mind. "We have volunteers who donate blood. It just would be nice to go out without worrying. To be able to attend a Broadway musical instead of lurking in the shadows."

"A musical? Really?"

"Did you think all we do is read *Dracula* and watch re-runs of *True Blood*?" Amusement sparked.

"Since I didn't know you existed until yesterday, I haven't had the time to imagine what your . . . social life is like."

"It's better than yours," he said.

Not about to dignify his comment with a response, she gestured to the area she had prepped. "Please stand—"

He was there before she finished her sentence. And the smirk was back. *Wonderful.*

Evelyn tried a number of different cameras, backgrounds, and techniques. Then she mounted her camera on a tripod and instructed him to keep still, hoping a long exposure would work. She set it for one minute, then five, then ten. Nothing.

Next test involved covering Gray's bare skin with make-up. He agreed and sat still as she spread the liquid foundation on him. Although his skin felt cold, it was . . . normal.

Feeling awkward with his proximity, she asked, "Why do you think your social life is better than mine?"

"Our queen has been interested in you for a year. We've been watching you to make sure your withdrawal from regular society wouldn't make waves."

Unease rolled in her stomach. "Withdrawal?"

"We are a close-knit group. We limit contact with outsiders to a bare minimum. Discovery of our . . . existence wouldn't be well received."

She huffed. "Are you sure? There's a reason books and shows like *True Blood* are popular."

"We're more concerned about the military."

"Oh." She considered. "My friends and family would be alarmed if I disappeared."

"Friends? Your only friend, Vincenza Salvatori, has successfully interviewed with *Good Morning America* to be their executive make-up artist. According to our sources, she has accepted the job and is scheduled to start next month. At a considerable higher salary than what you pay her, by the way."

Her hands stilled as his words sunk in like acid sizzling through her heart. *Why didn't she tell me? I would have been happy for her. Or would I?*

To avoid the hurtful truth, she said, "My mother will tear this town apart looking for me."

"When's the last time you talked to your mother?" he asked.

"Last week . . . I think."

"You don't know?"

"Do you know *exactly* when you last talked to yours?" she snapped.

"No."

"See?"

Gray gave her a flat look. "My mother's been dead over a hundred years. What's your excuse?"

"I'm very busy. Which your vampire spies should be well aware of."

"We are. And we also know that you haven't called your mother in over a month." He leaned back, looking smug. "So we have at least a month before your mother even realizes you're gone."

Evelyn clamped her mouth shut. Gray's blatant attempt to distract her wouldn't work. She finished covering him and snapped a few photos. When she pulled them up on screen, the make-up appeared as tan blobs.

"Give up?" Gray asked, peering over her shoulder.

"No. I've more things to try."

He swept her hair to the side and brushed his lips over her neck. A strange tingle shot through her, igniting fear and she'd like to say revulsion, but to be honest it was more akin to desire.

"It's two hours until dawn. And unless you have a bottle of A positive in your fridge, I'd better go before I rip into this lovely throat. Until tomorrow . . . " He kissed her neck and was gone.

She groped for the chair and collapsed into it, suddenly exhausted. Nothing she tried tonight had worked. At least she could rule out capturing a digital image. The next logical step would be to try her old film cameras. And that would require a number of items she no longer owned.

Wednesday

The studio door dinged, waking Evelyn. She had fallen asleep at her desk. Buzzing Olivia in, Evelyn handed her a list of supplies along with her company's—E. Mitchell Studios—credit card. She had been so proud when her company's name had been painted on the glass doors to her studio. It was simple and genderless and hers.

Renewed determination not to lose her business pulsed through her body. After Olivia left to go shopping, Evelyn sucked down an extra large cup of coffee and dug through old boxes until she found her thirty-five millimeter cameras.

When Olivia returned with the supplies, her assistant helped Evelyn clean out one of her walk-in closets.

"What are you using this for?" Olivia asked as she dragged out a dusty container of old photos.

"I'm converting it into a darkroom."

The girl paused and wiped her hands on her tattered jeans. "Darkroom? What's that?"

Now it was her turn to pause. "Didn't they teach you how to develop film in art school?"

"Not in my classes. I majored in new digital media and experimental photography. Not ancient history."

Evelyn suppressed a sigh. Despite her own troubles, she

wouldn't be remiss in her mentor duties. "Tomorrow I'll show you how to make pictures the old fashioned way."

Olivia wasn't quick enough to hide her frown, but she continued to lug boxes and even asked a few token questions about the process. After they had set up the darkroom, she sent Olivia home.

Loading her Nikon with black and white, thirty-five millimeter film, Evelyn lamented the demise of Kodachrome film. She could have hoarded a few rolls, if she had known . . . well, if she had known, then she would have kept her big mouth shut on Sunday night.

She hardly reacted to Gray's silent arrival. *Funny how you could get used to anything.* Evelyn glanced at her war photos. *Well, almost anything.*

He noticed the boxes littered around the studio. "Are you finally accepting your fate and packing?"

"No. I'm trying a new tactic tonight."

Gray examined the mess, picking through the piles of camera equipment. "Some of these are antiques. I remember when the Nikon L35 was first released. It caused quite a sensation."

When she connected that comment to the one about his mother, Evelyn realized he might have been around during the early years of photography. She asked him a few questions and soon they were discussing the evolution of the camera—a subject that fascinated Evelyn.

With a genuine smile, Gray said, "I don't know why you're so resistant to working for our queen. You'll be among people with similar interests."

It was as if he had thrown ice cold water on her, snapping her to her senses. Once again, he had distracted her.

"If you please . . . " She swept a hand toward the backdrop.

With a sigh, he posed with his arms crossed. "I don't know whether to admire your determination or point out the fact that you're wasting time."

Ignoring him, she took a few test shots to familiarize herself with the camera. Evelyn then burned through ten rolls of film.

After Gray left, she was too exhausted to do more than crawl up the stairs to her apartment and fall into bed.

Thursday

"Uh, Evelyn? I think I did something wrong again." Olivia passed her a negative. "I'm not sure 'cause it's hard to see with this red light."

She peered at the image. Shirt, pants and boots on an invisible man. No Gray. They had been developing film all day in the darkroom, and the results were the same. All ten rolls.

Dejected, Evelyn sent Olivia home, glad to be alone. The girl had complained about the smells, the chemicals, the red light, and how labor intensive it all was. Evelyn would have enjoyed returning to her photographic roots in the darkroom if the stakes hadn't been so high.

She slumped in her chair and scanned her studio. Covers for every major fashion magazine in New York, Paris, London and Rome covered her walls. *Vackra* had been the only one who hadn't hired her to shoot a cover. And she just couldn't let that one go. Oh no. She had to chase after it. Now here she stood facing a lion with a butterfly net.

Out of ideas, Evelyn called her mother.

"Evie, it's so good to hear your voice," her mother said without a trace of sarcasm or even a guilt-inducing inflection, which Evelyn fully deserved.

"I was beginning to worry about you, sweetie, but I never know when to call you. I'd hate to disrupt an important shoot."

"I'm sorry I haven't called."

"What are you working on?" her mother asked.

"A very difficult assignment and I'm stuck about what to do next."

"Why don't you ask that professor you liked so much in graduate school? The one who helped invent that bluescreen thingy?"

"Chroma keying," she automatically corrected, but her mind raced. The chroma key technology made things and people invisible on TV and the movies like Harry Potter's invisibility cloak.

"Didn't you say there was nothing he couldn't do with a camera? Maybe he can help you."

"Professor Duncan passed away last year." Genuine sorrow filled her.

"Aw. Too bad." A pause. "Didn't he write a textbook or something?"

Stunned, Evelyn gripped her phone tighter. "He donated all his research to the School of Visual Arts' library." Equipment, notes, computer. Everything. "Mom, you're a genius!"

Her mother demurred, but Evelyn could tell she was pleased. Evelyn promised to call more often, then hung up. Grabbing her purse and jacket, she dashed out to hail a taxi before Gray arrived.

The library was open until midnight. As a distinguished

alumni, Evelyn had full use of the facilities, and was soon tucked into a quiet corner, searching through Professor Duncan's research for the next several hours.

Taking notes, Evelyn devised a rough plan that used a video camera and reversed the chroma key graphics. Would Gray agree to wear a blue body suit?

"Find anything interesting?" Gray asked.

She jerked. "How did you know I was here?"

He wore a jacket, gloves, hat, scarf and sunglasses. No doubt to hide from the security cameras hanging from the ceiling. "Was your mother happy to hear from you?"

Evelyn rubbed her eyes. "Vampire spies. How could I forget? Did you listen to my conversation?"

"Of course, sweetie."

Surging to her feet, she confronted him. "That's illegal."

He shrugged. "Call the police. Good luck proving it."

"I can prove it right now." She reached for his hat.

But he snagged her wrist, stopping her before her hand came close to his head. "I don't think you fully realize the danger you are in." He tightened his grip.

Pain ringed her arm as panic ringed her chest. Thinking fast, she said, "If you break my wrist, then I'll be unable to take photos and the bet will be put on hold until I'm healed. I'm sure *your queen* will not appreciate *you* causing a delay."

Gray released her even though he was clearly unhappy. "I'll be waiting for you outside."

Score one for the photographer. She returned to her notes. At midnight the library closed and Gray escorted her home. No need to fear being mugged with a vampire bodyguard.

Evelyn spent the rest of the night searching Craigslist for the video and computer equipment she'd need. Gray left, Olivia arrived, and she sent Olivia to pick up her multiple orders before collapsing.

Friday

"You want me to wear this?" Gray held up the blue garment. "Is this a joke?"

"Think of it as a Halloween costume," she said, gesturing toward the changing room.

He paused. "I always go as Count Dracula for Halloween."

She laughed. Call it exhaustion or sleep deprivation, she couldn't help it.

He grinned and studied her. "So nice to see you smile. That scowl you favor doesn't belong on your beautiful face."

Sobering in an instant, she shooed him into the changing room. She wasn't going to fall for another delaying tactic. Yet she tucked her hair behind her ears. When she had been in college, many of her fellow photography students had asked her to model for them. They'd called her a classic blond beauty. But that was ten years ago, and, although they'd flattered her, she found the experience utterly boring. Far better to be behind the camera.

When he returned clad only in the skintight bodysuit, Evelyn pressed a hand to her mouth to keep a fit of giggles from bubbling out. For the first time, he appeared uncomfortable and that cocky smirk of his was nowhere to be seen.

And she would know since the suit left nothing to the imagination. Nothing. A flush of heat spread to areas of her body that hadn't felt anything in years. Perhaps living with Camilla's nest of nasties wouldn't be so bad.

Focusing on the task at hand, she instructed him to pull the hood over his head. "Cover your face as well, it will only be for a second."

"You don't have to worry. I don't need to breathe."

"Oh." Curious, she asked, "How much is true? You mentioned blood and dawn, what else is right?"

"Are you planning to attack me with garlic and a wooden stake?"

"You're too fast and strong. I wouldn't get near you, would I?"

"No. And I'm not telling you our secrets until you're part of the . . . nest." He gazed at her with a predatory intensity.

"Or is it because you're afraid I might win the bet?"

"I'm not afraid of anything." He yanked the hood down over his face.

Liar. But she wasn't going to waste anymore of her precious time. After she filmed a few minutes of video, she asked him to pull the suit down to his waist, exposing his upper body. He smirked as she recorded another couple minutes. She wondered if his attitude was a defense mechanism to keep people at a distance.

God, she had lost her mind. Who cared about a soulless demon? Once she took his fricking picture, she would never have to see him again.

He stayed as she ran the video through the computer program, hoping to reverse the process. Nothing but blue filled the screen.

She closed her eyes and rested her head on her desk.

Gray put his hand on her shoulder. "You should be commended for effort. I'll ask our queen to allow you to call your mother from time to time. She owes me a favor."

Sympathy from a vampire. Could she go any lower or was that the bottom? No, she wouldn't give up.

Evelyn shrugged off his hand and stood. "I still have two more days. I'll see you tomorrow." Without waiting for a reply, she headed to bed. A good night's sleep should help clear her head. She hoped.

Saturday

With panic simmering in her chest, Evelyn spent the day going over all the techniques she had tried this week, trying to find inspiration. When that failed to work, she surfed the Internet for information about Camilla D. Quinton, Grayson Windsor, and *Vackra* magazine.

No surprise that there were no pictures of Gray, but there were dozens of Camilla all taken prior to 2000. A memory tugged. She recalled a campaign by the magazine to find the most beautiful man and woman in the world to mark the new millennium. The staff traveled all over the world, including some very exotic lands. Perhaps they found more than they could handle. They had eventually featured a stunning couple, but after that, Camilla withdrew from the spotlight.

She searched for more information, but found nothing. Switching to her favorite photography websites, she spent a few hours looking for ideas. Googling "how to photograph a vampire" produced a number of interesting results, but none of them amounted to anything useful.

When she started reading articles written by paranormal investigators on how to capture ghosts on film with a hybrid digital/film camera, she knew she had gone beyond desperation. She scanned her studio and wondered how many boxes she'd need to pack it all up.

Evelyn was slumped at her computer when Gray arrived. He wasn't alone. Standing by his side was the Demon Queen decked out in the latest name brand fashion. She noted the woman's pale skin and how much younger and prettier she looked than her photos from the nineties.

Camilla greeted her with the mock/air kisses to her cheeks. "Evelyn, my dear. So nice to see you again." Her gaze swept the messy studio. "Grayson tells me you've been resistant to holding up your end of our little bet."

Little? She glanced at Gray, but he stood behind Camilla and kept his face impassive.

"You took advantage of my inebriated state," she said.

"Oh hush." Camilla waved long fingers at her. "You would have boasted just the same had you been sober. You know I'm right."

Evelyn considered. "Probably." But not now.

"No probably about it my dear. You've been chomping at the bit for an assignment for *Vackra* magazine and I gave you one. One that you couldn't fulfill."

"I still have a day."

Camilla pished at her. "It's impossible. It's the magic and the curse of the transformation."

"Which means the task you set was unfair and renders our bet null and void."

"Nice try, my dear. But you said *anyone*."

"Yeah. Anyone *living*."

"Then you should have been specific. Too late now." Camilla circled the room, avoiding the mirrors. "I certainly hope you don't plan to renege on our bet."

"What if I did?" She challenged.

"Grayson," Camilla said.

He crossed the room in a nanosecond, grabbing her. His fangs pricked her neck before she could draw a breath. Then he froze. Her false bravado shattered as her attention focused on his teeth on her skin.

Camilla stepped into her view. "He drinks and you disappear. That's what happens."

"But . . ."

The Demon Queen waited.

"I still have a day," she said.

"You do. Grayson, release her."

He closed his mouth, sucking on her neck before setting her down. She touched her throat.

Gray's arms remained around her. "It's just a nick. I couldn't resist."

"Grayson," Camilla snapped.

He returned to his position, leaving Evelyn to stand on her unsteady feet. Her world was quickly spinning out of control. She latched onto the one inconsistency.

"Why does he obey you?" she asked. "He's older than you. Why are *you* the Demon Queen?"

Camilla shot Gray an annoyed frown. "I found him and his nest mates living in self-imposed isolation on a tiny island in the middle of the Pacific. The modern world had defeated them more effectively than vampire hunters with wooden stakes. But I had enough money to offer them a life a luxury if they changed me." She preened. "My magazine empire was the perfect hide-out for a bunch of gorgeous people."

"Except for being unable to be photographed," Evelyn said.

"It makes it difficult, but it's a small price to pay for eternal life."

Touching her throat again, she asked, "Are you going to make me one of you?"

"Oh no. Creativity is snuffed out during the transformation, but in exchange we gain heightened senses, beauty, and intelligence to name a few. I need your talent, my dear. You will be well taken care of in my nest."

"Gee, I feel *so much* better now."

"Now, now. Don't be like that. You're the one who agreed to the deal. Tomorrow I will send Grayson to fetch you. Please be ready." Camilla swept out with Gray in tow.

Evelyn remained in place. Camilla's visit was meant to intimidate her, and it worked. Yet, it gave her a renewed determination to prove the Demon Queen wrong. Or was that a new surge of desperation?

Back at her computer, she re-read the ghost articles, jotting down details about the hybrid camera. Yep, that proved it. It was desperation.

Sunday

Consuming mass quantities of coffee and sugar, Evelyn had searched for information all night. But she couldn't get past the fact that neither the digital, video, nor the film cameras worked. Therefore, a hybrid wouldn't work either. She needed a different lens or medium. Or a miracle.

What else? She pulled out all her old photography textbooks and flipped through the pages. Listing everyone who had any knowledge of photography, she dug deep into her memory. Old jobs, ex-boyfriends, colleagues.

What else? kept repeating in her mind like a mantra.

Around noon, the answer popped into her head. She dismissed it for a split second as insane. But like Vee had said, desperate people do desperate things. Back at her computer, she looked up information on an old acquaintance, before heading to Best Buy for a new and secure cell phone.

As the phone rang on the other end, Evelyn tried to come up with an explanation that wouldn't make her sound like a lunatic.

"Hello?" a man's voice said.

"Hi, Antonio, it's Evelyn Mitchell. I know it's been ages, we used to work together at—"

"Evelyn! How the hell are you?" he asked.

"Truthfully, not good. Are you still in the business?"

"Yes, why?" His friendly tone had turned cautious.

One knot in her stomach eased. He still had access.

"I've a big problem and I need a huge favor."

Silence, then, "What do you need?"

The request came out in a rush of words. There was a long pause on the other end.

She jumped in before he could say no. "I won't tell a soul, and if you do this for me, I'll take pictures of your kids every year for the rest of their lives. I'll hire them as cover models if they want. It's vital, Antonio."

No response. But he hadn't hung up.

"I'll pay—"

"No money," he said. "If I do this for you, will you photograph my daughter's wedding in exchange?"

If it worked and she was free. "Of course."

He chuckled. "You used to scoff at wedding photographers."

"I've a new perspective on life."

"I see. And this is a onetime request?"

"Oh yes. I won't ask again. I promise."

"Okay. When do you need it?"

"Now."

"Uh. That could be a problem."

She sank to her knees. So close!

"Hold on," Antonio said. "Let me talk to my wife."

Sunday Night

After meeting Antonio uptown, Evelyn spent the rest of the day building a hybrid camera of her own. Using her new lens and thirty-five millimeter film, she prayed it would work. She couldn't test it until Gray arrived.

As daylight faded, Evelyn raced around her studio, piling a few boxes and dumping a couple of empty suitcases next to them. At least it would look as if she had packed.

Gray appeared. He glanced at the pile, then at the rest of the studio. "You didn't get much done."

She brandished her new camera. "Very last try. One roll of film."

Suspicion creased his forehead. "How long?"

"Two hours at most. Please."

"And then?" he asked.

"If it doesn't work, I concede defeat and will go . . . quietly."

He harrumphed. "I doubt the quietly part. All right. Two hours."

Evelyn didn't waste time. She snapped twelve pictures and then grabbed her coat.

"Where are you going?" Gray asked.

"CVS. There's one down the street. I can't develop film and print pictures that fast. But they can. Are you coming?"

"I guess I have to." He frowned as he donned his coat, hat, and sunglasses.

When they arrived at the store, Evelyn was fully prepared to bribe the tech to do hers first. But the processing department had been slow and the tech promised to have prints in an hour.

Her hands shook as she dropped the canister into his hand. God, he looked like he was twelve. Her life rested in this single roll. Ironic.

"Now what?" Gray asked.

"We wait."

"Here?"

"Yes. I'm not letting that film out of my sight."

He sighed, but didn't argue. What followed was the longest hour in her entire life. Sweat soaked her bra and her shirt clung to her. When the prints were ready, she paid for them then tore open the package.

Gray snatched it from her. "Wait until we get back to the studio."

She almost ran back. When they were inside, he handed the envelope to her. Wiping sweaty palms on her jeans, she pulled out the stack of photos.

A joy like no other spread through her. She felt as if she'd just been told she'd been mis-diagnosed and she was going to live after all. Evelyn whooped and danced around a confused Gray.

With a huge grin, she handed a picture to Gray. "Here, give this to Camilla. Proof that I won the bet."

He stared at his image. It was all there. The little smirk, the black hair, the muscular arms, the whole hot package.

"Is this me?" he asked, gazing at her in shock.

"Yes. Don't you recognize yourself?"

"It's been over a century. And the transformation changes you. I've seen it happen to others, but never really thought about how I'd changed. I look . . . "

"Gorgeous."

He smiled. "Young. I was close to fifty when I transformed."

As Evelyn watched him, she wondered what it would be like to never see your refection in a mirror. Rather difficult, she guessed.

She gave Gray all the photos. "You only need to show Camilla one. You can keep the rest. Will she be upset?" Fear dampened her high spirits.

"About losing?"

"Yes, and about me knowing your secrets."

"Oh yes. Camilla has never lost a bet before."

Despite her unease, Evelyn noted how he had used her name. Interesting.

Gray tapped the picture. "How did you do this? She'll want to know."

"Trade secret."

"She's not going to be happy."

"Too bad. It's business," she said with more bravado than she felt.

After Gray left, she picked up her hybrid camera. Popping open the back, she picked up a pair of tweezers, and extracted her life-saving lens.

The human eyeball had started to dry and was nicked where she had secured it inside the camera. She grabbed a glass jar filled with formaldehyde and dropped the eye in. It sank to the bottom, turning so its lifeless brown iris stared at her. Thank God Antonio still worked at the funeral home.

Despite her knowledge of photography, the solution had been simple. After all, she could *see* Gray.

Monday

Getting back to her routine, Evelyn felt good about the day's work. She even handled Vee's resignation with professional aplomb. However, her brush with Camilla taught her that there was more to life than photographing models. She planned to cut back her hours, travel more, and visit her mother.

Evelyn was in the process of cleaning up the mess from the week before, sorting equipment into boxes when Gray appeared in her studio.

She straightened as a sick feeling swirled in her stomach. "Are you here to—"

"No. Relax. Camilla's angry, but as long as you don't cause trouble, she'll leave you alone."

Not convinced, she waited.

"I called in that favor," he said.

"Then why are you here?"

"I brought a few friends with me."

"Friends, as in—"

"Yes."

Not good. "What do they want?"

"They want you to take their picture."

HOW GALLIGASKINS SLOUGHED THE SCOURGE

ANNA TAMBOUR

So long ago that the roads were topped with the dung of ass and ox, in a land rich in short days and mouldy shadows, in the town of Ranug-a-Folloerenvy, lived a master argufier named Werold but known as Galligaskins for his old-fashioned knee-high socks that (in the heat of argument) he was always hitching up.

In this out-of-the-way town called by the low, just plain *Ranug*, where the bakers sold more day-old bread than fresh, and the tailors worked all night—in this tumbly-down filth-paved town, all the men (save Galligaskins) wore long, leg-hugging fine-skein hose white and delicate as the foot of the petal of a rose. These stockings showed best in winter when the lacily laddered knit exposed a wealth of leg-skin glow—puce, blue, crimson, suet—according to the state of the wearer's chilblains.

Galligaskins' hose were loose and thick, and brown as feast-day pancakes for the poor. And they ended folded over just below the knee, where he tried to tie them fast but they always slid past his garter of a cord—a shocking sight but one that persevered and was accepted as something that must be; as a rainy day, which cleans the streets.

For Werold was Ranug-a-Folloerenvy's only argufier, as necessary as the glove maker. He had much to do with the rich and would have died a slovenly but relatively wealthy ancient, if the rich hadn't got themselves into such a muckle.

It happened this way:

One day a drab nullness of a man called Bladsteth who unnoticed, had left Ranug some time before, returned—a new man—from, he said, far Ghovenir. Or rather, that is what some people *said* he said, and though they knew not this mouthful-of-stones, they did not question where? but tsked and answered with an impatient nod and a quick "So? Yes, yes. Go *on*." For the question wasn't where he went, but what he *wore* now that he'd returned.

The ladies swooned, to be brought to life only with a clod of chicken scat up a nostril. Men secreted themselves, unbuttoned sleeves as fat and slashed and colourful as candied-fruit-stuffed pheasants, and blew their noses into the embroidered cloth. Each man was suddenly as ashamed to be seen in what he stood in, as Adam was in the garden that suddenly wasn't Paradise. Tavern braggarts, cock-strutting swaggarts, lute-picking peach-firm swains, grandfathers with faces like empty sacks, all men alike— each man then counted out his wealth (which took not long) and matched that to his wits to find a tailor to make up, without much lucre, a suit like that which had caused the swoons. Now such a time began!

The children who just a moment ago, it seems, were little versions of their fine-clothed parents, now wandered free, undisciplined, unfed. And in what wear? Whatever rags they pleased. The town's air shimmered with the cries of women, and their tearful honks. Their grief melted the starch in pleats that were once so proud, they could hold the women's heads up from the strength of style alone—till that traveller, Bladsteth, blessed and cursed be he, the cause of all this wilt.

Every woman of any worth cursed Bladsteth's cheek, for he'd returned alone. No lady did he bring with him, nor key, nor word to what a lady's wear would be to mate the splendour of his cockscomb finery. Not only that, but the menfolk's wear would beggar a dromedary caravan. And the most foudroyantly furbelowed dames, instead of crying, screamed. If only a *she* had come to town, a *Desidora* instead of *he*. For no Ranug man in normal times would risk his health ignoring the gentler sex's cry, lady to lady: *Be mode as me, you wish! On my own man's worth, you shall not be. Be modish, you who challenge me, as an old dried pea.*

And so, what with the men consumed by fashion with no time to think of else—and the women consumed, first with grief and then with hunger (for when his tailor took the whole of each man's all, what man had time to notice women, children, or even his stomach's need?) whatwith all this, there came to Galligaskins such a drying-up of arguments that finally, he had None.

Though the town resounded with grief, Galligaskins' sniffs could pick out not one rumour that added up to a dispute that he could eat from—not even one petty snivel of an accusation that the greatest troublemaking miser in the town would have normally ordered, to be paid for with a promise. As Ranug-a-Folloerenvy's only guilded disputationist, the doubly-good sums he was accustomed to taking from both sides of any case were now, many times over, doubly lost and missed. Starved, his leather inkpot shrivelled till its sides met, skint as gentle ox's cut-purse. The worthy citizens were too busy. For the master argufier: a ruinous state.

So Galligaskins spent a coin on a pair of boots so practical, they must have been pawned by a traveller. Wearing the best (least torn) of his two mangy shirts, a once-fashionable jerkin that was now a chest-warmer with one button, and something he considered a cape but no self-respecting ass would bear tossed over its shoulders, he left the place he had been born. His hobnails rang on the cobbles in a mockery of a fare-thee-well.

By mid-day he was so hungry that when he came upon a stunted medlar tree at the top of a hill, he braved it—a rash action. Being winter, the tree was bare of leaves. Every fruit that had met the wind had fallen, and had been eaten in the snow by creatures who knew not that the fashion for these fruits had ended generations past.

The tree had one stolid trunk and many arms, their elbows hooked together like a poor man and wife in front of the landlord. But the arms of a medlar sport sword-sharp thorns. Galligaskins bared himself, and wielding his body like a key, he stuck his arm in. Thorns raked his flesh and pricked his wrist as he stretched his fingers forth . . . and plucked the last remaining fruits.

Eleven medlars did he glean, a handful. Burnished and dry-pimpled as Winter's cheeks, as ripe as weeping boils, they smelled of musty spice. Famished, he sucked them dry, spitting skin and stones till just after the tenth medlar when his shrunken belly, delicate from starvation, whined at this rotting richness. Galligaskins, mad with rage at this contrariness, madder still with hunger, regarded the last suppurating medlar, the most dangerously swollen of them all. Then he ravished it, swallowing every bit—its weeping tear, its tannic skin, its gassy flesh, its five rock-hard, rough-edged stones.

Now the last medlar was gone. His tongue tingled from the dry sharpness of that skin. He breathed into his hands to catch the last wisps of smell from that rank, sopped, scented flesh. Oh, he regretted his haste. His stomach turned, but as he dressed himself, he paid it not the slightest heed. He was just pulling up his right galligaskin when his gut growled a most unfamiliar note.

And with no ado, the eleventh medlar spoke.

"Walk fifty-and-seven steps," it said, and though its voice was rusty, each syllable was quite precisely paced, "with the sun warming the right side of your face. Then cut across the field till you come to a place where there are five rocks that you can see poking from the soil at the base of the barley stalks. And," said the medlar from deep within Galligaskins, "If you see no rocks because they have walked away or because they lie, then continue as you please until you need to stop and eat.

"Continue on, and one day you will come to another kingdom. You will know this because of the clothing—*keep still! Mind my counsel.*"

Galligaskins rubbed his stomach. If the medlar only knew the stab of *clothing*.

"As I was saying," said the medlar, pausing frustratingly, so like a master argufier when interrupted that Werold held his breath in awe.

The medlar must have felt Werold's admiration. "Mind you," it said, chatty as if they were feasting at juicy gossip. "The people in the kingdom I speak of wear jerkins, surcoats, cloaks, skirts, mantles, codpieces, wimples, bodices, great pumpkin sleeves, guimpes as crisp as toasted eggwhite froth—clothing from top to toe, including galligaskins white as icing—all bought fresh every morning, and served with the morning cup by the serving class. *Thems that serve wears the yesterday's, or the day before's,"* the medlar sing-songed as if it had heard that rhyme ever since it was a bud.

"And them that are too poor to serve," it said, reverting to its russeted professorial cadence, "deck themselves out in the castaways tossed from the same windows as open for the overturning of the chamber pots."

"But!" the medlar rasped. "On your fortune do not ask why there is no water in their morning cup, nor any goblet to hold drink. And though you may smell high, cover yourself with spice rather than take a bath or anoint yourself with unguent—though there be trays clotted with rose petals or rivers flowing with cardamom-scented almond oil, or lakes of water clear as tears, or."

"Or?" said Galligaskins. *"Or?"*

He beat his stomach, but all he got from it was groans. The last medlar was silent, or maybe silenced. When next it spoke, its words would be lost in the trumpet calls of sooty rye, the worse half a half-rotten onion, that year-old shard of dried-peas pudding. Galligaskins cursed his gut. Now he would never know why, but follow the medlar's orders, he knew he must. For when had a fruit ever spoken? *And speak it did, to me.* And besides, he had nothing else to do, his way to find a crust in that style-fevered town all dried up. He turned around and spat on the ground as a curse and riddance to that worthless, worry-induced peace he'd left behind.

He set out . . . and though it took a long time, whatwith his pulling up his galligaskins at every seventh step, and the wrong turn he made at the beginning . . . one bright morning, emerging from a dark thicket, he espied a river soup-thickened with fish so fat they floated. He walked on them easy as upon a path . . . and when he stepped upon the other bank and saw the people and the land, his nose cried: *You are Here.*

His mouth filled and overflowed as if the river of saliva could run down his cheek, fall upon his jerkin, drop down to his galligaskins, slither down to the toe of his boot, and from thence to the riverbank, where it could surround and drown and pull the catch back up—but how could it? Werold grabbed at his calves, but the fat slovenly hose had slipped down to his ankles again. For a moment, his mouth hung open and glistened, stupid as a dead fish, as he tidied himself with desperate speed in this place of undoubtable good fortune.

That he was always *Here* and never *There* was a lesson he'd learned only too well on this trip. At last, however, Here was where he had been sent, for here was somewhere that only the likes of a lecturing medlar would think real, and not just mischievous leaf whisper.

He bent down and peered at the ground, then picked up a scrap of brown stuff with white stripes. He sniffed, and shoved it in his mouth before he had time to obey his mother's deathbed warning: *Never shove somewhat you dun know in your gob. It's like ter poison your blood and cause your hair to frizzle orf.*

Gingerbread!

Gingerbread with thick white swirls of icing! No one from Ranug-a-Folloerenvy who could have afforded this ambrosial cake would have thought to eat it—not when there were capes to seek, and new lace caps. Their treats were only what could sit from head to feet, on them. Their insides were never seen, so had to abide with day-old-bread made by bakers who made no cakes, and nothing fresh.

Before he knew it, the argufier Werold—weary, starving, workless—ate so much gingerbread that he fell asleep with an ache in his stomach and a smile on his face—having eaten his way through the scraps of twelve nightshirts, thirteen socks, a filmy guipure sandwiched between two caps, one-half of a too-stale boot, innumerable delicacies of bodices, a stodgy codpiece, a jerkin so padded its owner could stand with his chest puffed out at Cupid. And a slice of a detachable sleeve that truly was as big as (the medlar had foretold true) a pumpkin. Although even the meanest shred of underclothing was the most heavenly food he'd ever stomached, with a smell so divine he wanted never to be out of the presence these rags, he had been able to be picky, being all alone on the bank with not a soul in sight.

When the shadows lengthened, instead of trying to eat all the skirts that lay around, he made a bed of five of them and tossed one into the river where the fish it landed on picked a hole in it large enough that Werold could see one of the fish's protruding eyes, and the profile of its thick lips with a hint of double chin. The river that was visible between the fish was clogged with sodden clothing scraps, much as lichen hugs the rocks in a path. Every few moments, a fish barely moved its body and opened its mouth—encompassing a scrap of used apparel.

It wasn't dawn yet when Werold woke a changed man.

He sniffed the skirts and put his hands together in silent thankfulness to the wise medlar. *It must be the cloves*, he thought. No longer starving, knowing that he was sent here for his fortune, he was invigorated and ready to take on any argument. *Versuith aey!* Werold the argument-maker who hailed from that silly tumbledown, fashion-chasing town so far away, was now set for better things, Sharp as a clove, he walked to his unknown destination not caring a jot for the picture he made. *Up!* he commanded his galligaskins, and though they did not obey any more than they ever had, he felt as if they jumped to his raised eyebrow.

The road led to a gated town, but with no one to challenge him. Instead, the path before the gate had a pattern in white stones that said in swirly letters:

Welcome!

The townspeople, though dressed in mouthwatering display, were so obliging that he immediately felt at home. Everywhere he went, people wanted to help.

"I wish to have a sign painted," he said. No one asked him why, but he was taken to someone who said it could be done and took his order, refusing money "for the pleasure" (not that Werold knew what coin they took, even if he had any to hand out).

Werold next sought a place to set up business, and he was led to a narrow but luxuriously furnished shop and room above on Market Square, with a place to secure a sign so that it hung out over the street and would be seen by all. "As if I were a king" he protested in so few words that it would have shamed him, if he had been quoted in his Guild of expert exponential argufiers, but he was assured that he was the first argufier to ever have graced these parts. Indeed, no one had ever heard of argufiers, but all agreed that they must be very necessary, since he was one.

So.

Just before sunset on his first night in what the townspeople were pleased to call Pleasanz, the town's newest inhabitant hung his sign. It said:

for all your
ARGUFIER, DISPUTATOR, PILPULIST, DISCEPTATOR,
LOGOMACHIC, BELICOSSIC, WRANGULUMENTOR
~needs~
Werold of Ranug-a-Folloerenvy, MoA, HLD, GKoB

From the sign hung three iron rings framing objects finely wrought. In the left ring: a fork-bladed backstabber dagger. The middle held a scene as fine as lace: a man spitted over a small bonefire, flames curling from the eyes of the topmost skull. Suspended in the right ring: a simple vial. Each object in its ring was barred diagonally with a red-enamelled banner.

After Werold hung the sign he looked for a place to eat but didn't find one, nor a place to buy anything to eat. So, lit by stars, he crept out of town and visited the riverbank again, where he ate his fill and made another bed hidden by a hedge, as now that he had position in Pleasanz, he could not be seen to be slumming. *Tomorrow,* he said to himself as he snuggled into the fragrant bedding, *I'll find the measure of Pleasanz.* But just before he closed his eyes, he spied a scrap of bodice within arm's reach, and dropped it into his waiting mouth where it dissolved and trickled down his throat in a manner like gold down a wishfulfilled miser's. *If,* he mused as his throat convulsed on the remains of the taste of its tail, *this toothsome thing is not a Pleasanz cake, what marriage could there bake when a Pleasanz cake and wine, and my mouth meet?* (For Werold was at heart, a misunderstood poet.)

He woke bathed in sweat, and tried to jump off his bed, but his hands pushed through three skirts and stuck, and his chest pulled away the topmost's elaborate decoration so well that he looked like he'd aged twenty years and grown a mat of curlicued white hair.

He had to use his arms like flails to beat his way out. Torn skirts flew everywhere, hitting the ground with thuds. He ran to the river's edge where he jumped onto the backs of the nearest two fish and bent down to wash the icing off his chest. It was as hard to scoop up unsullied water as gleaning the mice from the rye in an opened barrel. He scraped at his chest, grabbed at his ankles where his galligaskins lazed—and was poised to run back to town, but the sight of the fish kept him longer, longer than he had meant, longer than he would have wished. They glistened in a slow turbulence, gulping their scraps of sodden clothing in such a desultory manner that he could see from the way their lips drew back: disgust. They lay on their sides, each fish's one bulging eye so lacking in expression, it lacked only the flattening that death brings. All these bloated creatures almost still as paving stones seemed to yearn that fate of slow choking in a basket, to lie on a slab at the monger's.

On an impulse, Werold tore the button from his jerkin and

threw it out between the banks where the fish were so massed, the river was hidden below them. Before the button had a chance to hit a body, the river shattered upwards. Fish jumped as high as his shoulder. Bodies as big as his arced up and slapped down, roiled the water and rolled in the river, their great mouths snapping, fighting for that button till the banks were slick with water and mucked with sticky, slippery brown bits as shiny and toothsome as a rotting mushroom.

Werold turned away, sickened.

His stomach was now upset as a sober man's. *I ate used clothing, like a fish!*

On dry land, he spent an hour looking for just the right yesterday's clothes, enough and good enough to make an outfit that could pass as fashionable, and fresh. When he finally found shoes modish enough, he next found a plain undecorated cloak. Then he stripped himself bare laying his cape, hat, jerkin, shirt, and boots upon the cloak. He balled his galligaskins and shoved them in his boots. Then with a look back at the fish, who he didn't trust, and a unanswered question about the future—What of the people in this town to come, the limits of their discontent? In case he had to run, he shoved the bundle into the hedge as far as he could reach, at shoulder height. Only then did he dress in his strange but magnificent clothes. These new galligaskins were thick and soft, and stood upright as toy soldiers.

Back to town he walked, no longer needing pause to bend.

The morning was just getting a move on when he stood under his sign, where he was immediately surrounded by curious Pleasanzers—so many that he had to mount a barrel to explain what an argufier does, and what he could do to improve the lives of all who flourish here, in this *most pleasant town, if I may pun*, he smiled. His audience smiled back, but there were some raised eyebrows. "Perhaps you do not pun," he bowed, in case some in the crowd were inclined to take offence. They looked so physically capable—if they spoiled to fight. He pointed out each swirly word in his sign and explained it bare. No one had ever heard or seen an Argufier, Disputator, Pilpulist, Disceptator, Belicossic, or Wrangulumentor.

To illustrate the wonders that his advocacy would bring, he then pointed to the iron-circled red-enamel bannered wrought-iron objects creaking merrily under the sign. His explanation had always worked before because what they showed, and their barring, spoke plainly to everyone who couldn't read in Ranug-a-Folloerenvy (and that meant pretty much everyone). But the people in Pleasanz, though most fragrantly and exquisite equipped, knew nothing of barring, let alone backstabbers, fork-bladed or not (Someone held up a butter knife and asked, "You mean us to use our fingers?"). They smiled and clapped when Werold said "bonefire", and an elder showered compliments at the graceful curls of flames shooting from the topmost skull, but this could not cover up their embarrassment of befuddlement at the bonefire itself and the man slowroasting over it on the spit, which they thought he was clasping, an urge they assured the newcomer they were free of.

And "No wine?" asked one worried Pleasanzer about the vial. Poison was too foreign a something for them to understand.

So Werold ended up saying that these portrayals were too ancient for him to know, but that the work he did was too modern and necessary for anyone in Pleasanz to be concerned about such old ways, *so consider them effuzlements of portriment, he said. That, invermore, by the by when all is said and done . . .*

The Pleasanzers were most pleasant, but they were drifting off. Werold had begun to treat them as he did an argument from a rich man, *by the word impregnable.* Panicking, he employed yet another argument without meaning, but this one contained the word *today.*

The result was faster than a new fashion sighted in Ranug-a-Folloerenvy.

Werold learned in moments that *Today* was the Pleasanzers' most important word, concept, creed, bond, promise, source of panic, pride, and aspiration. Everything in Pleasanz revolved around *today.* So much so that he got so much work that first today, and the next, and the next, that he had never been so busy.

They paid well, too: anything he asked. They didn't want to bargain, never cried poor. Pleasanzers carried wads of paper money that they liked to stuff their clothes with, pulling notes from sleeves and hat brims as often as a pocket.

Within days, Werold the Argufier had forgotten he'd ever been called Galligaskins. He was rich, and not only that—so well respected! Since no one had ever had a dispute here, they left them all to him. He proposed, and they paid. He crafted arguments that spread a web across Pleasanz more interconnected and elaborate than that of the most flamboyant spider. So complex were his arguments, so refined that sometimes he cried reading them, they were so perfect.

Like all perfections, however, this was flawed. Each Pleasanzer wanted Werold to argue: for each, an argument a day. If they could not get him to make an argument, they wanted what they considered the next best things, in the order of his sign: a disputation, pilpulation, or . . . If he was too busy to make them one of those, a . . . And if he couldn't fit any of those in, everyone settled for a wrangulumentation because, as everyone said within a week of his setting up, "Fie if anyone this side of the firmament is as great a wrangulumentor as Werold of . . . where this Master hails."

Within two weeks he had so much work that he had no time to count his money and no time to buy a trunk, so he began to stuff it in his chimney. He was so happy at first that he had no time to worry. On the twenty-second night, however, for no reason attached to the number 22 as far as he knew, the fault faced him, as big as that crack opens between your feet on the upper story of your house, and yawns wider . . .

Everyone in Pleasanz just hired him to be agreeable. No one cared about what arguments he made. "They pay me to see the pleasure in my face," he grizzled, grabbing a wad of money clogging the fireplace, and tossing it in the dusty air tinged, as always, gold from the Pleasanz dust of disintegrating gingerbread: rye, cardamom, ginger, cloves, cinnamon, mace. Werold guessed the rest, but he had never found any place where Pleasanz cloth was made, let alone where all the gorgeous raiments were created. He never even found a poor, cross-legged Pleasanz tailor. And what town doesn't have a wealth of those?

Though he sought, wandering alone in the hours when the population slept, those places of creation—cloth and clothing— they were not the only places he sought but never found. They were minor searches, to satisfy his curiosity. Sating hunger was something else. Being a prominent new citizen, as everyone assured him that he was—he could not say to anyone, "If you please, where do you buy your meat and cakes?" The market that he stared out at, only sold shirts and skirts and cloaks. Not an egg. Not a hen. Not a fish or cake nor cabbage. He could not find another market.

As to a place where he could drink a drop of ale, that was hidden, too. He could smell, at times, a glorious ferment that insinuated itself past the stench of gingerbread—but could he find a tavern? No. Nor a place to buy a slice of pease pudding or a pig's knuckle; nor could he even hear a woman selling pies. Werold could find not a scrap of food in Pleasanz, and was so well bred, everyone said, that he was too encumbered by respect, to ask.

At night, instead of following Pleasanz custom and tossing all his wearings of the day out the window onto the street below for the rubbish collectors to take out to dump at the river—every night he ate just enough to sate his hunger without causing his stomach to revolt. He had to pinch his nose as he ate. To stare at the beauty of the collar of the day, a lace of crisp rolled wafers hung together with suspended loops of icing—then to break it apart wafer by wafer and shove them in his mouth, where his teeth crunched the brown lace, and the loops melted on his tongue while he tried not to retch. A fine shirt, he bunched into a ball and squeezed till it was a pill that he swallowed. At first, these were the easiest to digest, the thicker clothing being too hard to keep down, but by the twenty-first night, he was so hungry he ate a whole padded jerkin, and then worried himself to sickness at the thought that a collector might notice that he was not discarding his dailies as he should.

Maybe the rumour would go around that he did not dress freshly. Maybe he would be unwelcome soon. Maybe he would starve here, in abject wealth. For he had nothing to spend the money on, except for his daily order of wearables—the richest available, only what was expected of him—delivered as was the custom, on the doorstep at dawn.

Come the next night, the twenty-second, he could not eat a thing. He picked up a brilliant argument and tossed it to the floor.

Then he picked up a wad of money, and tossed that upon the argument. He turned his head to the door, opened it and did not look back. He met no one as he walked out of Pleasanz, and his gingerbread soles made no sound on the cobblestones. Out of the town gate he went without looking back at its great smiling face. Along the road he went, till he reached again, the riverbank.

He stripped, tossing everything into the river, and rolled on the dew-laden ground till the revolting smell of Pleasanz had rubbed off.

Then he reached into his hiding place in the hedge and pulled out his bundle.

Rain had made its way past the thorns and leaves. The cloak had been sopped as bread in milk, then dried as a crust. Then it had split, and its pieces grew a velvety coat of blue-green mould. He opened it on the grass. There were his travelling boots, mouldy but still good for a thousand leagues. Their outsides stunk of gingerbread, but tucked inside each was a galligaskin, the hose soft and thick and unable to stand as ever, and though spotted with mildew, not smelling at all of Pleasanz. His shirt, jerkin, cape, and hat stunk. Though the gingerbread cloak was also green with mould on its inside, the smell of those hideous spices stuck to the clothing like an evil curse. In a fury, he tossed shoes, shirt, jerkin, cape and hat high, over the hedge. Then he sat on the grass and shoved the balled stockings in his face.

These galligaskins were moist and rich with the scents of his unwashed traveller's feet.

He dropped one ball in his lap and tore at the other one till he ripped it into pieces in the more worn and rotted places, the feet and inner calves. He stuffed a piece into his mouth. He sucked it, rolled his tongue around it and through the holes in the knitting. He put his hand up to his mouth so that he could breathe out upon his palm, and inhale.

His eyes were shut in rapture when the moon came up. A sibilance made him open them.

Some fish had come up onto the bank like a pack of eels, and had arranged themselves with their tails to the river and their eyes toward him. He continued to eat the one galligaskin that he had torn into pieces. It was not an easy thing to chew. Though rot softened it, particularly underfoot, its yarn caught between his teeth. This slowed his greed.

The moon showed through to the luminous back of the watchers' eyes, making them into mirrors in which he saw himself eating as he never had—with such joy, and sadness that there was only so much to this meal. The fish took no liberties, nor made any sounds that he could hear, but they must have communicated some way, for soon the bank was so covered with fish, each head pointing in his direction, that he choked.

The first stocking, the one that held extra savour at its crusty top from a time that he fell and tore his knee, he'd gulped the last stitch of, but he could not eat more with these silent lookers-on. Tears stung his eyes.

He ripped the top of the undevoured hose with his teeth so that the knit unravelled on his tongue. Swallowing his excess saliva and his appetite, he pulled the knitting asunder and made a yarn ball, as the fishes watched. Then he stood up, naked as he was born. Walking amongst them, he broke the yarn into pieces and dropped a piece into each of the uplifted mouths.

As he broke and distributed yarn, there was no fighting amongst the fishes, even though, to give each fish a portion, he had to break the yarn into shorter and shorter pieces. When he had fed the last fish, the one whose tail lay in the river, he was unsure what to do. The fishes watched him, but if they'd turned their heads away he wouldn't have been able to see himself in so many mirrors. There he stood on a riverbank—unclothed and without a coin of any realm.

Why did I take that medlar's counsel? he asked himself, striking his tripe-white knees with both his fists till all were red as a maiden's lips. Who should know better the value of what is free? He didn't ask the fishes, of course, any more than he would have asked a mirror. They remained as they were—expressionless but still as a playwright's wished-for audience as Werold hit himself, then wept a bit, then pondered, sitting naked on the grass. The only sound was the slow woosh of gill-moved waters.

Werold became very still and increasingly vacant-eyed, till suddenly he slapped his head. "I know!" He scrambled up, wiped grass and mud from his skinny backside, and did a little dance. "The medlar," he sang, stamping three times. "Valued as most blessed" *stamp stamp stamp* "what *medlars* wish."

Werold's deliberations had led him to this conclusion: Any medlar would anoint itself with the scent of gingerbread if only it could, for that is almost how a bletted medlar smells, but never quite.

Every medlar is rootbound. "But I have legs!"

Werold laughed, an action this master argumentitioner had never been seen to take. Even now, he thought, that goodnatured medlar might be living richly in its imagination, as it travels in the shoes of the traveller it told the way to happiness. Whether the medlar assumed that the scent of gingerbread is all for everyone, is something Werold didn't try to fathom.

He had made up his mind, with no argument that it brought forward. The fish had eaten his galligaskin kickshaws with the same delight as he—not to be polite, not to be agreeable. "We do agree!" he said, expecting not a wriggle of understanding, not a blink of their lidless eyes.

For now it was time, Werold decided. He would meet his end here, as he could go nowhere naked, but could not bring himself to don the litter on this land. "Perhaps you'll find me tasty," he said to them, "you poor creatures who have never tasted worms."

He jumped from the bank.

Werold the argufier will be no more, he thought as calmly as he could, as his nose met the water. He could not swim, so hoped his end would come before he lost his mind.

His toes touched the soft thick bottom of the river, but only once. Every fish must have raced into the water. They bumped up against his chin, hit his chest and legs and back. They flayed the water from the river, from him, using their solid bodies, their lashing tails and fins. One big fish slipped under his feet and flung him free of the river. He sailed into the air and tumbled back upon the back of another giant. Without thinking, he grabbed that fish's fin. It turned its head back toward him, and he saw himself in its eyes. Werold, wearing a smile to rival the happy face on Pleasanz' gate.

The fishes would not let his head slip into the river, but they pushed him so that his body hung in the depths. Then began a procession in which each fish rubbed against him backwards, and they rubbed him everywhere below his head, from his neck to the undersides of his feet. Soon he was as covered with a thick coat of scales as they, though the arrangement was somewhat Galligaskinish—saggy and slovenly next to the tight, neat patterns on the fish.

His coat and leggings needed constant adjustment, but the fish took care of that. His new profession—and the fishes greatly looked up to him—was to lead them up the great unexplored river where he pulled the worms off boys' hooks in every new fishing hole. If there was a fishermen's net poised to throw upon the river, Werold stood up, on a long sinuous fish's back (this was the only treat the fishes still squabbled for) and dazzled and intimidated all the two-legged landlivers with his shining raiment. Whenever fishermen saw the wondrous man of the river with their own eyes—the man who was coated in a fish's rainbowed mail—they rushed to their huts and then back to the river, where every fisherman emptied a bucket of offerings. The waters swirled the most at worms, but also liked were pig's knuckles, roasted hens, buttons and buckles and belts, soft slippers, and the lees of ale. The action of leaping fishes and man was so looped and wet and active that no one could say for certain whether the man ate worms or only hens and bacon.

Two-legged landlivers watched, drool-mouthed. And that night in the house of every civil citizen who saw that the man was not a myth, everything wearable though it be new as the morning egg, was ripped and cursed and piled in a heap—from gold-embroidered shirts to hose as fine as spider webs. On fine streets, it was impossible *not* to hear the rich men wail, and grizzle, answer their ladies' cries with sharp replies; and kick their dogs, and moan and keen and weep.

In rude huts, fishermen tore their hair, worried over whether their offerings were rich enough; whether the visitors had gone their way sated or having left a curse upon the nets.

The glittering vision on the river, the unattainably clothed man—though looking just the same from year to year, from sighting to sighting—left fashion in a leap.

So this is almost the end of this true story, except for what I pass to you.

At night, those days, only scoundrels and the wretched were not in bed at home. At campfires along the river, fierce arguments flamed over what the man on the river droned, for on moonlit nights the one they called Silverlips was seen to sit on the back of a fish, spouting a stream of endless words. About one thing though, every loud-mouthed vagabond agreed. That each word might have made some sense in some other order, but the arrangement from the mouth of Silverlips made "nonsense."

My great greeaaaaat grandfather, a wretched poet, watched the fire and held his tongue, but while others were sleeping, he'd slip to the riverbank and cup his hands around his ears. The river was slow and deep, never a babbler, so when one violet dawn he heard a drone, he knew it was Silverlips. He caught the stream coming from the river, answered back in like, and penned the story with the quill he carried, and his own hot blood. A fine procreator, he passed down his talents and this tale.

AVANT-N00B

NICK MAMATAS

Olivia got that witchy feeling frequently, but never so powerfully as the time she spotted a particular garment while thrifting at Dog and Pony on Guadalupe. It was a weird interstitial moment—the owner, Star, was in the back and Olivia was the only customer in the usually crowded store. She didn't even know what she was looking at, and had nobody to ask, but was sure the item would make for a great blog post. Olivia was fashionn00b, her blog was fashionn00b.net, and its slogan was "Clothes Blogging Live From Austin—We're the America of Texas!" It was her father's joke, and Olivia had appropriated it the way she had liberated any number of her mother's old dresses and shoes from the early 1990s, after mom had abandoned them. The clothes, and Olivia, that is. This garment was generous in its own way, stretching across two hangers. Its lines and folds were crazy. Was it some sort of sarong, but with sleeves, and in a half-faded black with a silvery lace gimp, instead of the more typical patterns and plaids of Asia? Anyway it was only ten bucks, and according to NextBus. com the bus was coming now!, so she decided that it was hers. Olivia left two crumpled five-dollar bills on the counter, shouted back to Star, "Hey, I bought the impossible garment on the two hangers!" and ran out of the store, with the garment in her arms. It was Saturday. Olivia didn't hear Star calling her back, didn't see Star leaning out the door to shout, "No, wait, not that thing!"

She slammed into some big kid with greasy hair on the corner, mumbled an apology as she ran, and just made it.

Everyone knows that the best time to make a blog is Monday morning, as the whole world gets up first thing in the morning to catch up on, and with, the Internet after a weekend of doing whatever. But bloggers do a lot of whatever on the weekends, including prep work for the Monday blogs. Saturday night was a wash, because Olivia went to the movies with her father—some artsy Japanese thing about the year in the life of a family she wasn't interested in except for the sailor fuku the girl character wore. Olivia preferred the winter outfit with the long sleeves and white scarf to the summertime version, which carried way too much sexualized baggage thanks to dirty old men and anime boys.

That was a problem, even in Austin, Texas, which was totally liberal and friendly, with decent weather most of the time. The male of the species and its dull, if hungry, gaze. The blonde cheerleader look was still the default, and most of the other girls just dressed like ugly boys as a form of sullen rebellion. Then there were the ironic cowgirls, with cleavage! and hats! So for Monday, Olivia picked out a ridiculously oversized sweatshirt she had thrifted a while ago, and tiny shorts nobody would see because the shirt came down past her knees, a New Wave belt, and black stockings, and what she called her *My So-Called Life* boots. She imagined hurling herself out the window of fifth period Social Studies and flinging her arms out, the sleeves stretched like the patagium of a flying squirrel, and gliding safely to the endzone of the school's football field. And the shirt even read DRAKE UNIVERSITY—put a bird on it! was always good advice. Look assembled, photos taken and properly cropped. Then the witchy-smelling garment.

"What the HECK is that THANG?" Olivia said, affecting a goofy hick accent for her own amusement, five minutes later. Unfolded and unfurled, the piece was over twenty feet long. It zig-zagged across the floor of Olivia's already cluttered room. The center of it was insanely narrow, but the fabric was stretchy, like nylon. Something a boa constrictor might wear, with a huge poofy bottom and a top that was a petaled flower of shoulder pads and seemingly random spikes. And the sleeves-slash-pant-legs-slash-huh, what?? She snatched up her phone to take some pictures. There *would* be a Sunday night posting to fashionn00b. net. The hardcore Olivia thought of as the ladysphere was always online.

The comments flooded in, but nobody knew what the hell it was.

Bibian Bestwould guessed: Like a bicycle-built-for-two, but a garment.

Joan of Park(Place) wondered: Some sort of circus outfit? You should get some stilts and see if it fits then! But which holes are for which appendages, eh?

MsCantBeWrong tried: Snuggie Couture.

Three other bloggers announced that they were totally going to change their screen names to Snuggie Couture, and everyone had a good laugh. It was nice to have friends in every time zone, people who really understood a girl, even if nobody understood what was on the floor at Olivia's feet. The pictures were tumblrd and tweeted around a bit. With luck, by Monday morning someone would be able to identify the piece as something other than a horrific factory error or a prank on Olivia's part. Then, at the stroke of midnight, when Sunday turned to Monday, there was a new comment. Olivia always slept with her phone. It blazed to life, and she read:

YOUIDIOTDOTCOM: INSIDEOUT!!! *On t'a bercé trop près du mur?*

Olivia had a strict policy about deleting griefers and trolls, but she knew not a word of French and hoped that it would be some sort of clue, so she decided to let the comment stand till morning. Olivia took Spanish, because it was easy and the maid could help when it wasn't, but she could ask a French teacher, or maybe a student. *But what if it was something* nasty, *or dirty?*

"Nice shirt!" a pimply fifth-year senior shouted as Olivia walked down the hall to homeroom "Planning on gaining three hundred pounds?" It was the greasy kid from the other day, Olivia realized.

She turned to him, stepped right up and said, "I'm going to give you one minute to come up with something more entertaining, all right?" She had a Swatch—1990 Robin Gj103, day-glo green and pink with little Kirbyesque superheroes decorating the band—on her left wrist and made a show of rolling up the sleeve of her sweatshirt to count down the seconds.

"Uhm . . . more like Drake Cakes University?" he tried. "Heh heh, get it?" He looked around for support, but only got a sneer from a Chinese girl on her way to the honors homeroom, and a shrug from her obedient boyfriend. The senior smiled at Olivia, and even pushed his bangs from his face. "Hey, you're all right. I'm sorry."

"Okay, thank you," Olivia said. She would have left it at

that, but something witchy his way stunk, and it wasn't just his Hatebreed T-shirt. So Olivia found herself asking him, "What language are you taking?"

"Why?"

"Is it French?"

"Yeah. My mother's French, so I took it all four years. Why?"

"Because you already have a negative opinion of me for no reason, thus I don't care at all what you think." She produced her phone, found the comment on her blog, and said, "Could you translate this?"

"Uhm . . . you've been rocked too close to the wall? Something like that. You're in a cradle and it was rocked too close to the wall as a baby. so you kept smacking your head against the wall. It's the French version of 'Were you dropped on your head as a child?' "

"Well," Olivia said. "Okay, thank you." And she turned on her heel and left. The senior called after her, "My name's Bobby!"

"Thank you, Bobby!" she said back, over her shoulder.

Class was tedious, lunch tasted like lead and felt like concrete in her stomach. What a nasty little comment, but it was definitely a cut above the average troll—they generally only managed *Ugly bitch suck my balls lol* and the like. *Hey Titless Wonder, ever consider dressing as an ironing board for Halloween? Oh, too late!* was about as clever as they got. Olivia wondered if it was her fault somehow, that a smart person had gotten so mad at her. Then came Social Studies and rather than looking out the window as she usually did, Olivia looked at the phone on her lap. One anonymous commenter wondered if the piece wasn't a garment at all, but some sort of celebratory, or even funerary, bunting or wall-hanging made from clothing. Tatterdemalion's Roar made a joke: "For Siamese twins that have grown apart . . . and a part!" And then, another in French, from YOUIDIOT.COM: *Vous avez le corps d'un chien et le QI d'une durée de cinq ans! INSIDEOUT!!!*

"Let's hear from Ms. Higginbotham," the teacher, Mr. Crain, said. He had his hands on his plastic belt, like always.

Olivia was appalled already. "Hmm?"

"The Nazis, Olivia," Mr. Crain said. "Could it happen here? Could Americans all sign up and start goose stepping around in a fit of racist and anti-Semitic rage, or are we free and democratic and thus immune from such impulses. You appear to be the tie-breaking vote in the class."

She glanced around the room, quickly trying to determine who voted for what, but everyone shared one expression—joy that the daydreamer was squirming. "I say . . . yes." It was a risky gambit. Olivia was already on the edge. She saw her future flash before her eyes. One more Needs Improvement grade, one more "If only she applied herself" lecture at parent-teacher night and then it would be UT and not FIT in New York, and from there a generic marketing major, Texas for life, and nobody to look forward to but scrawny unsuccessful musicians in frayed and mustard-stained T-shirts. Forever and ever. She should have said no, should have said no. There was no sweatshirt large enough for her to sink into.

"And why is that?" Mr. Crain asked.

"Well," Olivia said. She licked her lips. Then remembered something she had read on the ladysphere and decided to go for it. "Hugo Boss."

Mr. Crain's eyebrows crawled to the top of his forehead. "Go on."

"I mean, Hugo Boss—very popular company, for men and women. They have casual wear, premium garments, they make bespoke suits for the wealthy. Everyone here can dress in Hugo Boss and not hurt their looks at all, if they wanted to and had the disposable income." Olivia glanced around the room again, confirming that she had confused everyone. "But he was a Nazi—the original Hugo Boss was, I mean. All the sharp tailoring and angles people like, those are right out of the SS uniform. We don't wear swastikas anymore, and nobody even has that dumb little Hitler mustache, but once you eliminate the iconography, people are still lining up to buy Nazi fashion from a Nazi company, and they think it's awesome. It's military wear, and it's all the same except for people at the very top who can afford to be different, and we don't even realize that it's happening. Uhm . . . that's why we need to do what all the bumper stickers say: Keep Austin Weird." She was hoping for a generalized giggle, but didn't get one.

The room was silent for a long moment. The fantasy of jumping out the window and gliding away came back to Olivia now, but feverishly. She dared not break eye contact with Mr. Crain. Then he said, "I'll buy that. Aesthetics as politics, politics as aesthetics. But please put your phone away, Ms. Higginbotham."

Olivia had study hall after Social Studies and wanted nothing more than to get on one of the library computers. Google Translate was the plan, but Bobby was already in study hall, with two sophomores. One was wearing velour, the other had a T-shirt celebrating the Super Mario Bros. Bobby was apparently part of the intersection between heavy metal longhair and Dungeons and Dragons weirdo, and was leading the small group in some sort of paper-and-pencil game. She walked past them, and got online. The latest French insult translated literally to, "You have the body of a dog and the IQ of a five-year." An IP lookup turned up nothing but an anonymous proxy—YOUIDIOT.COM was registered to a cybersquatter, and the insults seem to have come from a couple of webpages featuring popular French slurs. Then Olivia felt a finger on her shoulder. It was the boy in velour, who whispered silently that she should join Bobby's table.

Bobby and the boys weren't playing a game at all, or at least no game with rules. Instead, they had created a ouija board of sorts out of piece of foolscap, and had an origami planchette, with two pencils under it allowing it to roll. Bobby introduced the boys as Tyler and Charles, and then pointed to the results of their work so far.

BRING GIRL HERE.

Charles had been keeping the notes.

"Who are you supposed to be talking to?" Olivia asked. She wasn't a skeptic, but the whole thing seemed rather ludicrous. Ouija boards worked best when made from fancy wood rather than by Hasbro in some Mexican factory, and when used in dark rooms by a circle full of earnest girls. Three dudes under the fluorescents using plain old paper couldn't really get anything going. But Bobby did get Olivia's witchy-sense a'buzzin', so she took a seat.

"Robert's grandmother," Tyler of the velour shirt said. His arms looked like little pipe cleaners.

"French?"

"Yes," Charles said. Bobby wasn't saying anything, just peering intently at Olivia.

"What languages do you guys take?"

"Spanish," said Charles.

"I tested out," Tyler said. "I did take Latin when I was in Catholic school." Everyone looked at him. "Long story."

"Are you on my blog?" Olivia asked the piece of foolscap before her. It seemed as good a place as any to direct her query. The boys put their hands on the planchette and it moved to YES.

"Well, that means that one of you guys are pranking my blog, nothing more."

"Ask her something else," Bobby said.

"Who are you and what do you want with me?" Olivia crossed her arms and looked at Bobby. "To make things easy for you, answer in your native language, okay?" She took the pencil and paper. "I'll transcribe."

The boys moved the planchette slowly but confidently to M, then to A, then hesitated and moved it to R. Then the bell rang and study hall was over and the spell was broken.

"You guys are jerks," Olivia said.

"No, it's not like that!" Bobby insisted.

"What was her name?"

"Marthe. Rufus," he said. "My maternal grandmother."

"That's why they don't have the same last name!" Tyler offered as the study hall monitor came to sweep them out. Everyone just stared at him. "Ah, nevermind," he said.

Marthe Rufus was an odd enough name. Sounded French, Olivia supposed, and not like something someone would make up on the fly, like FiFi La Rue or whatnot. She cut seventh period and walked the long way to get the city bus. On her phone, she Googled "Marthe Rufus" and there were a few English-language hits. A very slim Wikipedia entry was the first one. It had little more than dates of birth and death, and a brief note. Rufus was an avant-garde clothing designer and mother of one who had died in Vichy France during the Second World War, of "an apparent suicide." There was a citation link but it was dead, and in French anyway, and even archive.org didn't catch a cap of the site when it did exist. The other useful link was to a few weeks ago, and was for an obituary in the *Westlake Picayune*. Bobby's mother, it sounded like, had killed herself. *Poor kid*, Olivia thought.

She got home and was alone. Her father wouldn't be back till late, so she defrosted some breakfast tacos, though that was against house rules, and got online immediately. She asked around after Marthe Rufus, and got a few responses, and even a picture of the one surviving garment from the encyclopediast MsCantBeWrong. The look was very Rodarte, but with an industrial tinge due to wartime rationing and materials. It was weird and flowy, except for the short skirt with an angled hem. The top of the dress was organic, with an odd texture as though decorated with bundles of tightly twisted wheat, and then there was that gimp along the edge, just like the impossible garment. Then FashionBOG sent in another picture. Same garment, on the same model, except the garment was upside down. The skirt was actually made stiff, and acted as a strapless and cylindrical tube top. The flowery top was now a bottom with a very narrow hem, and the model had to pose with her legs tightly shut as one would when shoving two legs through a hole meant for one's neck. The garment looked stranger, but just as good, as it did right-side up.

Or maybe the second picture was the garment right-side up, and the first one was upside-down. Either way, it was reminiscent of the ten yards of weird fabric snaked across the floor of Olivia's bedroom.

Olivia had another question: *Anyone know anything about ouija boards?* she typed. What she really wanted to type was *I wish we could be friends in real life, and that you could all come over and look at this thing and help me figure it out. And could someone bring a ouija board? And some pizza?* She wished she had somebody to call who would just drop by and keep her company.

MsCantBeWrong had the answer: There's an app for that.

A dozen people chimed in to say that they were so excited to see a ouija board app and that they were all going to download it immediately, but Olivia actually did. According to the whimsical instructions on the app, the mass worldwide connectivity of the Internet and mobile environments had made "legacy" boards with their "analog displays" and "manual communication" systems obsolete. All you had to do was select a language, type in a question, and wait. Olivia was feeling very witchy, like in the moments before a storm, when the air smelled like the sea.

She typed her question in English, and set the language to French. And she waited. She went to Facebook and played a little Bejeweled Blitz. She checked back to the discussion of Rufus, but nobody had much to say about her except what anyone could Google. Nothing came through on the oiuja board app, so she Googled the app to look for reviews, but they were the usual mix of five-star fantasies from morons, and one-star rants from even bigger morons who were actually upset when the free download didn't come bundled with actual magical powers. Best most people could figure was that the app distributed questions to random users, and it was users who input the answers to one another. Not that anyone on the whole Internet had come forward to say that they had answered any questions, or even to describe how one could find the textbox *for* answering questions.

Olivia's father came home. She did her homework, which wasn't much. As her father put it, "Hey, it's Texas." He'd been born in Texas and escaped! to New York! for grad school, but now he was back and taught Shakespeare at the community college. "Apparently," he said over a dinner of Trader Joe's vegetarian lasagna, "he was a sexist! And a racist! Every reaction paper agreed, so it must be true, right? No notion of changing times, or mores, or that there is even more than one way to be a good person." Then he laughed, and Olivia grew worried about UT and marketing majors again. They watched some movie on the Sundance Channel that was subtitled even though it was already in English and then retired to their respective bedrooms. Olivia chose tomorrow's outfit—definitely the dark-rinse high-waisted jeans since things were getting a little intense for tights and skirts with Bobby and the boys, and an old man cardigan and a tuxedo shirt with ruffles for underneath it. One silk flower for her hair, another for the top buttonhole in the cardigan, which was missing its button anyway, and pictures were taken and cropped and prepped for the Tuesday morning post.

And at midnight, Olivia's phone went on again, as did her monitor. It was the ouija board app, spewing out some French. She copied and pasted the output into a Word file and saved it, then headed over to Google Translate. There was a liquid ton of calumny—Olivia was stupid, and shit, and could eat shit, and probably eats shit every day, and was an idiot, and Olivia's mother sucks off bears in the forest and it took Olivia's mother nine months to take a shit, in the woods, among the bears, and thus Olivia was born . . . and that was all stuff from the French insult webpages, as though someone was just copying and pasting from them. But interspersed with the insults was a set of instructions on how to wear the garment. One wears it inside out. So to be as beautiful inside as one is outside.

That is, Olivia read, one soaks the garment in a tub and twists one end of it tightly, as though wringing it out. Then swallow it—with a note to Olivia to swallow it like her mother was probably swallowing all sorts of things in hell now. There was a special lubricant in the gimp and otherwise limning the muslin that made the garment easy to swallow. It would snake through the small and large intestines and the stomach and then "come out." Marthe Rufus, for all her foul insults, was surprisingly discrete about from where the garment would emerge. The bottom would be worn like a skirt. The top would wear like a "vest-blouse-display," at least according to Google Translate. It was a true exercise in *avant* fashion—nobody had ever even conceived of dressing the body's interior organs—but it was also practical, as "the model could not eat or drink while in the garment, and thus would not stain it, or grow fat like a pig." Then there were some insults about Olivia's father, who was also a pig who birthed a stupid idiot daughter who didn't understand the first thing about style.

Olivia sat there in her chair, burning with every swipe of the cursor and click of the mouse. This was some horrific troll. There could be no other answer. Someone had made this garment, planted it in the Dog and Pony, knew Olivia would find and buy it, and then unleashed all of this crap on her. Everyone had to be in on it—even the other members of the ladysphere who'd given her advice and made their jokes and led her to the app were just part of an all-encompassing cyber-bullying ring. Even Star from the store was likely in on it. So Olivia was alone, a friendless waif who didn't even have any Internet friends, and everyone who saw her blog hated her and wanted her to die, and she was agreed. She just wanted to die too.

She supposed that one way to die would be to simply follow the instructions, and swallow the garment. And then something occurred to her. An impossible garment couldn't be created by a far-fetched, if possible, hoax. Anything was better than the idea that the whole world, online and off, was arrayed against her. It was easy to wallow in teenage angst, hard to do something about it. Witchiness! roared up inside her.

As beautiful inside as out? she typed. *So you tried it and choked on it, didn't you Marthe, because you're an ugly bitch inside, right?*

There wasn't a long wait for the answer this time. The virtual planchette scooted right to the left-hand side of the board. YES.

And maybe your daughter too—though I bet that was your fault too, for being such a bitch to her when she was alive.

A swifter answer: NO. The planchette shivered like it was angry.

I suppose living under Nazi occupation had something to do with being a bitch, Olivia typed. *But she finally tried the dress after bringing it to America and it didn't work. It's not so witchy as you thought it was.*

YES.

I'll wear the dress, Olivia typed. Then she shut down the app and went to the kitchen to get a pair of pliers from the junk drawer.

Olivia wasn't much for social studies, but she wasn't half-bad at biology. And she knew better than to hang her clothes on wire hangers—*No wire hangers, ever!* as she had learned from an old movie—so she had them going spare. It took an hour to untwist the necks and straighten out the hooks, and Olivia scratched herself on the tips more than once. She'd be a raccoon by morning, but that was all right, she decided. Dark baggy eyes could be accentuated with make-up, and would go well with the look. The jeans were going back in the dresser.

By dawn she was done. Fifteen hangers refolded and crimped together to form a three-dimensional maze—a little cage that came up to her knees She stood in the middle of it. Then Olivia took what she perceived as the bottom of the garment, put the hanger-labyrinth in and started slowly working the long nylon stretch through it, turning it over and over in her hands, tugging and yanking. The fabric was tough; it snagged, but never ripped. Finally, the long boa constrictor of intestine was wrapped around the wire hangers. She jumped out of the assemblage, took off her baggy sweatshirt and shorts, and threw on a slip. Yes, she'd be wearing the same tights two days in a row, but if anyone was looking at that, she had done something very wrong with the rest of her outside. She stepped back into the maze, lifted it up around her hips, and then held the top of her garment over her chest. It looked fine, covered everything, and even looked cool, so she pushed herself up against the wall to hold it in place while she reached for the bottom of the garment and moved it up to cover her back. Olivia had been ready to staple the two ends together if need be, or to use a dozen safety pins on each shoulder, but what at first appeared to be random ribbons worked perfectly as straps to make the top the front and the bottom the back.

It was a good look. Half-Black Swan, half-Frank Gehry tutu, and the slip and tights were okay. Olivia wouldn't be going to school in it—one more cut day wouldn't ruin her life or anything, she decided—but the look would definitely make fashionn00b. net's Google ranking skyrocket. Olivia had a story to tell, about ghosts and death and style and important life lessons, but she decided to keep it to herself, for now anyway. She took some pics, cropped them, put them up, and by way of explanation wrote a simple caption: *Figured out the impossible garment. Just doing my part to Keep Austin Weird.*

Then she added, *Ever notice how all the* Keep [City] Weird *bumper stickers always use the same font and color scheme, no matter which city is supposed to be the weird one?*

INCOMPLETE PROOFS

JOHN CHU

Next autumn's proof of Gödel's incompleteness theorem tailored itself to Grant's body. A three section proof, the trousers grew snug around his waist and shortened to break against his feet. The shirt buttoned itself as it tightened against his chest, arms, and shoulders. Jacket sleeves shrank to reveal his hands. The proof looked retro rather than elegant, not at all what Grant expected from Duncan. Grant wondered what the buyers and journal editors on the other side of the curtain would make of it. He hadn't verified a proof for an audience this important in years.

His own jacket, shirt, and trousers pooled around his feet. Duncan's stylists stopped fussing with Grant's face and hair, pronouncing him fit for the runway. They scooped up his clothes, patted him on the back for luck, then left him alone to focus.

The cutting edge mathematics that held the proof together permeated Grant's brain. He felt its structure, how each lemma and proposition stitched together to support the conclusion that no axiomatic system could be both consistent and complete. Either some truths were unprovable or the system could erroneously prove falsehoods. This time, Duncan had proved the theorem through computability theory.

The audience's quiet murmur bled through the curtain. Grant took a deep breath, then cursed himself for letting himself become a cog in Duncan's machinations again. His grad students had been having the time of their lives watching mathematicians verify proof after proof. Otherwise, he'd have told Duncan's stylists to go stuff themselves when they asked him to verify the final proof of the new Duncan Banks autumn collection.

Grant exhaled. His feet tested the runway's sprung floor as he stepped through the curtain. Where other theorem houses placed safety nets for their mathematicians, a trench of spikes lay on either side between Grant and the audience. Nothing was too over the top for Duncan. Journal editors thought he was potentially the best mathematician since Gauss or Euler. People had worn their proofs, or ready-to-wear copies thereof, for over a century. Editors expected the same from Duncan.

The audience hushed except for his students: Marc and Lisa. They stood, cheering and waving their arms in the air. The silence surrounding them made their excitement sound ironic. He resisted the urge to bury his face in his hands. Instead, he launched into the first steps of the proof: a tumbling pass down the length of the runway.

The jacket, shirt, and trousers exploded apart at their seams into their constituent lemmas and propositions. They swirled in wide arcs around him as he twisted and spun through the air. Pain spiked his knees and shocked through the rest of his body each time he landed. Air whooshed past him and flapping lemmas surrounded him on all sides. Each somersault, jump, and handstand evoked the logic and reasoning that stitched pieces of proof together. The body canvas and chest canvas slipped inside the jacket's shell and gave the jacket its retro shape.

The proof danced in counterpoint exactly as he expected his

logic and reasoning to animate them. As he flipped through the air in a pike position, the trousers slid onto his legs. One section proved, two to go. He stepped to the far end of the runway. The shirt weaved around his arms then settled on his torso. It buttoned itself as Grant ran, building up speed for the proof's final steps. Focused on proving the theorem, he danced with the jacket.

It flew toward him from the side rather than from the back. Its sleeves reached out as if it wanted a hug. Rather than sliding onto his body, it was about to tangle him in mid-air, knocking him into the pit of spikes. If he lined himself up with the jacket, it'd slide onto his body but, in the process, he'd tumble off the side of the runway into the pit of spikes. No valid proof took a mathematician off the runway. Either he repaired Duncan's proof right now, or he'd be impaled by rows of sharp spikes.

Grant stretched his mind out to the jacket. He'd already started his front triple layout when he realized the jacket's shape was subtly off. Duncan hadn't intended the jacket to feel retro. Its chest was prone to collapse and the lapel rolled too easily. The proof's linch pins, the body canvass and chest canvass inside the jacket's shell, were fine by themselves, but they didn't hold this proof together. Grant need stronger intermediate results.

The jacket sideswiped him as he started the second revolution of his layout. If this were a valid proof, he'd be wearing the jacket now. Instead, he thought back to where the proof had gone wrong. The jacket split on its seams into pieces. It flowed around him rather than tangling him and knocking him into the pit of spikes. He landed, then tumbled an extra pass, flipping and twisting in the air. Through that reasoning, he proved stronger versions of the lemmas Duncan had used. The body and chest canvasses morphed in response from what Grant was given into their proper shapes.

The math was so complicated that the reasoning took longer than the length of the runway. As he hit the end, he front tumbled towards the curtain he'd started from. His lungs burned with each breath. His heart pounded not from nerves or even fear of death but from exhaustion. His legs wanted to crumble each time they hit the runway. The jacket reformed, now swooshing towards him from the front. He dove and the jacket rushed onto his body just before he rolled to stand next to the curtain.

Grant stood, his arms stretched overhead, the jacket, shirt, and trousers crisp on his body. His students stood again and hollered, their arms pumping. This time, applause did fill the space. He nodded to half the audience, pivot turned, then nodded to the other half. Disconcertingly, the applause seemed to be growing. They had to have noticed the jacket he wore now wasn't the jacket he'd started with, but that didn't stop anyone from cheering.

Duncan strode onto the runway to receive the applause as Grant left. The two passed each other. Grant glared. Letting this proof onto the runway was no accident. At the latest, the theorem house should have caught its flaws during the run through. Duncan trapped Grant in his arms. He whispered into Grant's ear.

"Hi, Tsai." Duncan always called Grant by his last name. "I know you're angry at me. Meet me in the dressing room after the show. I'll explain everything."

Grant hung the proof of Gödel's incompleteness theorem on a rack with the other proofs verified tonight. His own clothes lay in a heap on the dressing room table next to some proof that hadn't been put away. His wallet and cellphone fell out as he pulled out his shirt. Wisps of thread jutted where there should have been buttons. One sleeve dangled from its seam. His trousers had been rent into strips. That explained how the stylists had undressed him so quickly. They'd assumed he'd worn a proof to the show and could fix the damage. His clothes, though, were just clothes, ready-to-wear.

The proof still on the table had an apology in Duncan's handwriting pinned to it. Grant recognized the work, a proof of Fermat's last theorem Duncan had created during grad school. Its asymmetrical curved seams emphasized Grant's musculature. He didn't feel clothed as much as he felt like an anatomy chart. Spent, he slumped into the chair next to the table and waited.

Duncan strode into the dressing room wearing the proof of the first significant problem they'd solved together: ten was a solitary number. A critical triumph, the proof never sold well. Too few people had the body to pull it off. Duncan had, and damn it, he still did.

To Grant's dismay, Duncan wore the proof better now than ever. His brawn no longer fought to burst out of the proof. Rather, the proof now exposed his beautiful proportions. He was still the mutant spawn of the sun and lightning. If the sun had passed its zenith and the lightning was now the lament of distant thunder, he still made any room feel too cramped to contain him.

"You couldn't have asked me for help before you put the proof on the runway?" Grant was determined to stay angry despite Duncan's smile. "You invited Marc and Lisa here, all expenses paid. It's not like you didn't know how to find me."

"You wouldn't have come, much less helped, if I hadn't brought your students here." Duncan sat on the table. "The proof of Gödel's incompleteness theorem is the signature piece of the fall collection. No one understood its flaw much less how to fix it. I brought here, the only way I could, the one person who could fix it."

Grant stood. He folded his arms across his chest. With Duncan sitting on the table, they saw each other eye to eye. Duncan's gaze burned, but Grant met it.

Duncan was right, as usual. Grant wasn't above refusing to help just to spite him.

"The one person who could fix the proof? Give me a break. And what were you going to do if I'd failed or died trying? Let the fiasco destroy your theorem house?"

Buyers and editors were a fickle lot. One tumbling pass that wasn't parallel to the sides of the runway was enough to cancel orders and deny publication.

"Like you could have failed." Duncan shook his head. "I don't risk my theorem house on just anyone." He pulled out his cellphone, tapped at it, then handed it to Grant. "I'm about to offer the man in this video a job. Tell me what you think of him."

The screen filled with a beefy guy jumping, spinning, and twisting up and down a runway. He used computability theory to prove Gödel's incompleteness theorem, a corrected version of Duncan's proof. The man reasoned with a strength and incisiveness that made Grant's jaw drop.

Grant might quibble with the handful of moves that were not textbook perfect, but the result was superior to Grant's attempt. He wanted Lisa and Marc to see this version.

"You should have gotten him to verify your proof tonight. If you already had this, why did you show the flawed proof?" Grant handed back the cellphone. "Never mind. I no longer have to understand or care about your machinations."

Duncan stood. He bore down on Grant. His head and shoulders blocked the room from view. The musk and leather of his cologne enveloped Grant.

"Tsai, this is video from tonight. That's you correcting my proof." He held the phone in front of Grant's eyes. "When I say you're the one person who could fix the proof, it's not flattery. As hard as you are on everyone else's work, you're even harder on your own. God knows how you sell yourself in interviews. Are you surprised you can't find another job?"

Grant's face burned. He pushed the phone away. His gaze fell to the floor as he sat.

"What makes you think I'm looking?" Grant slid the chair away from Duncan.

"Your department is eliminating its graduate program and some of its non-tenured faculty. Your student evaluations are . . . bi-modal. A small number of students will register for anything you teach. Everyone else writes comments like 'Dr. Tsai can't teach a cow how to moo.' "

Being a force of nature had its advantages. By the time Duncan had worked over the department's administrators, they probably thought that Duncan was doing them a favor by letting them show him Grant's evaluations.

"You used to be charming, Duncan." Once, Grant would have done, hell, he had done anything Duncan wanted.

"I still am." Duncan flashed a quick smile. "But you no longer trust me when I'm charming and I need you to work with me."

"Yeah, right." Grant forced himself to match Duncan's gaze. "The first Duncan Banks collection got published in all the major journals and sold to all the major buyers. Everyone wanted to work with you. You didn't need me anymore and I might as well not have existed."

"You're never going to forgive me." Duncan seemed to deflate a little. "I'm not who I—"

"Make your damn offer."

When the semester ended in a few months, Grant would be out of a job. Besides, his legs felt like marble. Otherwise, he'd have walked out.

"I have the outline of a solution for P=NP. Flesh it out with me. Please?"

Grant sighed. Whether P=NP was one of the remaining great unsolved problems. Proving that P=NP meant biologists could quickly compute the structure of a protein rather than guessing its structure then checking for correctness. It meant computationally tractable ways to find optimal solutions to all sorts of packing and scheduling problems. No industry would be unaffected. Grant and Duncan would be heroes for the ages.

"Show me." Grant tried to sound bored.

The proof of ten as a solitary number transformed into pieces of muslin. They changed shape as they slid around Duncan's body. A lemma around Duncan's back fortified two results on his shoulders. What covered his chest seem to stay there out of sheer faith that someday something might hold it in place. He'd built it on conjectures Grant didn't recognize. After a minute, Duncan wore something that fit roughly on him, pinned together by hope and determination more than it was stitched together by mathematical theorems and logic.

"Well?" Duncan showed his palms to Grant. Rather than casting his light on the world, Duncan looked as if he were in eclipse.

Grant let the outline inhabit his mind. Not enough hung on Duncan to prove anything. Grant wasn't even sure what it actually proved, but the bits that were actually stitched together dazzled. The intermediate results, if verifiable, would advance mathematics nearly as much as the conclusion. What was missing defined the structure as much as what was there.

Grant's hands gripped the chair. He forced himself not to engage with proof. Math hadn't excited him this much in years. But was it worth being burned by the sun and shocked by lightning again? They had never been, and could never be, just about the math.

"By the age of thirty-five, most mathematicians have already done their best work." Grant didn't see any reason to be harsh, not when Duncan had been thoroughly, if bewilderingly, non-toxic. "You'll want someone in his or her prime."

The outline transformed back into the proof of ten as a solitary number. Its austere elegance replaced the buzz of the outline in Grant's mind.

"Do you need to see your video again? This has nothing to do with age." Duncan frowned. "Tsai, I can't change how I treated you but—"

"I have grad students now." Grant's thighs burned as he stood. "I can't just abandon my kids."

Maybe that wasn't the real reason either, but like his age, it was the truth. Grant pushed himself to the door.

"Wait." Duncan's voice swung away from Grant, not towards. "The proof, it's as much yours as mine. You should write it up."

Duncan reached Grant with long strides. He offered the proof to Grant.

"You need the proof as a template for the ready-to-wear version." Grant could write it up from memory. "Send me a copy of the video instead?"

The video had its flaws, but it was a proof verified at a major show. More importantly for the job search, it was available right now.

"I uploaded it just after the show ended." Duncan patted Grant's back. "Within a week, anyone with even half an interest in math will have seen it."

"I'll send you a draft of the paper to review in a few days." Grant forced himself away from the intoxicating heat of Duncan's desire.

"When you're swamped with job offers, don't forget who asked you first, ok?"

Grant wouldn't dignify that ridiculous thought. He just grunted a hoarse laugh as he walked out the door.

Stacks of boxes took the place of reference books, papers, and office supplies on Marc and Lisa's office shelves. The two grad students sat at their desk reading their tablets. What made Grant suspicious though was the missing junk food.

Either Marc and Lisa had gotten better at hiding their stockpile of chips, cookies, and whatnot, or they'd removed it. Hyperactive metabolisms be damned. They couldn't eat like crap forever if they expected to be able to verify their proofs at conferences. However, Grant had never expected them to believe him, much less do anything about it.

"Not that I'm complaining, but why is the office suspiciously clean?"

"We're leaving school, Grant." Lisa could make anything sound reasonable. "Everyone's seen that video of you in Dr. Banks's show. The word is you're going back to him. Nice of you to tell us yourself that you're dumping us."

Lisa looked hurt. Grant hadn't realized that was possible.

"One, I'm not going to make any plans without letting you know first." Grant put his hands at his waist. "Two, I can't believe neither of you bothered to check with me."

"You've been sending everything to voice mail." Lisa swiped then tapped on her tablet. It chimed a few times. She thrust her sent mail folder in Grant's face. "And you haven't answered any of my emails."

Grant fished his cellphone out of his pocket. The screen stayed blank when he tried to wake it. "Oh, I forgot to turn it back on."

His phone vibrated as it booted up. His eyebrows raised at the number of voicemails waiting for him. He checked his email. His jaw dropped at the backlog. He recognized the sender addresses: every theorem house of note, editors of all the important journals, and all of the best mathematics schools in the world, except one, Duncan's. Its mathematics department would have been formidable even without him.

"I may have other options." Grant leaned against a shelf. He swiped through his email, sorting his job offers. Duncan was right again, damn him.

"Why are you so surprised?" Lisa never let him get away with anything. "You fixing the proof on the fly is all anyone has talked about for days."

"I always disconnect my router when I write up a proof." Grant's gaze met her dismay. "Otherwise, I get distracted."

"Why the hell are you teaching here in the first place, Grant?" It was Marc's turn to rip into him. "You're not just good for your age—"

"Hey, I'm not even twenty years older than you."

"You're good." Marc held out the last word. "That last pass up and down the runway—" His eyes widened and his voice broke with awe. "Why don't you have your own collections?"

"That's why you let your funding lapse." Lisa's face lit with revelation. "You'd planned to abandon us."

"No, we're losing funding because I write really crappy grant proposals."

"Look." Marc stood, opening his palms to Grant. "Go back to Dr. Banks. If he wanted me to work with him, I'd ditch you in a second. It'll be fine. I've started auditions for *Project Prove It*."

"No." Grant straightened up. He breathed deeply expanding his chest as he crossed his arms and subtly flared his lats. Stealing a page from the Duncan dominance display playbook was shameless, but he hadn't found another language Marc understood yet. "Auditioning to get on the reality show will eat up the rest of the semester. If you get in, all being on *Project Prove It* will demonstrate is that you can create trivial proofs within twenty-four hours for people with more money than aesthetic sense. You can't build a career on that."

Actually, Marc probably could. Grant just wasn't about to let him settle. Marc sat down, a bit stunned.

Lisa wasn't the least bit impressed with dominance displays. If anything, she grew louder. "I can complete all the math for my dissertation by the end of the semester even while looking for a job. After that, it's just writing. A full time job won't get in the way of that. I have a whole year after you leave when you can still sign my dissertation."

"Oh, Lisa." Grant had expected no less than her full-throttled self confidence. "You have no idea how much work you have ahead of you."

Grant's cellphone buzzed. He shut it off again.

"If you ever answered your phone or read your email, you'd probably find some way to fund us." Lisa shrugged. "All I know is if I had a research assistantship next semester, I could afford to stay in school."

And that was why Grant never ever dismissed Lisa. She had more sense than he did.

"Give me a few days. I'll think of something."

Grant locked himself in his own office. Towers of books surrounded him. He sped through his email and voicemail. When he'd caught up, he stretched away the back strain then hid his face in his hands. After that video, the universities clearly expected him to bring money in, not need support for his kids.

Wherever he ended up, they could follow him, but they wouldn't if he had no way to support them.

People who distracted themselves from their dissertations never finished them. If he didn't secure a future for his kids, they'd secure one for themselves and their hard work would never come to fruition. Lisa's plan to finish was unworkable and Marc wouldn't even bother.

He called Duncan and left a message with his assistant. Maybe Grant was just capitulating to Duncan's master plan, but he couldn't think how else to secure funding before his kids did anything stupid. He'd get them their doctorates before Duncan could discard him again. Security, job or otherwise, could wait.

Grant's flip-flops squeaked against the just-mopped floor. Water that clung to him from the shower chilled off his skin. He dropped his towel in the middle of the bench then unjammed his locker door. The pounding reverberated through the locker room. He pulled his gym bag out then dropped it on the floor.

"Tsai, are you in here?" Duncan's voice echoed off the metal. "I'm sorry my assistant wouldn't put you through to me. Never happen again. I've fired him. Your kids said that you work out every night but I didn't see anyone in the gym."

"Over here." Grant took a deep breath. "Fund my kids until they complete their dissertations and I'll do anything you want."

When Grant looked up again, Duncan stood just in front of the gym bag. No footfalls, much less squeaking.

Rows of lockers dutifully closed in on Duncan. The ceiling lowered and the walls collapsed as he sucked up all the space in the room. Maxwell's equations in differential form covered the front of his t-shirt. The symbols rippled as they curved around his body. The t-shirt caressed his beautifully powerful shoulders, chest, arms, and back. A wrinkled leather belt held faded jeans on his body. The slight stretch across his thighs did the same. Dust and wear had ground his boots gray. The messenger bag Grant had given him long ago hung off a shoulder. Every tear on the bag had been expertly mended.

"Hi, Tsai." Duncan's face registered Grant's gaze sweeping through him. "Something wrong?"

"No. I'd just forgotten what you looked like." That sentence had made more sense in his head. "Do we have a deal?"

"Tsai, work with me because you want to, not because you have to." He handed Grant a manila folder from his messenger bag. "The advance for the Gödel's incompleteness theorem proof will support your grad students long enough for you to line up proper funding."

Grant skimmed the contract in the folder as he dressed. Signing it wouldn't make him Duncan's slave or anything. He patted his pockets. Empty. He tucked the contract under one arm then found the pen stowed in his gym bag's outer pocket.

"Whoa." Duncan squeezed Grant's shoulder. "Have the contract looked at first. You'll find it fair, but I could be scamming you."

"You're not that kind of asshole." Grant shoved the folder into the bag.

"Thank you." Duncan sounded as if Grant had paid him a compliment. "Now we can focus on what you really want."

"No, I'm good." Grant felt bad about leaving right after getting what he needed from Duncan, but not that bad. "I'll send the contract back tomorrow."

Grant slid into his coat. He slammed the locker shut, picked up his gym bag then waved goodbye.

"No one knows you better than I do. You'll settle for funding, but that's not all you want."

Grant's soles squeaked on the floor as he turned and with each step away. So much for the graceful exit, not that it mattered. Duncan froze Grant with a single word.

"Tenure."

Grant knew the scene behind him. A slight smile leavened Duncan's face. His messenger bag slumped on the floor against a rusty bench leg. Duncan straddled the bench, leaning forward. His hands gripped one end of the bench. His arms braced his torso as if he were about to lift into a handstand. He presented the illusion of being perfectly relaxed while his T-shirt exposed every muscle of his torso.

"Where?"

"With me. Same university."

Grant turned around. His shoes squeaked again. He forced himself not to wince. Duncan looked as exactly as he imagined.

"Isn't that overkill?" Grant glared down at Duncan. He had so few chances to do that. "With tenure, how will you get rid of me when you don't need me anymore?"

Duncan lifted his torso and legs parallel to the bench. His smile faded as his gaze focused onto the bench's graffiti. "You know, you get older, you realize the first guy you first bounced ideas off of has ruined you for everyone else since. So you change."

270

His hands thumped against the bench as he walked himself away from Grant. "You become what that first guy wants."

Duncan straightened into a handstand, lowered his legs, then stood upright on the bench facing one end. He backflipped off the bench landing to one side. The control required to avoid crashing into the lockers was intimidating. His hands spread in front him as if to ask, "Well?"

The day Duncan didn't look confident was the day the world would end. However, the years had abraded the smugness from his demeanor. His blistering gaze had always been inquisitive, but it now also yearned. Grant had walked away from the smug Duncan, but this one taunted him with possibilities he'd long convinced himself didn't exist.

Grant pursed his lips. His hands gripped his gym bag. He'd ask for the ridiculous. That ought to cool Duncan's ardor.

"For a start, the university will matriculate my grad students."

Not only did he want the university to fund his students, but he wanted enough funding from Duncan's theorem house that he could buy off his teaching responsibilities. No reason why undergrads should suffer. Grant set down his gym bag and for what felt like minutes detailed his dream job.

"Done." Duncan unzipped Grant's gym bag.

"What?" Grant felt sucker punched. "My demands aren't reasonable."

"Done." Duncan teased the manila folder out of Grant's gym bag then handed it to Grant. "I told you. No one knows you better than I do."

Grant studied the pages he'd glazed past the first time. They met his conditions term for term.

Duncan had changed, but he hadn't become what Grant wanted. Life hadn't taught Duncan any humility. Rather than scaling his self-assurance down to match his achievements, he'd scaled his achievements up to match his self-assurance.

"It's up to you, Grant." Duncan walked towards the locker room exit. "Refuse my offer and I'll never bother you again. I promise."

Grant stuffed the folder back into his bag. "Tell me this, Duncan. What are you really trying to prove?"

Duncan turned around. His gaze pressed against Grant. He looked as if he were intuiting the right response from how Grant's bag pressed against his back, how Grant hadn't tucked in his t-shirt or how off-kilter Grant had knotted his boot laces.

"I should have known you'd see it right away even if I hid the conclusion from my outline." Duncan shrugged. "But I knew you'd find proving P=NP sexier."

"You've jumped ahead a few steps again. Back it up, Duncan." For years, saying that might as well have been Grant's full-time job. If Duncan expected mere humans to understand him, he needed to take it step by step.

This time, Duncan had skipped past surprise and straight to wistful. As he sighed, he seemed to deflate. Grant had never seen him look this mortal before.

"P≠NP. Or maybe I'm wrong." Duncan took a deep breath. "Rehashing old results in ever more elegant ways has done so well for me, I don't have to be practical. I can do real math now. You know, throw yourself into unsolvable problems. Get lost in every twist and leap the way young mathematicians say they'll do until they realize they need to eat. It's time to tackle the impossible and . . . I just thought you'd want to do that too. With me." Duncan showed his palms to Grant again. "Like I said, it's up to you."

P≠NP meant that computationally intractable problems would always be intractable. The best anyone could do was recognize that then focus on heuristics and other approximate solutions. Mathematicians would care about that result, but no one else. The proof might become the most elegant anyone has ever seen but his theorem house would never sell it. No one, not even Duncan, had a body perfect enough to wear it in public without embarrassing themselves.

They held each other's gaze for what seemed like days before Duncan turned around. He started towards the door, his motion so perfectly controlled, Grant couldn't tell how Duncan felt.

"I think when we flesh out your outline, we may find that P=NP is undecidable." Grant allowed a small smile on his face. Duncan was at least capable of the truth on occasion. That was a start.

Duncan stopped, then pivoted around. Grant made a note to ask Duncan someday how he did that without squeaking.

The puzzled look on Duncan's face melted into one of realization then resolve. "Perhaps." He shrugged. "Let's discuss it over dinner. My treat."

Wind swept across the parking lot. A hoodie coalesced around Duncan. His giddy smile outshone the stars and the moon. The light poles seemed bunched together, corralled by the encroaching Jersey barriers. Not even the parking lot could contain Duncan tonight.

No wonder he was so happy. Grant had done exactly what

Duncan wanted. Maybe Duncan had discovered the virtue of telling Grant the truth. Maybe Duncan had maneuvered Grant here the way he'd maneuvered Grant back onto the runway. Grant only knew one way to find out what was true. Take Duncan on. They'd tumble and swirl around each other until either they covered each other or Grant fell into the trenches of spikes.

Grant suspected he could tumble on the runway forever and never really know. Not everything that's true had a proof. No consistent formal system was complete. He wouldn't be a mathematician though if he didn't want to find out.

ABOUT THE AUTHORS

Holly Black is the author of bestselling contemporary fantasy books for kids and teens. Her titles include the Spiderwick Chronicles (with Tony DiTerlizzi), the Modern Faerie Tale series, the Good Neighbors graphic novel trilogy (with Ted Naifeh), and the Curse Workers series. Holly has been a finalist for the Mythopoeic Award, a finalist for an Eisner Award, and the recipient of the Andre Norton Award. She lives in New England with her husband, Theo, in a house with a secret door.

Die Booth is a fan of pencil notes and analogue film and can most often be found lurking in abandoned buildings in the English countryside. An award-winning author who writes mainly horror and slipstream, Die has most recently worked on a co-edited anthology of traditional horror stories entitled *Re-Vamp* and is currently editing a second novel.

Richard Bowes has won major and minor awards, published seven books and many, many stories. His Lambda winning novel *Minions of the Moon* will be reprinted by Lethe Press in late 2012. Other recent and forthcoming appearances include *The Magazine of Fantasy and Science Fiction, Icarus, Apex, Jenny* and the *Million Writers Award: The Best Online SF & Fantasy, After, Wilde Stories 2012* and *Blood and Other Cravings* anthologies.

John Chu designs microprocessors by day and writes fiction by night. His fiction has appeared in *Boston Review*.

Zen Cho is a Malaysian writer living in London. Her fiction has appeared in various publications including *Strange Horizons, GigaNotoSaurus, Steam-Powered II,* and *Heiresses of Russ*. Her short story "First National Forum on the Position of Minorities in Malaysia" was nominated for the Selangor Young Talent Awards and the Pushcart Prize.

Shirin Dubbin is known as a "chic geek," and she likes the sound of it. Especially since she's secretly a closet wallflower (a fact her gusto for karaoke belies). When not working in graphic design, Shirin spins tales of urban fantasy and sci-fi, both with romantic edge. The battle between good and evil, humor, and break neck action are ink to her imagination.

Kelly Link is the author of three collections of short stories, *Stranger Things Happen, Magic for Beginners,* and *Pretty Monsters*. Her short stories have won three Nebulas, a Hugo, and a World Fantasy Award. She was born in Miami, Florida, and once won a free trip around the world by answering the question "Why do you want to go around the world?" ("Because you can't go through it.") Link and her family live in Northampton, Massachusetts, where she and her husband, Gavin J. Grant, run Small Beer Press, and play ping-pong. In 1996 they started the occasional zine *Lady Churchill's Rosebud Wristlet*.

Nick Mamatas is the author of several novels, including *Bullettime* and the forthcoming *The Last Weekend*, and of over eighty short stories, some of which have appeared in *Asimov's Science Fiction, New Haven Review, Tor.com*, and *Weird Tales*. His fiction and editorial work have variously been nominated for the Hugo, World Fantasy, Shirley Jackson, International Horror Guild, and the Bram Stoker award—the last five times in five different categories. His anthology with Ellen Datlow, *Haunted Legends*, won the Stoker. A native New Yorker, Nick now lives in California.

Sandra McDonald is the award winning author of the collection *Diana Comet and Other Impossible Stories*, a *Booklist* Editor's Choice for Young Adults. She also writes adventure novels for gay and straight teens and science fiction romances for adults. Her short fiction has appeared in more than sixty magazines and anthologies. She currently resides in Florida with a backyard full of wild things. Visit her at www.sandramcdonald.com

Sharon Mock's short stories have appeared in *Realms of Fantasy, Clarkesworld Magazine, Fantasy Magazine*, and *The Mammoth Book of Steampunk*. She is a graduate of the Viable Paradise workshop. She lives in Southern California with her husband, the writer and artist Zak Jarvis.

Maria V. Snyder switched careers from meteorologist to fantasy novelist when she began writing the *New York Times* best-selling Study Series (*Poison Study, Magic Study*, and *FireStudy*) about a young woman who becomes a poison taster. Born in Philadelphia,

Maria dreamed of chasing tornados and even earned a BS degree in Meteorology from Penn State University. Unfortunately, she lacked the necessary forecasting skills. Writing, however, lets Maria control the weather, which she gleefully does in her Glass Series (*Storm Glass, Sea Glass,* and *Spy Glass).* Maria returned to school and earned a MA in Writing from Seton Hill University where she is currently one of the teachers and mentors for the MFA program. Her published young adult novels include *Inside Out,* and its sequel, *Outside In,* both are about the dystopian and fully-contained world of Inside. Her latest release is *Touch of Power,* which is about healer dealing with a plague stricken world. Readers can find more information on her books, including the first chapters of all of them, a number of free short stories, and maps on her website at www.MariaVSnyder.com

Rachel Swirsky is a graduate of the Iowa Writers Workshop and Clarion West, two writing programs with much emphasis on how to style words, and almost no emphasis on how to style clothing. She makes up for this deficit by obsessively watching Project Runway, collecting books on fashion design, practicing fashion illustration, and never wearing white after Labor Day. Her short fiction has been nominated for the Hugo, the Sturgeon, the World Fantasy Award, and other honors, and her novella "The Lady Who Plucked Red Flowers Beneath the Queen's Window" won the Nebula in 2011.

Anna Tambour's other stories published in 2012 include "The Dog Who Wished He'd Never Heard of Lovecraft" in *Lovecraft eZine,* "King Wolf" in *A Season in Carcosa* edited by Joseph

S. Pulver, and "Marks and Coconuts in *Memoryville Blues* (PS Publishing). A novel, *Crandolin*, that David Kowalski described as "A fairy tale Dostoevsky would have liked . . . It's like it was written by a demented chef" will be released by Chômu Press later this year, for the feasting season.

Genevieve Valentine's fiction has appeared or is forthcoming in *Clarkesworld, Strange Horizons, Journal of Mythic Arts, Fantasy, Lightspeed*, and *Apex*, and in the anthologies *Federations, The Living Dead 2, Running with the Pack, After, Teeth*, and more. Her nonfiction has appeared in *Lightspeed, Tor.com*, and *Fantasy Magazine*, and she is the co-author of *Geek Wisdom* (out from Quirk Books). Her first novel, *Mechanique: A Tale of the Circus Tresaulti*, won the 2012 Crawford Award. Her appetite for bad movies is insatiable, a tragedy she tracks on her blog, genevievevalentine.com

PUBLICATION HISTORY

ABOUT THE EDITOR

Ekaterina Sedia resides in the Pinelands of New Jersey. Her critically acclaimed novels, *The Secret History of Moscow*, *The Alchemy of Stone*, *The House of Discarded Dreams* and *Heart of Iron* were published by Prime Books. Her short stories have sold to *Analog*, *Baen's Universe*, *Subterranean* and *Clarkesworld*, as well as numerous anthologies, including *Haunted Legends* and *Magic in the Mirrorstone*. She is also the editor of *Paper Cities* (World Fantasy Award winner), *Running with the Pack* and *Bewere the Night*, as well as forthcoming *Wilful Impropriety*. Visit her at www.ekaterinasedia.com.

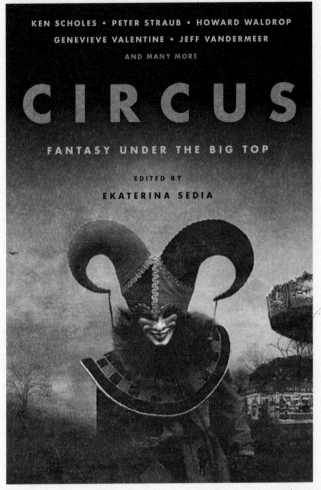

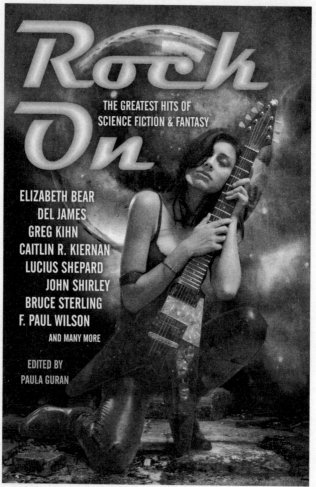